BOQUILLAS CROSSING

Rawles Williams

iUniverse, Inc.
Bloomington

Boquillas Crossing

iUniverse books may be ordered through booksellers or by contacting:

iUniverse
1663 Liberty Drive
Bloomington, IN 47403
www.iuniverse.com
1-800-Authors (1-800-288-4677)

Because of the dynamic nature of the Internet, any Web addresses or links contained in this book may have changed since publication and may no longer be valid. The views expressed in this work are solely those of the author and do not necessarily reflect the views of the publisher, and the publisher hereby disclaims any responsibility for them.

Any people depicted in stock imagery provided by Thinkstock are models, and such images are being used for illustrative purposes only.

Certain stock imagery © Thinkstock.

ISBN: 978-1-4697-3925-0 (sc)
ISBN: 978-1-4697-3926-7 (hc)
ISBN: 978-1-4697-3927-4 (e)

Library of Congress Control Number: 2012900552

Printed in the United States of America

iUniverse rev. date: 3/14/2012

Cover art painted by Crystal Allbright: http://crystalallbright.com

Boquillas Crossing is dedicated to my father, Major Billy Joe Williams.
Billy Joe died in Viet Nam in May 1970.

Why do I write? I write to entertain my friends
and to exasperate our enemies.
To unfold the folded lie, record the truth of our time
and of course to promote esthetic bliss.
— Edward Abbey

PREFACE

BOQUILLAS (BO-KEÉ-YAHS) IS a Spanish noun for which we find various interpretations in translation. I have heard *boquillas* translated to mean many things, including, "little mouth," "cigarette holder," "mouthpiece of a musical wind instrument," "nozzle," "rumor," "a piece of gossip," or a "chisel." Spend time in the shadow of the Sierra del Carmen on the Mexican bank of the Rio Grande, and boquillas transforms from a noun to a feeling.

West of the Pecos River lies the Big Bend region of Texas. The Spanish called it El Despoblado, the uninhabited wasteland. It is hard country embraced by empty savannas and sky island mountain ranges cradled by the northward bend of the Rio Grande along the Texas-Mexico border.

My first pilgrimage to the Big Bend was in December 1976 as a botany student from Stephen F. Austin State University. I arrived in the Chisos Basin in the wee hours before dawn. Stars pulsed in the inky black sky, and volcanic spires reflected starlight. After a five-day hike through the Chisos Mountains on the Dodson Trail in Big Bend National Park, and a long soak at Langford's Hot Springs at the mouth of Tornillo Creek, I waded across the Rio Grande to Boquillas for supper. The restaurant owner and defacto mayor, José Falcon, invited me to play dominos with him and a Mexican *aduana*—customs—agent, who wore a pistol on his belt. We ate tacos and burritos—three for a dollar—drank cold beer served with *sotol* poured into cow horn shot glasses, and watched sunset paint the Sierra del Carmen. My life was forever changed.

Don José Falcon made Boquillas special. José was one of the most observant, intelligent people I have ever known. He was a gracious host, a good friend, and a talented domino player; however, the man ran Boquillas from his wheel chair with a tight fist. José taught me to see the Big Bend from a Mexican perspective.

Although *Boquillas Crossing* integrates historical characters, it is strictly a work of fiction that in no way represents any actual persons living or dead.

It has taken ten years to finish this novel, and the list of folks who helped me get it done is very long. Thank you to all my wildland fire *compadres* who tolerated me as I rambled on and on about this damn book for the better part of a decade.

I am eternally grateful for the near-constant emotional, literary, and technical support that I received from my beautiful, intelligent, and kind wife, Aimee Michelle Roberson. Without her, this story would still be untold. Aimee constantly inspires me with her capacity for loving compassion. Aimee is many things in my life: muse, loving wife, best friend, yoga teacher, and editor. Aimee, you rock my world. I love you forever.

Many people deserve acknowledgment for their help and encouragement. Bill Green read generation after generation of the original drafts, providing valuable input. Bill was a great resource for the historic details of life in Terlingua circa 1915. My older brother Aubrey served, as he always does, as a reliable bullshit meter. Marcia Hilsabeck generously provided a critical edit. Jean Hardy counseled me with sage advice about the business of novels. Crystal Allbright designed and painted the cover artwork. Carol Fairlie photographed the book cover. Steve Anderson graciously contributed a much-needed edit to the final draft. José Aguayo translated my version of the Adelita song. Thank you, all.

In addition, I have to offer a special thank-you to my mother, who has been patiently waiting to see this story in print.

A Brief Chronology of the Mexican Revolution of 1910

1910

- Francisco Madero defeats Porfírio Díaz in presidential election
- Madero drafts the Plan of San Luis Potosí, calling for the overthrow of the Díaz Regime
- The Revolution begins in northern Mexico

1911

- Under Madero's direction, Pancho Villa and Pascual Orozco attack federal troops in Ciudad Juárez
- Díaz resigns
- Emiliano Zapata drafts the Plan de Ayala denouncing Madero

1912

- Orosco breaks his alliance with Madero
- Villa and Victoriano Huerta attack Orozco's army

1913

- Huerta leads a coup against Madero and assumes the presidency
- Venustiano Carranza drafts a Plan de Guadalupe accusing Huerta of treason
- Villa attacks Huerta in the Second Battle of Juárez

1914

- Woodrow Wilson sends US troops to occupy Vera Cruz
- Carranza declares himself president of Mexico
- Villa and Zapata break from Carranza

1915

- Álvaro Obregón under the direction of Carranza defeats Villa at the Battle of Celaya
- The United States recognizes Carranza as the president of Mexico

1916

- Villa murders seventeen Americans in Chihuahua
- Zapata is defeated in Morelos by Carranza's forces
- Villa raids the United States at Columbus, New Mexico
- Pershing leads the First Punitive Expedition into Mexico yet fails to capture Villa
- Villista sympathizer Captain Ramirez raids Glenn Spring, Texas, triggering the Second Punitive Expedition into Mexico
- Zapata captures the water supply for Mexico City
- Villa seizes Torreón

1917

- Pershing retreats from Mexico
- Mexican Constitution drafted
- Carranza elected president

1918

- The Spanish influenza epidemic sweeps Mexico, killing thousands
- World War I ends with German defeat

1919

- Villa is defeated at the last Battle of Juárez
- Zapata assassinated
- Obregón declares himself a presidential candidate

1920

- Carranza attempts to assassinate Obregón, who escapes and rebels against Carranza
- Carranza assassinated in Puebla
- Obregón becomes president of Mexico

1923

- Villa assassinated in Durango
- The United States formally recognizes Mexico's new government

PART 1:
Arriving

I am a brother of dragons, and a companion of owls.
— Job 30:29, King James Version

1

CHAPTER 1

Texas, West of the Pecos River

January 14, 1915

DANIEL TAYLOR WOKE to the sway of a moving train and the sound of an old man talking. It took him a moment to orient to his transient surroundings. He sat upright and yawned.

"A good morning to you, sir," called the gray-bearded conductor from two rows forward in the train car where he had been chatting with another passenger.

Daniel acknowledged the conductor with a nod. "Good morning." He looked past his own reflection in the darkened window, where the pale orange glow of daylight reflected a menacing line of blue-black clouds along the northern horizon. "What time is it?"

The conductor fingered the gold watch that dangled from his wool vest and walked toward Daniel. "Ten minutes past eight o'clock."

Daniel turned up his jacket collar and stared through the drafty window. "That looks like a storm coming."

"It does indeed. That storm looks and feels like a blue norther'," said the conductor. "It was seventy-five degrees here yesterday, and today it might snow. The damned weather here in the Big Bend appears to have a mind of its own."

Daniel smiled at the old man's joke and pulled a blue glass bottle from his jacket pocket. As he did so, a piece of paper fell to the floor. Daniel retrieved the fallen paper, a telegram from Samuel Jenkins. Samuel had been Daniel's army companion in Cuba. He now claimed

2

to be a commodities broker, trading cattle for munitions with Villa's army. Although Daniel suspected that much of Samuel's business included contraband, he had allowed his old friend to entice him into accepting employment as a smelter engineer at a quicksilver mine in Terlingua, Texas.

"Why is this place called the Big Bend?" asked Daniel, stuffing the telegram back into his pocket.

The conductor laughed. "Can you picture a map of Texas?"

"Yes I can," said Daniel.

"As the Rio Grande flows from El Paso to Del Rio, it forms a large elbow before running to the Gulf of Mexico; therefore, Texans call this region of the Texas Trans-Pecos, the Big Bend."

"I see," said Daniel. "What time are we due to arrive in Marathon?"

"Around four o'clock this afternoon," replied the conductor. "Your accent sounds Appalachian."

"You're correct."

"Where are you from, sir?" the conductor asked.

"I was born and raised in Eastern Tennessee, near Johnson City."

"What brings you to Marathon?"

"I have employment in Terlingua."

"Terlingua?" said the conductor. "How did you manage to find employment in such a remote location? Do you know people here?"

"A friend from El Paso secured my employment."

"It's good to have influential friends."

"Yes it is, if their intentions lack subterfuge," said Daniel with a laugh. In dealing with Samuel, Daniel had learned to anticipate a certain amount of pretense.

"What is your profession?"

"I'm an engineer."

"You look more like a soldier than an engineer," said the conductor.

"I was a soldier, but now I'm an engineer." Daniel laid an arm over the seat rest and twisted to one side, then the other, adjusting his spine with audible cracks.

"Did you serve in the Philippines?"

"Yes, and in Cuba," said Daniel.

"How exciting!" the conductor exclaimed.

"Not really. War is a terrible business, regardless of the cause."

"Did you fight with Roosevelt?"

"Not under his direct command, but in the same vicinity."

"Is this your first trip west of the Pecos?"

"Yes," replied Daniel, lifting his brimmed hat and running a hand through his gray-streaked auburn hair, currently longer than he normally wore it.

"Settlement has changed things a great deal," said the conductor, launching into a boredom-inspired monologue. "For instance, when I first arrived in the Big Bend there were no trains. A man had to walk or ride a horse to get from one place to another. It was the winter of 1884, and the Mescalero Apaches were angry about our government's insistence that they stay on their reservation in New Mexico. Why in those days …"

Only half-listening to the conductor's long-winded story, Daniel opened the blue glass bottle he had been holding and drank two swallows of the bittersweet laudanum. The conductor talked without interruption about far-west Texas while Daniel's mind drifted to arriving in Marathon—the anticipation of a decent meal, a hot bath, and a good night's sleep between clean sheets.

Yawning, Daniel returned the laudanum bottle to his jacket pocket, nodded at the talkative conductor, closed his eyes, and embraced the narcotic bliss of dreamless sleep.

CHAPTER 2

Marathon, Texas

"Marathon, Texas!"

Daniel sat upright on the wooden bench, gathered his hat, and admired the white steeple of a neatly kept church surrounded by a tight cluster of ramshackle adobe homes. Outside the train, a lone cowboy hurried past, guarding his eyes against the wind with his hand, his scarf tied tight around his face.

"Marathon, Texas!" called the conductor again as he passed forward through the train.

Daniel followed the conductor onto the platform, held his hat by the brim, dipped a shoulder into the wind, and turned toward the baggage car to collect his freight: saddle, rifle, lariat, rain slicker, bedroll, and saddlebags that contained a change of clothes and other necessities. He could carry all of his possessions if the distance was not too far.

After collecting his baggage and squinting against the wind, Daniel moved toward the station and fought the wind as he opened and then closed the station door. Inside, he piled his gear against a wooden bench. The station lobby was empty except for a crackling cast-iron stove. Daniel pulled off his gloves and warmed himself at the stove. Through the barred ticket window, he heard muffled quips of the conductor's conversation with an unseen man inside the station office. Rocking on his boot heels in front of the stove, Daniel alternately warmed his hands, and then his backside.

"Safe travels, sir," called the conductor, passing through the station lobby and back onto the train.

Daniel nodded at the conductor then turned again to face the stove.

The stationmaster was perched on the stool behind the ticket counter, his trousers barely containing his poorly buttoned white shirt. He picked at his bald head and examined the newly arrived stranger. This stranger stood with a straight spine. He was lean and muscled, six-feet tall or more. His face was weather beaten, but he was not like the local desert folks. With obvious curiosity, the stationmaster asked, "Are you in need of a horse, mister?"

"Why? Have you got one back there you're in need of selling?" said Daniel, enjoying the warmth of the stove, not turning to face the stationmaster.

"No, sir, I didn't mean to pry. You certainly don't appear to be a man looking for day labor."

"No, I'm not," said Daniel, his steel-gray eyes glancing over his shoulder at the stationmaster.

"I mean, although you look like a man familiar to hard work, you don't present yourself like the typical sun-baked cowboy around these parts."

Daniel continued to look at the stationmaster but did not respond. He rubbed his hands together in front of the stove, then turned and stared past his reflection in the window, studying the storm.

The stationmaster cleaned his glasses with a white kerchief, inspecting his spectacles against the window light. "What is your destination?"

A cold wind rattled the windowpane. "Terlingua is my final destination."

"I see," exhaled the stationmaster. "Terlingua isn't exactly on the way to any place in particular. You must have a good reason to justify such a journey."

"I was hired to install a furnace at the Chisos Mining Company."

Daniel watched the westbound train climb the low pass into the Del Norte Mountains, the black line of smoke bent by the constant north wind. The station clock rang four times, marking the time.

Stepping into the lobby from inside his office, the stationmaster pulled two short fat cigars from his shirt pocket and introduced himself. "My name is Edgar Clemens. Welcome to Marathon."

Turning to accept the offered cigar, Daniel considered how the simple act of sharing tobacco created a momentary bond between unacquainted men. He leaned forward so that Edgar could light the cigar. Exhaling a cloud of smoke, he said, "Thank you."

"Am I correct in assuming that you have a need for a horse?" asked Edgar.

"Yes, I'm going to need a horse."

"Well, the local cow-men around here generally prefer the stockier quarter horses over the rangy little Mexican ponies, but I recommend that you select a Mexican pony. Besides, it will cost you less."

Daniel nodded and smiled.

Edgar pointed his cigar at Daniel.

"You're a government man, aren't you?"

Daniel bit down on his cigar and reached for his gear. "Thanks for the cigar. I appreciate the hospitality, but I should find the hotel before it starts snowing."

"As it might," said Edgar.

"Where will I find the Chambers Hotel?"

"Walk east along the tracks. The Chambers Hotel is the only two-story building on the south side of the railroad track." Edgar opened the door for Daniel and said, "Remember what I said about Mexican ponies."

"I appreciate both the cigar and your sound advice about horse buying." Daniel adjusted his gear on his shoulder and left the station.

⁓~⁓

Edgar closed the door and watched through the large windowpane as Daniel walked toward the Chambers Hotel. "That man isn't an engineer," he whispered to himself. "He's a filibustering soldier of fortune if I ever saw one."

⁓~⁓

Outside, Daniel moved to the lee side of the railroad station and wrestled his saddle higher on his shoulder. Shoved by the wind, he followed the footpath across the railroad track to a boardwalk leading to the Chambers Hotel. The lobby smelled of fresh coffee and wood smoke.

Relieved to be beyond the wind's grasp, Daniel set down his gear beside the reception desk and surveyed the hotel lobby. He touched one of the ladder-backed chairs and admired the carved oak table covered with dated newspapers and dime novels. The boldest headline on the top newspaper read: "Congress Votes Down the Right to Suffrage for Women."

From over his shoulder, a tentative voice called Daniel from his contemplation.

"May I help you?"

"Yes." Daniel turned to greet the man who had appeared behind the wooden reception counter, his shirt sleeves rolled up, a chewed stub of a pencil in his right hand. Daniel tamped his cigar on a boot heel and slipped it into a jacket pocket. "Howard Perry was supposed to have a room held for me."

The hotel clerk examined his register. "You must be Daniel Taylor."

"I am."

"Yes, your room has indeed been arranged. I'm Anderson."

The men introduced themselves and shook hands. Daniel signed the register, and Anderson handed him the key to his room.

"Room number nine is up the stairs and down the hall on the right. Although supper is served between six and seven, Maggie prefers for guests to be seated by six thirty."

"What would it take to arrange a hot bath?"

"Consider it done. Maggie will give you an exact time at supper. Typically, bathing hours run between seven and nine, depending on how many takers there are. Please let me know if I can be of assistance during your stay."

"Thank you." Daniel nodded to the man and shouldered his gear. He climbed the stairs and made his way down the hall, where the door to his room stood open. Pushing his way inside, he dropped his gear on the worn Navajo rug and hung his hat and jacket on the iron coat hooks on the back of the door. The room was clean and smelled of soap.

Sitting on the quilt-covered feather bed, Daniel pulled off his boots and gazed at his reflection in the mirror above the chest of drawers. He considered the lines etched on his face before he lay down on the bed and closed his tired eyes. Sleep was a constant nightmare.

~~~

Daniel runs along a canal gripping a carbine in his right hand. His left hand braces field glasses against his chest. The thick tropical air is hot and humid. His face pours sweat, and he can feel each individual drop as it trickles down his spine. Running with a dozen men, each struggling to maintain the panicked pace, he feels the men's labored breathing, the scraping of brush, his own heart pounding in his burning chest. Tiny puffs of white smoke mark the staccato crack of targeted rifle fire from the shadows of the overgrown hardwood forest beyond a battle-scarred field of burnt sugar cane. The lethal song of a single bullet precedes each soft, sickening thud: lead colliding with human flesh. Men fall dead. The men run through a rain of bullets until they collide with the Spanish breastworks.

~~~

Determined knuckles on a wood door shattered the dream.

"Mr. Taylor."

It was a woman's voice.

Daniel sat upright, "Yes, ma'am?"

"You'd better get to the table while it's hot."

"Just a minute," called Daniel.

Opening the door, he encountered a stout woman wiping her hands on a yellow dishcloth. She wore a pressed white apron over a blue gingham dress and smelled of lavender soap, wood smoke, biscuits, and bacon.

It took a couple of breaths for Daniel to find his voice. "Good evening, ma'am."

"If you're hungry, wash up and come eat. If you're not hungry, I could wrap a plate and leave it at the front desk."

"No, don't do that. I will wash up and be right down."

"You're not from Texas, are you?"

"Is it that obvious?"

"I can tell that much from a man's voice."

Daniel looked at his socks and self-consciously ran a hand through his hair.

"Ma'am, are you the person to ask about a bath?"

"It has been arranged, Mr. Taylor. You can bathe after supper, which is on the table."

"Thank you." Daniel nodded his head in response, a habit of politeness he had acquired from his father. "I will be right down."

Descending the stairs, Daniel heard argumentative voices long before he entered the dining room where he discovered several men already seated at the table: Mr. Anderson the desk clerk, an army captain, two men in woolen suits with starched white collars, a big man dressed in bib overalls, and the inquisitive stationmaster, Edgar Clemens. Anderson stopped talking midsentence when Daniel entered the room.

"Good evening, gentlemen," said Daniel. Every man said hello in return, each in his own fashion. Daniel joined them at the table, filling his plate with a thick slab of beefsteak, pinto beans, coleslaw, mashed potatoes, brown gravy, pickled okra, a large biscuit, and a generous spoonful of fresh butter.

Anderson waited for Daniel to begin eating before he rekindled the interrupted conversation. "You never answered my question, Captain Henry. How does protecting the international bridge at Presidio keep Mexican bandits from raiding into Texas?"

"It doesn't. Everyone agrees that the situation along our border with Mexico is both frightening and confusing. The federal government is doing everything possible to protect the local citizens. My commanding officer, Colonel Langhorne, is building new camps and requesting more soldiers. Why, just today I dispatched a second lieutenant fresh from West Point to take command of the garrison at Glenn Spring. This single act exemplifies President Wilson's earnest commitment to border security."

"That's exactly the point I'm trying to convey. What good are a few additional soldiers now that Carranza is receiving military aid from the Kaiser himself? How could President Wilson ever find a reason to financially and politically support Carranza when he is allied with the Germans?"

"I can't answer that. No one can predict the result of the war in Mexico. I am a simple soldier, not a historian." The captain softly laughed and said, "I'm certainly not a politician, sir."

"How can President Wilson distinguish who holds legal claim to the head position in the Mexican government, and who we are supposed to fight? When Carranza and Villa united to fight against an illegitimate central government, it was much easier to tease the good from the bad. Now, Carranza and Villa are fighting one another. Not to mention Zapata or all the second-tier generals."

"Northern Mexico appears to incubate bandits like Villa, and henchmen such as Chico Cano, both of whom are revered by the barefoot peons along the Rio Grande as modern-day Robin Hoods. Yet, until the banditry directly threatens the many industrious American citizens who are ranching, mining, and timbering in Mexico, even with this threat of violence, it is unlikely the US Army will become involved in the hostilities." The captain exhaled a long burst of wind before declaring, "But, if we should ultimately invade Mexico, for whatever reason, it will be a quick and simple operation."

Daniel frowned and rolled his eyes.

"I take it that you hold a different opinion?" asked the captain, noticing Daniel's reaction.

"My opinion doesn't matter," said Daniel.

"That's one opinion our friend here doesn't seem to share," replied the captain, causing a nervous ripple of laughter to circle the table.

"What brings you to Marathon?" asked the captain, shifting the conversation to a less-sensitive issue.

Daniel poked at his food. Ignoring the question, he asked, "Where are you posted?"

"Marfa, Texas. I'm a staff officer for Colonel Langhorne."

"And Marfa is where?"

"Marfa is about sixty miles due west of Marathon, some twenty miles west of Alpine."

Looking to Daniel, Anderson asked, "What are your thoughts about the war in Mexico?"

Daniel paused; however, he could find no reason not to speak his mind. "I agree with the captain, mostly. Mexico's regional heroes field large armies of soldiers who are more loyal to their local generals than a central Mexican government. Now that Villa's General Angeles is marching on Saltillo and the oil fields near Tampico, it will be interesting to see what happens next. All I know is, the Mexicans aren't done fighting, or so it seems."

"That is both an interesting and educated perspective, sir," said Captain Henry. "What is your solution to the situation in Mexico?"

"Carranza should have accepted Villa's offer that they both commit suicide," said Daniel with a smile.

Everyone at the table laughed, except the well-dressed men sitting at the far end of the table, one of whom shot Daniel a contemptuous look. For men with money to invest there was nothing humorous about the thought of either Villa or Carranza committing suicide. Mexico needed weapons. Europe required beef. Trading one for the other was a profitable venture. The well-dressed men exchanged offended glances, excused themselves from the table, and carried their coffee into the lobby.

Maggie came through the swinging kitchen door with a pecan pie and placed it on the table. She poured fresh cups of coffee, gathered the empty plates, and doted over the men for a few moments before returning to the kitchen.

Anderson waited for Maggie to leave the room before he said, "If what I hear from Presidio about the army and the Texas Rangers is true, folks down south are leaving the area because it's not safe to stay on their ranches."

Edgar raised his hand for emphasis before interjecting, "I heard that even Langford is thinking about moving his family to El Paso until the war is settled."

Narrowing his eyes, the captain did not respond. A tense silence settled upon the table.

Daniel ate a generous slice of pecan pie and silently considered Anderson's remarks. He could not decide if Anderson was genuinely possessed with a fear of the war in Mexico erupting along the Texas border, or if he actually enjoyed baiting the captain. It made sense there would be friction between local residents and an army of occupation, even if it were the US Army.

Abruptly, Captain Henry stood. "Gentlemen, if you will excuse me, I need to get something for my digestion." As he left the room, the captain scowled toward Anderson.

Edgar watched the captain leave the room before placing his right hand on the shoulder of the big man dressed in overalls seated at his side. "Daniel, this is Ben Stapleton. He has a horse for you."

"Glad to meet you, sir," said Daniel, shaking the man's calloused hand.

"You are here to collect the horse that Howard Perry paid for?"

"Yes, sir, I am."

Anderson excused himself and left the table.

"I've got just the horse for your needs."

"Thank you, sir."

"The horse I have in mind is a three-year-old gelding that was foaled down south. He is mostly Mexican stock, a good trail horse with a bit of an attitude, which I take as a positive trait."

"I appreciate your opinion," said Daniel. "When can I see him?"

"Any time after first light will do." Finished with both his supper and his business, Ben rose from his chair and excused himself. He pulled on his wool coat and settled his felt-brimmed hat on his head. Ben opened the door, and snow swirled into the room. The night air was thick with wildly swirling snowflakes, and a thin blanket of snow had covered the yard.

Edgar stood with a spring and worked his hands along his belt in a failed attempt to keep his shirt and belly contained. "It will be a spell before you eat like this again."

"It might."

"Good luck with your horse and your business in Terlingua."

"Thank you."

Edgar set his chair back under the table and left the room.

Daniel turned in his chair to the frost-laced window and stared into the snow-covered night. There was a thermometer nailed to the outside window frame. It read nine degrees. He could feel the cold as it seeped through the thin windowpane. His mind drifted to the young, inexperienced second lieutenant that Captain Henry had dispatched south ... how the young man was all alone, possibly for the first time in his entire life, in an unfamiliar place, in this brutal winter storm.

Daniel failed to notice that Maggie had slipped back into the room. She cleared her throat before she spoke quietly. "Your bath is ready."

"Thank you, ma'am," said Daniel, turning to face Maggie.

"You worried about that storm?"

"No, ma'am, I was thinking about that young lieutenant."

"You know him?"

"Not personally, ma'am. I just can't help but feel that once upon a time, a very long time ago, I was him."

~~~~~

Daniel eased into a brass tub of hot, soapy water.

The conversation at the supper table, and the idea of that young lieutenant riding south to his first posting, had stirred old memories of Cuba. He knew from personal experience how fervently young soldiers dream of war. West Point does that to a man. Daniel's own military career had been a chaotic medley of opportunity, success, and misfortune.

The USS *Maine* had mysteriously exploded in the Havana Harbor in February of 1898, and in May, Second Lieutenant Daniel Taylor arrived in Havana fresh from West Point with the initial deployment of American infantry. His first assignment had been overseeing the logistics of receiving and sorting men and supplies, and he had been desperate for a reassignment to a cavalry troop. Angry at his rotten luck, he could not tolerate the idea of spending the entirety of this fine little war counting heads and shouting directions at soldiers and horses.

Daniel reached for his pewter flask of Tennessee whiskey and took a long drink before sinking deeper into the soapy embrace of the steaming hot water.

For eighteen hours each day, Daniel had documented and distributed cargo, signed inventories, and organized civilian work details to unload and reload the enormous fleet of cargo ships. By the end of his first week in Havana Harbor, Daniel was constantly complaining about his disappointment to anyone who appeared to listen, although not a single fellow officer sympathized with his attitude. His peers were quite happy with the duties of port logistics, which kept them safe from the rigors of combat. Daniel expressed his frustration to his commanding officer, Captain Thomas.

Captain Thomas was a nervous man. He would shake his bent right index finger in the air in response to Daniel's complaints and stammer, "Don't be a fool, son. You should spend this lovely war drinking rum, dancing with pretty women, sleeping in a good hotel bed, and eating three meals every damn day. Cuba is nothing more than a damnable, disease-ridden, insect-infested jungle. Not to mention all those Spaniards and barefooted peasants taking shots at a person both day and night. I plan to survive this war. And you would be well advised to do the same."

Fate had intervened; word arrived that Samuel Jenkins was to arrive in Havana with a detachment of Teddy Roosevelt's Volunteer Cavalry. Daniel and Samuel had been roommates at West Point. Born and raised in El Paso, Texas, Samuel was a small man with large hands and big opinions. Daniel remembered Samuel as a man who was quick to pick a fight. When Samuel and his men came ashore, Daniel was standing at the bottom of the gangplank. That very same night, in a smoky cantina crowded with drunken soldiers, Daniel explained his frustration to Samuel, who agreed to help his friend secure a more interesting posting. It took Samuel only two days to negotiate Daniel an immediate assignment with C Troop of the Tenth Cavalry, the famed "Buffalo Soldiers." The enlisted men and noncommissioned officers of the Tenth Cavalry had all been Negroes, whereas the officers were strictly white men.

A sharp, single knock on the bathroom door beckoned Daniel from his daydream. Before he could speak or properly react, a portly Mexican woman entered the bathing room. The old woman was an apparition shrouded in steam, and her shoulders were stooped by her burden—a fresh pail of hot water.

Daniel acknowledged the matron's sense of business and relaxed. "*Gracias, señora.*"

"*Da nada, señor,*" said the old woman, never looking up from her task of adding the water to the bath.

In order to avoid a scalding, Daniel moved to one side as the old woman poured the pail of hot water into the tub. When she was finished, she left the room. Daniel settled back into the tub and closed his eyes.

He had not intended to remain in Cuba after the war until he discovered Rosa. Love can alter a man's expected course. It had happened during a patrol along a coconut tree–lined beach. Rosa had stood barefoot in the shadow of the veranda of her father's summerhouse, slowly combing her freshly washed, raven-black hair. His mind grasped at the memory of her white cotton dress clinging against her damp buttocks. The spark of romance between them had been immediate and intense. They were married three weeks after meeting. His favorite memory remained—Rosa dancing naked in their open-air bedroom. Oh, how she had laughed with the sheer joy of uninhibited desire. Rosa passionately and intelligently contested his version of history. They argued constantly about politics and history. How he missed her soliloquies, her lengthy oratories spoken with emotional authority about the French Revolution, her lamentation over the dilution of Carib culture through slavery, and the unfortunate results of too many years of European and American colonial interventions. Rosa had infused his life with passion. Daniel had loved Rosa unconditionally. It had shattered his soul when she died in his arms, four months pregnant. The fever quickly took her. In the short span of a few hours, she was gone forever.

Daniel reached beyond the tub for the bottle of laudanum. Liquor helped, but only opium dissolved the painful image seared in his mind—the Angel of Death carrying Rosa away. He unscrewed the lid and took a long drink. Closing his eyes, he sank into the hot water. His heart remained unhealed after all the years.

CHAPTER 3

Second Lieutenant Jack Thompson

SECOND LIEUTENANT JACK Thompson left Marathon before daylight, excited to be in the field and headed to his first official posting since leaving West Point: D Troop of the Ninth Cavalry at Glenn Spring, Texas.

Living the dream, the lieutenant rode onto a vast savanna of grass, brush, and mesquite trees beneath a spectacular canopy of predawn stars. He stopped to water his horse at Peña Colorado Spring, where daylight revealed a menacing bank of clouds lining the northern horizon.

Nurturing an escalating sense of concern about the impending storm, the lieutenant glanced nervously over his shoulder as he continued to ride south. He repeatedly cursed the fast-moving clouds as they settled upon the desert. By midafternoon, the advancing storm clouds had obscured the upper portion of Santiago Mountain, casting an eerie twilight. When the snow finally came, it pelted his head and shoulders.

Accepting the inevitable, the lieutenant stopped his mare to put on his rain slicker, and then continued south at a much slower pace. The snow thickened, covering both man and horse as daylight receded beyond the western mountains. Shivering, the lieutenant leaned forward against his horse, finding solace in his mother's favorite prayers.

A single raven flew past riding the cold north wind that sculpted deepening snowdrifts over the two-track road. It soon became impossible to see beyond his horse, and he worried that four years at West Point had not prepared him for this moment. The lieutenant was scared and did not know what to do, except to push on. He was delirious with fear.

Crossing a snow-covered arroyo, his horse stumbled and threw him to the ground. Stunned from the fall, the wind knocked from his lungs, he watched the spooked mare disappear into a curtain of snow.

"Damn it to hell," the lieutenant cursed, shaking his head. He pushed himself onto his hands and knees, and struck the ground with his fist as he struggled to regain his composure. After slowly rising to his feet, he tried to follow the mare, but she was lost to the storm. Even her tracks were gone, buried in the rapidly accumulating snow.

Cold and confused, the young soldier sought shelter against a rock ledge beneath a thicket of mesquite and considered his options. His shoulder and chest ached from the fall, his feet felt frostbitten, his hands were numb, and his damn horse had run off into the blinding snowstorm! What a fine way to begin his first assignment.

Gathering his nerve, he built a fire and waited.

The storm lifted not long after midnight. The night air turned bitter cold, and the sky throbbed with stars. There were so many stars in the coal-black sky that it took a very long time for the discouraged lieutenant to locate a single constellation. After an exhausting search for familiar stars, he found Orion. The presence of the warrior with his hunting dogs confronting Taurus the Bull brought a sense of comfort to the frightened young man. Using Orion as a starting point in the night sky, he identified the familiar stars of the winter circle. There were Castor and Pollux in Gemini; Capella in the constellation Auriga; and Sirius, the brightest object in the night sky.

The lieutenant poked at the fire with a stout mesquite stick and considered another attempt to look for his horse, but he could not find the courage to leave the fire and its lifesaving warmth. He tended the fire until Scorpio rose in the eastern sky. Only after the rising sun breeched the southeast horizon did he step away from the fire.

The muffled desert landscape appeared transformed. Snow clung to the tallest yuccas like carefully placed Christmas tree decorations. Purple-hued prickly pear cactus penetrated through the delicate quilt of snow that embraced the desert. The long cold night had humbled his pride.

Stomping his feet for warmth, the lieutenant walked a short distance to a low hill that rose above the open valley. The weak winter sun sparkled against the snow, causing him to squint as he looked for his horse.

"She had to have gone north toward Marathon," he said aloud, too tired to complain about what needed doing.

Using Santiago Peak as a landmark, the lieutenant made his way north through the snow-covered desert. He no longer dreamed of the war in Mexico and the opportunity to lead soldiers into combat. All he wanted was to find his damn horse.

CHAPTER 4

Marshal Navarro

SERGEANT MCKINNEY CLOSED his eyes, slouched in the saddle, and listened to the bored chatter of the soldiers at the front of the moving column.

"Hawk," called Private Harlow, as Corporal Hawkins suffered a violent cough. Harlow waited for Hawkins to quit coughing but did not wait for him to respond. "You think Marshal Navarro enjoys trouble?"

It took Hawkins a moment to clear his throat. "What do you mean by trouble?"

"I mean, he drags us around after all these Mexicans, very few of whom are troublemakers, and seems to enjoy harassing them."

"Not all of them are as nice as those girls in Glenn Spring," replied Hawkins, laughing.

"You know it ain't against the law to carry sotol across the border," said Harlow.

"It is if you don't expect to pay taxes. Men who are smuggling moonshine liquor north will steal most anything when they are going south—be it horses, mules, burros, goats, chickens, and who knows what all else. Harlow, from the way Navarro tells it, most of these bandits would just as soon cut your throat as shake your hand."

"Ain't Navarro a federal marshal?" insisted Harlow. "Is it really his job to run down every chicken thief that runs for the border? Is it?"

"No, but he seems intent on making sure that every Mexican with a gun that crosses the Rio Grande is fearful of the very mention of his name," explained Hawkins, buttoning his tunic collar tight around his neck.

"You cold?" asked Private Owen.

"To the bone," said Hawkins.

"We're headed back to Glenn Spring tonight, aren't we?" asked Private Owen.

"Although it appears we are, I wouldn't bet on it," muttered Harlow. "Lately, I've been feeling like a prize bull with a brass nose ring."

Sergeant McKinney straightened in the saddle and cast a hard look across his shoulder, ending the men's conversation. He generally tolerated their complaints, as he too had grown weary of Navarro being in charge. These last four days in the saddle chasing rumors of armed bandits had consumed McKinney's limited patience. He was ready for the new lieutenant to arrive; however, he knew from experience that a greenhorn second lieutenant was not a proper match for Navarro.

Marshal Navarro raised his right hand, and McKinney repeated the signal. The column halted, and the soldiers sat on their horses in the gathering darkness.

McKinney followed Navarro's gaze toward the cloud-shrouded mesa paralleling the arroyo. In scanning the ridge for movement, he saw nothing but rock and cactus.

The bitter north wind had sharpened its assault upon the inhabitants of the sparsely populated savanna.

As night fell, snow suddenly began to fall, and Corporal Hawkins spit an inaudible curse.

An unseen coyote howled three mournful times.

McKinney signaled the soldiers to hold in place and rode to where Navarro sat his horse. "What did you hear?"

"I heard a rock fall," said Navarro, shouldering his rifle. He took careful aim and squeezed off a shot. The muzzle flash lit the night, and the explosion of noise startled the horses.

"Find a place to make camp," commanded Navarro, sheathing his rifle.

"You want us to check that ridge?"

"Like I said, make camp."

McKinney watched Navarro encourage his horse up the graveled bank and out of the arroyo, and then turned to the mounted soldiers waiting in the dry wash. "Corporal Hawkins!"

Corporal Hawkins rode alongside McKinney. "What did he shoot at?"

"He heard a rock fall."

"He shot at a rock?"

"Yeah, he shot at a rock," McKinney said, laughing.

"Did he see anything?"

"Hawkins, it is damn near impossible to say what that man sees in the dark. Take Owen and ride the creek until you find a suitable camp, then report back. Get it done before this damn snow sticks to the ground, Corporal."

"Yes, Sergeant," said Hawkins, saluting. "Owen," he shouted, spurring his horse south along Tornillo Creek.

As commanded, Private Owen followed in the wake of the corporal's horse.

CHAPTER 5

Samuel Jenkins

COLD, GRAY CLOUDS flooded the sky as darkness eased across the desert.

Samuel Jenkins ground-hitched his horse beneath a weathered outcrop of igneous rock and examined the gathering storm. The air smelled of snow. He beat his arms about his chest for warmth, then buttoned the top button on his denim jacket and tied a black silk kerchief around his neck, knowing that the scarf was thin protection against the frigid air.

Rifle in his right hand, Samuel made his way up the ridge through the broken rocks and thorn brush, being extra careful to avoid the spine-tipped clumps of lechuguilla. Upon reaching the caprock of the mesa top, Samuel squatted on his heels and peered through the veil of descending clouds into a failing light. He quickly spied the column of soldiers riding north along Tornillo Creek. The men looked tired in the saddle. A civilian rode some fifty yards in front of the column.

"Marshal Navarro," spit Samuel.

Sneaking along the rimrock, he followed the patrol's progress. Razor-sharp sotol leaves grabbed at his legs, and catclaw acacia snagged his jacket sleeves. Samuel stumbled, hitting his right knee on the rain-dimpled limestone caprock causing a fist-sized rock to fall from the cliff. He hugged the weathered limestone and held his breath as the rock crashed through the darkness.

When the rock stopped falling, a single coyote howled three times.

Samuel took a deep breath and raised his head to see a distant gunshot illuminate the darkness; an immediate explosion of limestone shrapnel peppered his right cheek. He collapsed onto his belly, grabbed his face and cursed, "Damn you, Navarro."

Wiping blood and small fragments of stone from his cheek, Samuel retreated off the rimrock. He hurried through the desert maze of thorns until a sharp jab punctured his left calf. Dropping to one knee, he carefully pulled the fibrous tip of a lechuguilla spine from his calf with a determined tug.

Hampered now with a significant limp, Samuel ran the final distance to his horse and sheathed his rifle. He rubbed his aching calf, calmed his breath, and listened for the sound of approaching horses. Hearing nothing except the rush of the cold wind and the muffled hush of falling snow, Samuel rose into the saddle and spurred his stallion.

The horse sensed danger too, and ran hard against the storm.

CHAPTER 6

La Familia Torreón,
Boquillas del Carmen, Mexico

MARIO TORREÓN WOKE to the sound of burros outside a shuttered bedroom window. The smell of fresh coffee made him smile. He sat up in bed and touched his face. It was an old ritual. Every morning, the instant he awoke, Mario always felt the thick scar that marked a curve that began at the tear duct of his missing left eye and ran downward across his check.

Sitting on the edge of the bed, Mario found his leather moccasins and reached for the wool poncho hanging from a bedpost. Stiff with age, he walked to the kitchen where his niece was toasting tortillas on a cast-iron comal.

"*Buenos días*," said Mario, yawing with an exaggerated stretch.

"Good morning, uncle," answered Ramona, pushing her long black hair behind her ears.

Mario kissed his niece on the crown of her head. "I had better check on the boys." Stepping outside, he cinched the poncho at his waist and allowed a moment for his one good eye to adjust to the star-blanketed darkness. He paused to consider the weather; the bitter north wind smelled of snow.

Walking to the rock dugout that served as a barn, Mario stopped to relieve himself against the dry-stack flagstone corral. He counted the loaded pack mules in the corral and listened to his oldest grandson

25

singing a *corrido* about marching to war. When he saw the unsaddled horses, he shouted, "Tomás! Is everything ready?"

Tomás stepped from the dugout rock barn and answered his grandfather. "The mules are ready. The horses are not. That was Chato's job, remember?"

"Where is Chato?" asked Mario, going to inspect the pack mules' rigging.

"Sleeping?" Tomás said. "I tried to wake him, but he refused."

Mario cursed and turned back to the house.

"That lazy bastard deserves a good beating," murmured Tomás. He filled his cob pipe and sparked a match before returning to his chores.

Inside the house, Mario jerked Chato from his bed. He pulled the twelve-year-old boy to his feet and demanded that he get to his chores. It frustrated Mario to no end that Chato took the rough treatment without complaining. He understood the boy's mind. The back of his grandfather's hand was simply the price he paid for sleeping late.

Escaping his grandfather's grasp, Chato raced through the house, grabbed a warm tortilla from the pile on the kitchen table, and ran to his neglected chores.

"Don't slam the door!" scolded Ramona.

Mario returned into the kitchen buttoning a blue, long-sleeved chambray shirt. He sat at the metal table. "Where are your daughters?"

"Ofelia is with Sergio. She will be here soon," explained Ramona, handing Mario a cup of coffee.

"And little Carmelina, where is she?" asked Mario, wrapping his hands around the blue enamel cup, comforted by the warmth.

"She is sleeping in my bed," said Ramona, rolling burritos into butcher paper.

"How old is she now?"

"Eight."

Mario silently reflected about his niece as he watched Ramona prepare breakfast. She was in her early thirties, the prime years of her life. Ramona was a most peculiar woman—beautiful, mature, well informed, and quick to speak her mind. She was more than capable of working alongside the men at any task, yet she appeared happiest in the kitchen caring for her extended family. She was almost three years a widow, and her feminine yet muscular body and piercing green eyes intimidated most men.

"You worry too much," said Mario, sipping his coffee.

Ramona turned and faced her uncle, who had kindly welcomed her into his house after her husband had died in a tunnel collapse at the Puerta Rica Mine. "I worry for my two daughters. And now that Ofelia is pregnant …" She glanced at the ceiling, making the sign of the cross. "There is so much responsibility since …" Unwilling to speak of her deceased husband, Ramona stopped midsentence.

"Now that Sergio has claimed her baby, our lives are already much calmer." Mario took a tortilla from the warm pile wrapped in a clean blue cloth on the table. He tore the tortilla into pieces and scooped up a combination of eggs and beans. "I will worry for both of us," said Mario, pulling on his thick mutton-chop mustache.

Ramona wiped the hint of a tear from the corner of her right eye and smiled.

Tomás returned to the kitchen.

"Is everything ready?" Mario asked.

"It's ready."

"Where is Chato?"

"Watering the mules," said Tomás, pouring himself a cup of coffee before he sat down at the table. "Why can't we leave Chato and take Sergio?"

"Because I'm going with you," explained Ramona. "And you know we cannot trust Chato to stay and watch the house." Ramona sat a plate of food in front of Tomás. "Eat so we can go."

Tomás scowled at Ramona but did as instructed.

Mario pushed his plate aside and sipped his coffee. "Tomás, what news do you have about the most recent events in Mexico City?"

Tomás sat upright in his chair. "They say President Gutierrez has fled the capital with ten thousand men leaving Roque Gonzalez de la Garza as his representative."

"Isn't de la Garza a *Villista*?" Mario asked.

"Yes," answered Tomás.

Chato returned from his chores and joined them at the table. Ramona handed him a plate of food and a cup of coffee sweetened with goat's milk and honey, just the way he liked it.

"Is Villa still sitting in Mexico City?" asked Mario.

"I think not, because just last week his General Angeles defeated Carranza's General Villarreal in the battle for Saltillo."

"Who is your champion now?" Mario asked.

"Certainly not Villa," said Tomás scowling. "Villa is a thieving, whoring bastard."

Mario laughed. "Have you just realized that Pancho Villa is a thief?"

Tomás had grown numb to the old man's constant sarcasm, yet he was compelled to defend his limited ideas of the war in Mexico. "Villa has always been a thief, and it's quite obvious that Carranza has gained the support of the American president, which is necessary for any real victory."

"I had hoped you would agree with your father, as he is fighting for Carranza," said Mario. "A family should not be at war with itself."

"Carranza is no better than Villa," said Ramona, interjecting her opinion without hesitation. "José fights with Carranza because he hails from Coahuila, not because he is a better man."

Mario smiled. Carranza was indeed a rapscallion, having schemed to commit general banditry in the lower Rio Grande Valley in hopes that the gullible Americans would recognize his claim to the presidency in exchange for a promise of law and order along the border. Although, listening to Ramona and Tomás argue about the war entertained Mario, it also saddened his heart. He knew that Tomás was a moth yearning for the flame of war. Inevitably, Tomás would slip south to join his father in the bloody war that consumed Mexico.

Ofelia entered the kitchen rubbing her eyes.

"There she is," said Mario. He pushed his chair back from the table and stood. "We had better get going. Samuel will be waiting."

CHAPTER 7

Cabron

DANIEL WOKE BEFORE sunrise, shaved at the basin in his room, dressed, and went in search of the privy. Stars blanketed the moonless sky. The crisp air crystallized his breath. He found the outhouse by following a woman's footprints crunched in the thin crust of snow, where a single candle softly illuminated his choice of two seats inside the well-maintained toilet. Daniel surveyed the interesting assortment of magazines and catalogs, some of which were in Spanish, all missing pages.

He picked up a newspaper as he sat down, intrigued by the bold print headline that read, "Angeles Defeats Carranza in Monterrey." The article explained how Carranza's army had fled, leaving behind three thousand prisoners, a dozen locomotives, and twenty wagons loaded with ammunition.

In Daniel's mind, the war in Mexico was both fascinating and confusing. It seemed impossible to determine who held the upper hand. Carranza, the most polished politician among the war leaders, appeared to have the most influence with the American government. Zapata and Villa appeared to have the most popular support. After hearing the lively conversation last night, Daniel was eager to gauge the effect of the war in Mexico on the local citizens, both Texan and Mexican.

Back in his room, Daniel washed in the porcelain basin and checked his pocket watch. He concluded that he could indeed be riding south by midmorning if the horse buying went smoothly. He organized his gear and went downstairs to the kitchen where he found Maggie and the Mexican woman who had refreshed his bath water last night. Together, they were scrambling eggs, flipping hot cakes, kneading tortilla *masa*, and making salsa.

"Buenos días, señoras," called Daniel upon entering the kitchen. "It smells good in here."

Maggie looked up from her work and returned his smile.

Out of habit, the older Mexican woman asked, "How did you sleep?" in Spanish.

"Acostado con mis ojos cerrados," answered Daniel.

"Your Spanish is better than most," said Maggie with a laugh, repeating the phrase in English. "On my back, with my eyes closed. Most Anglos don't know enough Spanish to solve her riddles." Maggie pulled a large iron skillet away from the hottest part of the wood-fired stove.

"Thank you, ma'am."

"Do you need something, Mr. Taylor?" Maggie asked while spooning eggs cooked with chilies, tomatoes, onions, cilantro, and bacon onto a large blue china platter.

"Yes, ma'am, I do." Daniel sheepishly held his brimmed hat with both hands. "Would it be possible to buy some refried beans, bacon, and tortillas for my ride south?"

"When do you plan on leaving?"

"That depends on how long it takes to do business with Ben Stapleton. I hope to be headed south around nine, no later than nine thirty."

"I will have some food packed and ready for you before nine," said Maggie, gathering the platter of eggs from the tiled kitchen table.

Daniel pushed open the swinging door to the dining room.

Maggie walked through the open door, pausing briefly to say, "Why thank you, sir. And as a reward for your good manners, I might surprise you with an apple muffin." She smiled, placing the platter on the table, and immediately took to helping the men seated at the table in passing the heaviest dishes.

Daniel was impressed with Maggie's transition from the kitchen to the table and her focus on the work at hand. On his way around the table, he smiled at the captain and patted Anderson on the shoulder. "Good morning, gentlemen."

Anderson looked up from his plate and smiled.

An older Mexican man entered the room and sat down at the far end of the table, placing his hat in his lap. His face was red and raw. Three more Mexicans, each dressed in denim britches, blue chambray shirts, and wool ponchos tied at the waist with braided cords of rope, joined the man at the far end of the table. Daniel recognized the men as teamsters—wagon drivers. The men were humble and quiet. They ate without making eye contact with any of the gringos.

"What do you think about the weather?" asked Anderson.

"It seems a fine day for traveling," said Daniel. "A bit cold in the morning and perhaps muddy this afternoon if the sun warms things too much, but otherwise it appears a most beautiful day for traveling south." Tearing a corn tortilla in half, Daniel scooped up a bite of eggs. He noticed that Captain Henry ate with a scowl and appeared quite irritable, eyes firmly gripping his plate. The man looked uncomfortable and out of sorts.

Anderson finished his breakfast, excused himself, and left the table.

The Mexican teamsters got up from the table before Daniel could engage them in conversation. Daniel watched the Mexicans through the dining room window as they walked to their wagons parked alongside the railroad track. The oldest of the Mexicans picked his teeth with a stick match while being verbally and physically harassed by the youngest driver. He considered their world for a moment, trying his best to orient himself to this place.

Daniel wiped his face with a cloth napkin, got up from the table, walked to the reception desk, and asked Anderson, "What do I owe?"

"All we need is a signature," said Anderson, opening his ledger.

"What about the food Maggie packed?"

"That is included."

"All you need is a signature?"

"That's it."

Daniel signed the invoice. "Should I take a copy to Perry?"

"No, that won't be necessary," said Anderson, filing the receipt.

"Those men at the table," said Daniel.

"The Mexican teamsters, you mean? What about them?"

"Where are they from?"

"Boquillas, Mexico," said Anderson.

"What are they hauling?"

"Iron ore from the Puerta Rica Mine."

"How far is it to Boquillas?"

"About one hundred miles, they say. It is confusing as there are actually two villages only a few miles apart, both named Boquillas."

"Seriously?" replied Daniel.

"Yes, sir," said Anderson. There is a Boquillas, Mexico, on the south bank of the Rio Grande. It is near the entrance to Boquillas Canyon, directly opposite La Noria, Texas. La Noria is where those teamsters load their wagons with iron ore from the Puerta Rica mine. The cable tram that spans the river that delivers the ore into Texas is a most remarkable engineering accomplishment."

"Interesting," said Daniel.

"And, there is a Boquillas, Texas, which consists of a store and some farms that raise produce for the mining community of Boquillas over in Mexico."

"That is confusing."

"No doubt," said Anderson with a chuckle. "Folks here often distinguish between the two communities by calling Boquillas, Texas, 'the other Boquillas.'"

Daniel nodded his head and smiled. He truly appreciated the information, but he sensed the man's anxiety to get back to his work. "Thank you for the hospitality."

"It's our pleasure to serve you," said Anderson.

Slipping on his jacket, Daniel tied a kerchief around his neck and stepped outside into the cold where he discovered Ben Stapleton tying a short-legged, chestnut-colored gelding to a hitching post.

"Is this the horse?" Daniel asked.

"It is," said Ben, rubbing his gloved hands together for warmth.

Daniel stood close to the horse and allowed the gelding to sniff at his hands. The animal was the color of freshly ground cinnamon. There was a fractured white star on the bridge of his nose between dark brown eyes. When the horse relaxed his ears, Daniel scratched his face.

"Would you mind if I take him for a quick ride?"

"No, sir. Take all the time you need to decide," said Ben. "I will go eat."

Daniel loosened the bridle reigns tied to the hitching post and patted his hands along the gelding's shoulder and flank. He judged the horse's breath, and then rose into the saddle.

The gelding startled but did not move.

Daniel spoke softly in Spanish to the horse and nudged it forward, reining the spirited gelding into the frozen field beyond the railroad tracks north of the hotel. He heeled the horse with the rowels of his spurs, and they headed north toward burnt-red mountains; man and horse galloped across a mesa of closely cropped bunch grass and stunted yuccas. After a good hard run, Daniel reined the horse to a stop and admired the view.

The gelding shook from head to tail, adjusting the position of saddle and rider on his back. Both man and horse breathed hard against the cold morning air.

Daniel wiped his forehead with a kerchief and laughed. "You remind me of an old goat my father owned when I was a kid." He thought for a moment then told the horse, "Regardless of what Ben called you, as of today, your name is Cabron."

CHAPTER 8

The Road South

DANIEL RODE INTO the Big Bend on his newly acquired horse. Cabron proved to be a fine companion, most responsive to commands given in Spanish.

The road south ran through a valley of exposed limestone flatirons, metamorphic rock bent into geologic waves turned upside down in places. Indian willow seedpods rattled the breeze. A cactus wren complained from a bent yucca. Daniel traveled as he pleased, taking the time to inspect an unfamiliar plant or unique rock formation as he rode through a desert grassland softened by an evaporating quilt of snow. Santiago Peak provided a gauge for his progress across the uninhabited savanna.

Midday, Daniel stopped for lunch under the shade of a weathered mesquite tree and ate the last of the food he had brought with him on the train. It was a simple meal of canned sardines and saltine crackers. After he ate, Daniel lay on his back, drank whiskey, and watched a red-tailed hawk twirl lazy spirals in the azure sky. In his solitude, he marveled at the sheer beauty of the broad sweep of majestic mountains that spilled across the Rio Grande into Mexico.

After wiping a mealy red apple on his sleeve, he pulled a long knife from his boot and cut the apple into quarter pieces. Cabron, who had been watching his new master with interest, nudged his shoulder, pushing him onto his side.

"So you like apples?" Daniel laughed and offered the horse a piece.

Cabron begged for more.

"Okay," said Daniel, giving the horse the last piece. "You are doing most of the work, aren't you?"

Cabron bobbed his head as if he understood, making Daniel laugh even harder as he rose and climbed back into the saddle. He tested the stirrups before nudging Cabron back onto the road south. He pulled the pewter flask from his jacket pocket and threw back the last swallows of his Tennessee sipping whiskey.

The road south remained frozen in the most shaded of places, yet it was quite muddy where it lay fully exposed to the sun's warmth. Riding across a long, open stretch of creosote brush draped in melting snow, Daniel noticed a lone horse standing in the road. Even at a distance, he could tell by the rigging that it was an army-issued horse. In assessing the situation, Daniel reached beneath his jacket and loosened the thumb strap on the pistol in his shoulder holster. Only then did he approach the obviously frightened animal.

The abandoned mare stood stiff-legged with her ears thrown back. Eyes flared, she sniffed the air.

Daniel slid to the ground and walked closer, speaking to calm the horse. "Whoa. Easy girl. There's no reason to be afraid."

Her ears pinned to her head, the mare took a half step backwards.

Slowly gathering the loose reins from the ground, Daniel allowed the mare to adjust to his presence before touching her neck. After gaining her confidence, he inspected the horse for signs of injuries. She seemed okay—a bit spooked but not hurt.

"Where's your rider, girl?" Daniel asked.

The mare snorted and shook her head.

Daniel brought the frightened horse toward his gelding and allowed the horses a moment to become acquainted. Continuing south, he rode with a renewed sense of alertness, leading the mare. It worried him to consider what calamity might have separated the rider from his horse.

Within the hour, Daniel spied a man walking north. The man wore a khaki army uniform with the insignia of a second lieutenant. It had to be the lost rider. The young officer looked angry as he watched Daniel approach. Daniel offered him the reins to the horse. "Is this yours?"

"Yes, it is." The lieutenant grabbed a canteen from his saddle and took a long drink of water.

"Are you okay?"

The lieutenant frowned. "My horse took a fall during the worst of the storm and she got away from me. My shoulder hurts, and to be honest, I damn near froze to death last night. Otherwise, I am fine … thank you," said the lieutenant, easing into the saddle. "Thank you for returning my horse, sir."

"You are traveling south, are you not?" Daniel asked.

"I am."

"Then we should ride together," offered Daniel.

"Sounds fine to me," said the lieutenant.

The men shook hands and shared introductions.

"I really do appreciate you finding and returning my horse."

"It's my pleasure." Daniel recognized himself in the young officer and wanted to put the man at ease "When did you graduate from West Point?"

The lieutenant's face flushed. "Is it that obvious?"

"For me it is. I graduated with the Class of '97."

"Well I'll be damned!" The lieutenant laughed. "I just graduated with the Class of 1914."

"Where are you from?" Daniel asked.

"Texarkana. And you?"

"Johnson City, Tennessee."

"Did you serve in the Philippines?"

"Unfortunately, yes."

"What a great opportunity!"

"For some, I guess."

"And your rank?"

"Full colonel," replied Daniel.

"What caused you to leave the army?"

Daniel looked at the lieutenant and considered his response. "That's a long story, but maybe I will tell it over a bottle sometime."

A broad smile creased the lieutenant's face.

"What are you grinning about?"

"I feel fortunate to have met you today."

"You would have found your horse, given time."

"After what I endured last night, I thought my luck had run out. There is a word for us meeting this way." The lieutenant looked up at the clear blue sky as if searching his mind. "*Serendipity* is the word I'm looking for. Our happenstance meeting here in the middle of nowhere does seem fortuitous. What with me fresh out of West Point and you done with the army and leaving it all behind. Last night, I doubted everything. Today, I'm excited to be a soldier again."

"One man's happiness is another man's misery," said Daniel. "You know that you aren't the first second lieutenant to have a rough go on his first assignment."

"What brings you into this country?" asked the lieutenant, ignoring the older man's sarcasm.

"I have employment with the Chisos Mining Company in Terlingua."

"Doing what?"

"I've been hired to install a new smelter at the mine."

"They mine quicksilver?"

"Yes, quicksilver—mercury," said Daniel.

"Were you an engineer in the army?"

"No, I was a cavalry officer."

"So, where did you learn about smelters?"

"Back home in Tennessee," said Daniel, weary of the frequent inquiries from everyone he met about his profession and personal history.

"Interesting," said the lieutenant. "Seems like a long reach to find an engineer."

"I have a friend who works with the owner."

"Is he an engineer too?"

Daniel removed his hat and ran his hand through his hair. "No, Samuel Jenkins is an investor."

Sitting upright in his saddle, the lieutenant said, "Investor, you say?"

"You seemed bothered by the mention of his name. You know of him?"

The lieutenant glanced at Daniel and said, "I have heard that name mentioned. My commanding officer said that Samuel Jenkins is a notorious smuggler and war profiteer … that he is a man not to be trusted."

Daniel shook his head and laughed aloud. "I don't honestly know much about his business, or if he truly merits the title of 'notorious.' All I do know is that he helped me secure employment with Howard Perry at the Chisos Mining Company. Samuel and I were classmates at West Point. In Cuba, Samuel rode with Roosevelt's Rough Riders, whereas I served with the Tenth Cavalry."

"The Tenth Cavalry—those were Buffalo Soldiers, were they not?"

"They were."

Unable to resist the young officer's enthusiasm, Daniel entertained the lieutenant with stories of Cuba. Mesmerized, the lieutenant plied Daniel with questions. Surprisingly, Daniel took a liking to the young man. He told the young officer about the frightening day when he led Buffalo Soldiers up Kettle Hill, and how he was wounded in the leg with a long-bladed knife by a dying Spanish colonel. Daniel lifted his pant leg to show the lieutenant the dead man's knife that he carried in his right boot. This was the first time Daniel had spoken about his war experiences since returning from the Philippines. He saw himself in this young lieutenant and considered how the mechanics of fate had pushed them together in such a wide-open place.

The men rode without incident and made camp under an overhanging ledge of wind-and-rain-polished limestone blackened by the smoke of many previous campfires. That night, Daniel dreamed of Cuba.

Sergeant Johnston is a good soldier who enjoys the respect of both his men and superiors. He keeps the men organized as they travel to war on the miserable, stinking boats from Guantanamo Bay to the long sandy beaches near the coastal town of Ocuial. The ship reeks of vomit and horse manure. A boson's whistle pierces the air, and sailors scream at the horses making them hurl themselves into the rolling ocean waves. Punished by the pounding surf, soldiers wade ashore desperate to hold their rifles high above their heads and keep their ammunition dry. Most of the men puke into the sea as they struggle toward the shoreline. Beyond the beach, the soldiers meld into the wretchedly hot, mosquito-infested hardwood forest swamps of the Sierra

Maestra, which actively resist their progress every step of the way. Each man's step echoes in the dream—the sound of shovels digging graves; a terrifying vision of Sergeant Johnston running through withering volleys of rifle fire as he leads their assault onto the Spanish ramparts atop Kettle Hill, where a bayonet pierces the brave man's chest. Enraged, Daniel shoots the man who killed Johnston. In that moment, he fully embraces the mayhem of war.

Daniel woke with a start. Sitting up, he wrapped himself in his blanket. A solitary owl called from the predawn darkness. Shaken by his dream, he tried his best to relax the emotional knot in his gut. He built a warming fire, made coffee, and watched sunrise paint the eastern horizon with light far across the river in Mexico. He was sincerely grateful to have lived when so many good men had died.

"Is that coffee done?" asked the lieutenant, rolling to face the fire.

"Yes, it is," Daniel nodded at the young man. "I was beginning to think you were going to sleep away the best part of the day."

The lieutenant threw off his bedroll and stomped around on one foot, then the other, trying unsuccessfully to pull on his frozen boots. Giving up, he dropped the boots and walked sock-footed to the camp's margin and urinated. Shivering, he brushed leaves and rocks off his feet and crawled back into his bedroll. "Damn, it's cold."

Daniel took the young man's cup and filled it with hot, black coffee. "This will help."

"Thanks," said the lieutenant, blowing the steam off his coffee. "Are you in a hurry?"

"Not at all," replied Daniel, hunkering down on his boot heels near the fire. "When do you expect to arrive at Glenn Spring?"

"Today, I hope."

"Are you hungry?" Daniel asked.

"Yes, sir," said the lieutenant, grinning.

Daniel greased a small iron skillet with bacon fat and filled it with already cooked pinto beans. Raking a pile of glowing embers to one side, he dropped six corn tortillas directly on the white ash. The men ate in silence as the warm rays of the sun crept toward their camp.

Finished with the meal, the lieutenant sat his tin plate on a flat rock and said, "Thanks."

"You're welcome," said Daniel, using his last piece of tortilla to clean his own plate. He reached toward the fire and asked, "You need more coffee?"

"Sure," said the lieutenant, holding out his cup.

Daniel poured coffee from the small blue enamel coffee pot.

"Thanks. I never thought the desert could be this damn cold."

"Be glad that the wind isn't blowing."

"You seem different from the others," said the lieutenant.

"What others?" Daniel asked, noticing how the smoke from their fire flowed like water across the desert.

"Well, men like Captain Henry, for example."

Daniel poked at the fire with a stick and considered this most simple ancient human ritual—men on the move camped beneath a rock ledge enjoying the warmth of a fire, sharing food and words. "I'm not sure what to tell you," said Daniel, looking from the fire into the lieutenant's face. "I do know that a soldier's career is measured by his campaigns."

The lieutenant pitched the dregs from his coffee cup into the brush at the edge of camp and gathered his gear. "I don't mean to be rude, but I have heard that same pearl of wisdom from countless instructors at West Point. You of all people must know how important it is to draw a good assignment early in one's career, and here I am, stationed in the middle of nowhere."

"My words afford little comfort."

"This damned assignment seems more misfortune than opportunity. What if the war in Europe ends soon?"

"For those who are killing and dying that might not be such a bad thing."

The lieutenant shook his head and bundled his bedroll.

"Things aren't always what they seem," said Daniel. "Give it time, Jack. Give it time."

~~~

The cold air hung close to the ground as the men rode south.

Thick clumps of bunch grasses lined the edges of the road where it ran through open valleys dominated by creosote brush and yucca plants taller than a man sitting on a horse. The arroyos were thick with gnarled trees covered in thorns.

Overhead, a red-tailed hawk carved tight circles in the pale-blue sky. The dramatic contrast of broken mountains against the azure sky was a spectacular site. Midmorning, they encountered a crudely painted sign that marked the side road leading to the low-water crossing at La Linda as well as the ore road that would take them south toward Boquillas.

In the dry arroyo leading into the low mountain pass, Daniel and the lieutenant came upon a Mexican teamster tending to the mules that pulled his freight wagon. As the teamster stood between a pair of mules untangling the rigging, he loudly sang a corrido in Spanish. He appeared unaware of the approaching riders.

Daniel stopped his horse, and the lieutenant did the same. They sat on their horses and listened to the man's song from a distance.

> *Adelita, la que me robó el corazón.*
> *La seguí de la cama a la batalla*
> *Un guerrero Villista y campesino.*
>
> *La Adelita dijo que me amaba*
> *Cuando el coronel se la llevó me la quitó.*
> *Todo el dia luchando en Ojinaga*
> *Hasta que la sangre corría por los calles.*
>
> *Mi amor, Adelita …*

The lieutenant shifted in his saddle. "I wonder what he is singing about."

"It's about going to war and leaving a woman behind."

"You understand him?"

"Mostly," admitted Daniel. "His dialect is rather thick, and I don't understand every word, but he is definitely singing a Villista marching song. Although the songs of war change in order to fit a man's memory—or misery—the basic theme is universal to men during war: drinking, fighting, and women."

The teamster looked up, following the distracted attention of his mules. He watched as the two riders approached, the younger man in a soldier's uniform, the older man riding a Mexican pony.

"Buenos días," called Daniel.

Stepping out from behind the mules, the muleskinner smiled and said, "Hello, gentlemen."

The lieutenant waved an unspoken greeting.

The teamster offered them a plug of chewing tobacco, which Daniel accepted, filling his right cheek with a noticeable bulge. The lieutenant shook his head, declining the offer.

Daniel sensed the lieutenant's frustration—that sense of not knowing what to expect, or how to react. He knew from experience that being unable to understand the local language would be a continuing frustration for the young man. The lieutenant had entered a world of which he knew little, and learning quickly might mean the difference between life and death.

The teamster sliced himself a chew then wiped his forehead with a faded bandana.

Daniel probed the teamster for information about distances and directions, and the man responded at great length. They chatted like the best of friends.

The lieutenant understood little of the conversation except for an occasional place name or exaggerated gesture. He examined the teamster, noticing the man's large hands covered by smooth deer-hide gloves that looked homemade. The Mexican wore Levi's overalls, was quite bowlegged, and sported an air of confidence. A large round sombrero hung down the middle of the teamster's back below a thick tangle of shoulder-length hair. He had silver coins sewn into his belt, and he sported large silver spurs on his boots. As he spoke, the teamster frequently used his hands for emphasis, and occasionally spat dark-brown streams of tobacco into the dust. A kind smile lay hidden beneath his drooping black mustache. The man embodied the newspaper photographs the lieutenant had seen of the war in Mexico.

Sliding to the ground, the lieutenant hitched his mare to the branch of a mesquite and moved far enough away to relieve himself with a sense of privacy. He buttoned his britches and returned to find Daniel shaking the teamster's hand. Without speaking, the lieutenant rose into the saddle, gestured good-bye to the teamster, and turned back to the trail.

After a prolonged good-bye, Daniel followed at a slower pace.

The lieutenant looked back to see the teamster pull on his mustache and watch the gringos depart. The wagon driver spit a thick stream of tobacco juice as he straddled the wheel mule, released the brake, commanded the team forward, and continued his song where he had left it.

The singing faded as the two men continued south through the low notch in the long arc of mountains that flowed from Texas into Mexico. Arriving at the crest of the Persimmon Gap Pass, the lieutenant slowed his horse and waited for Daniel to ride alongside.

"Where was that Mexican from?"

"Boquillas, Mexico," said Daniel. "Did you know there are two villages adjacent to one another along the Rio Grande, and both are named Boquillas?"

"Captain Henry mentioned that, but it made little sense at the time."

"One is in Mexico, the other in Texas."

"So it seems," said the lieutenant. "Did those empty barrels smell of kerosene?"

"They did."

"What was it for?"

"Machinery at the mine, I suppose."

"What was he hauling that weighed so much?"

"Lead ore from the Puerta Rica Mine south of Boquillas in Coahuila. He said there is a massive cable tramway that delivers the ore across the river." Daniel grinned. "He also told me that both Boquillas, Mexico, and the other Boquillas in Texas, host some lively fandangos, and the girls are known to enjoy dancing."

"That is all I need, huh?" said the lieutenant with a laugh. "Go and get myself shot by an angry Mexican father or drunken brother for dancing with some little *señorita*." Relaxing in his saddle, the lieutenant said, "This country likely grows on a man in a fashion. Take this landscape, for example. It is rather awe-inspiring."

"Yes, it is." Daniel replied.

"Those must be the Chisos Mountains," said the lieutenant, pointing toward the south where an island of mountains floated in the sky above the horizon, a faded shade of purple.

"They could be."

"Captain Henry said that the word *chisos* means ghost."

Daniel dropped to the ground to examine his gelding's left front hoof.

"That shoe loose?" asked the lieutenant.

"Yeah," said Daniel. "It's missing a nail."

Daniel reached into his saddlebag for his fencing pliers and a nail. He carefully raised the gelding's foot and set a replacement nail with two quick blows, bent the nail, and inspected the other three shoes. Satisfied with his work, he rose back into the saddle, pulled a cigar from his pocket, and lit it.

"You are headed west soon, aren't you?" asked the lieutenant.

"I believe so," replied Daniel. "Do you see those riders coming up the creek?"

"No."

"Look past where the road splits."

"Now I see them. They seem rather heavily armed for plain ranchers," commented the lieutenant; the nervous knot that had formed in the lieutenant's stomach rose awkwardly into his throat.

Daniel nudged his horse forward. "There is nothing wrong with being well armed, especially along this stretch of the border."

~⌒~⌒~

The men stopped their horses above Tornillo Creek, where the trail split: one road led west to the Terlingua mining district, the other road led south toward Boquillas and the remote ranching communities in the heart of the Big Bend. Somewhere along the road to Boquillas lay the cutoff to Glenn Spring.

"I count four riders," said the lieutenant.

"I count five."

Recounting, the lieutenant said, "You're right. Those mules are loaded heavy. I don't want to pass them coming out of that arroyo."

"I guess we wait here then," Daniel agreed.

Two riders soon appeared on the road, yet the string of mules continued north remaining hidden in the arroyo. The riders wore similar canvas britches, hempen blouses buttoned at the neck and sleeve, and wool ponchos tied at the waist with braided lechuguilla cord belts. Both riders sat confident in the saddle. Their horses were wet and lathered— wild-eyed animals that strained at the bit.

The first rider was an older man, short and muscular with a curved scar where his left eye should have been. He wore a round-brimmed straw sombrero cinched beneath his chin with a knotted leather cord. A Mauser rifle hung from his saddle in a beaded case.

Daniel stared at the second rider. Her long black was hair pinned up beneath a brown felt fedora, so it took a moment for him to realize that the second rider was a woman.

"*Buenas tardes,*" said the approaching one-eyed Mexican rider. His generous smile revealed several gold-capped teeth.

"Buenas tardes, señor," replied Daniel, distracted by the confident and strikingly beautiful woman, her strong thighs controlling a restless horse. She carried a short-barreled shotgun across the saddle horn, and crisscrossed bandoliers of cartridges accented her breast. Her fierce green eyes stirred his blood. The woman appeared both prepared for and capable of violence, yet the sight of her soft brown skin along the curve of her neck caused an emotional flutter in his gut.

"*Te hablas Español?*" asked the one-eyed Mexican.

"*Sí, lo hablo,*" answered Daniel.

"Good," grunted the old man. "What about the boy soldier?"

Daniel shook his head, indicating that the young officer did not speak Spanish.

The old man studied Daniel before he continued in Spanish. "So, your government now sends us babies pretending to be soldiers?"

"Seems like it, no?" agreed Daniel. "Where are you coming from today?"

"Boquillas," replied the old man.

"Which Boquillas?" Daniel asked. "I hear there are two villages named Boquillas."

The old man laughed and said, "Boquillas, Mexico."

"And your companion?" asked Daniel.

"She is my niece."

Daniel glanced at the woman. She wore men's clothes, yet he found her strikingly beautiful. The contrast of her clear, green eyes and dark black hair fascinated him, as did the way she proudly sat her horse. The woman returned his gaze without fear or intimidation, causing him to avert his eyes.

"And where are the two of you coming from?" asked the one-eyed Mexican.

"Although we each started in Marathon, we are traveling together by accident."

"You aren't from Texas, are you?"

"No."

"And you are not a soldier?"

"Not anymore. What are you hauling on those mules?"

"Mostly hides and candelilla wax, although we have some fine liquor if you are thirsty, amigo."

Daniel laughed but did not respond. He watched the lieutenant looking at the one-eyed Mexican's spurs. They were hand-tooled silver with oversized rowels. The spurs appeared to be very old, perhaps stolen, or passed from father to son more than once.

A sharp whistle cut the air. The one-eyed Mexican rose in his saddle and waved his quirt toward the north, where the pack mules melded with the landscape, swallowed by dust, distance, and limestone. "There is work to be done."

Daniel offered his right hand in friendship.

The one-eyed old man leaned close, shook Daniel's hand, and half-whispered, "Samuel will bring you a bottle tonight." Sitting straight in the saddle, he flipped the lieutenant an informal salute and kicked his horse into a hard run, departing with an explosion of dust and boisterous laughter.

The woman put quirt to horse and followed the old man.

A warm shiver traveled the length of Daniel's spine as he watched the green-eyed woman ride away.

Steadying his horse, the lieutenant asked, "Did he say what they were hauling?"

"Hides and candelilla wax."

"What is candelilla wax?"

"I'm not sure."

"Okay, I'm confused," confessed the lieutenant. "We encounter this stray Mexican running a string of mules loaded with cargo he obviously doesn't want us to get a look at, and just before he departs he speaks of your friend by name?"

Daniel measured his words. "Perhaps he works with Samuel. I don't know."

"Why would your friend be mixed up with a bunch of Mexicans?"

"Samuel simply negotiates and arranges business deals for men with money. In this country, not everyone is Anglo. If you are going to succeed out here, you need to adjust your perspective on things. Business is business, and the morality associated with the commodities being traded is a matter of opinion."

The lieutenant slumped in the saddle and exhaled a stale breath. "This place is more different than I ever imagined."

"You are going to have a fine stay. On my first assignment, it took me a long time to see things the way they actually were instead of the way I wanted them to be," said Daniel, glancing at the falling sun. "Stay focused on protecting the citizenry and don't take yourself too seriously, and you'll do fine. Just fine, I'm sure."

"I will try," said the lieutenant with a small smile.

The men shook hands, and then went their separate ways.

Riding west through a denuded badlands of rock hoodoos and goblins, Daniel crossed Tornillo Creek beneath a weak winter sun. He had enjoyed the lieutenant's company, but was content to be alone; although he worried that he had troubled the young man more than necessary.

Beyond Tornillo Creek, Daniel followed the trail across rolling hills of matted tufts of low-growing bunch grass into a gap in the volcanic mountains, as the sun sank beyond the serrated horizon. The trail naturally led to a pleasant camping spot above a flowing spring.

While turning loose his hobbled horse, Daniel noticed a faint glimmer of chipped flint. He bent down and picked up an arrowhead. Intrigued, he poked around in the dirt and easily discovered several knapped obsidian chips before kicking up a spear point—a palm-sized blade of expertly crafted stone. Fingering the spear point, Daniel inspected a large pile of burnt rocks, which he assumed were the remains of a primitive kiln. Hungry, he pocketed the spear point and gathered an armload of dry wood.

Daniel built a small fire and cooked a skillet of beans in bacon fat. He raked glowing coals from the fire into a pile, toasted his last three corn tortillas, leaned against his saddle, and ate. For desert, he enjoyed the apple muffin that Maggie had given him.

The clang of horseshoes on slick rock brought Daniel suddenly to his feet. He tossed the skillet to one side, pulled his pistol from his shoulder harness, stepped away from the fire's light, and waited.

An unseen voice soon called from a deep dark shadow. "Put that gun away and help me drink this bottle I brought you, Colonel."

"Well I'll be damned," said Daniel. Laughing, he holstered his pistol as his friend Samuel Jenkins stepped into the light of the fire.

The men shook hands and grabbed each other by the shoulders as old friends do.

"It has been a few years, no?" said Daniel.

"Amigo, it has been far too long." Samuel looked over his shoulder at his horse. "Let me get him hobbled. Here, take this." He handed Daniel a bottle.

Daniel rekindled the fire while Samuel tended to his horse. He sat down on his bedroll, leaned against his saddle, and waited for Samuel to settle.

"Open the damn bottle," said Samuel, returning to the fire.

Daniel did as instructed. He took a long drink; the smoky-tasting liquor seared its way down his throat. "What kind of liquor is this?"

"Sotol," said Samuel. "It's made from the root of those waxy-leafed, grass-looking plants with razor edges. You know, the ones with the dried-out wooden stalks sticking up from them."

"It tastes like a day-old campfire."

"It has got a kick, no?"

Daniel smiled. "Like a mule with a bad attitude."

The men passed the bottle back and forth a few times before Samuel asked, "Are you glad you quit the army?"

Daniel looked into the fire for a long time before he answered. "Yeah, it was the right decision under the circumstances."

"You could have made general. You know that?"

"Yeah," groaned Daniel. "What happened to your face?"

Samuel touched the scabs on the side of his face. "I was scouting an army patrol and I knocked a rock loose while I was running in the dark along a cliff. The local marshal got a lucky shot closer than I would prefer, and I took some rock shrapnel to the face."

Daniel shook his head and grinned. "I'm not sure if that qualifies as good luck or bad!"

"A bit of both, I guess." Samuel took a drink from the bottle. "How long did it take you to get home from Manila?"

"Almost twenty months."

"I want to hear that story someday, okay?"

"Someday I will tell it, but not tonight." Daniel paused before he confessed, "There wasn't much reason to go home."

"Never is at our age," said Samuel.

"I'm not sure what I was thinking."

"Oh, go easy on yourself. You thought your father was still alive."

"I suppose, but after what happened at El Moro ..."

The two men lapsed into silence and passed the bottle.

"Cuba made sense, at first," said Samuel. "Someone blew up the *Maine* and we made it right."

The men nodded and exchanged a knowing glance. The bottle passed again.

"War is like that, isn't it? We beat the Spanish then turned on the Cubans. It was the same in the Philippines," said Daniel.

"Except them being Muslims allowed us to behave even more vicious." Samuel took a drink and exhaled a long hard breath. "Killing people never bothered me like it does you."

"It isn't the killing that bothers me. I have killed more men than I dare count. It is the reason behind the killing that is important. If the reason is a lie, it's wrong."

"You didn't always think like this."

Daniel took the bottle and a drink. "No."

"It was your Cuban wife who changed you, wasn't it?"

"I've heard that said, but Rosa and I argued constantly about our beliefs and philosophies. It was only after she died that I felt what she had been saying may have been right. Only after I participated in the army's atrocities in the Philippines did I change."

The men sat in silence, allowing the past to recede. The level of sotol in the bottle was considerably lower than it had been.

"What is your commitment to the Chisos Mining Company and Howard Perry?" asked Samuel.

"I promised to install the new furnace and get it fully operational."

"No long-term commitment?"

"No."

"Good," declared Samuel, taking another drink. "I have a business proposition for you."

"I don't know."

"It's easy money."

"Is it? What about that marshal who damn near shot you? Look, Samuel, you need to know that I'm more interested in mining opportunities than war profiteering."

"A man can earn more money selling guns and ammunition to Villa in a week than you will make engineering in a whole year."

"That might be true, but I simply don't want to have to worry about dangling from a short rope or being lined up in front of an adobe wall in a town without a name, shitting my pants, and catching bullets from a firing squad of barefoot revolutionaries." Daniel took possession of the bottle with a quick swipe of his hand.

"A man shouldn't waste his time worrying about things," said Samuel with a grunt. "Besides, until their war is over, you could get killed either way. This is a damn good business opportunity. Nobody cares what we trade, as long as Marshal Navarro receives his percentage. Even Perry is paying us with ammunition for the mine timbers we get from the Villistas."

"Is that one-eyed, gold toothed Mexican your partner?"

"Mario? I trust him with my life."

"What about the woman?"

"Ramona?" Samuel laughed again and took back the bottle. "Did she pique your interest?"

Daniel shook his head. "I will think about your offer, okay?"

"Good enough. There's a lot of money going through this country; we're running guns, ammunition, cattle, hides, furs, wax, even liquor.

And that doesn't include the demand for wood, charcoal, and mine timbers in the Terlingua mining district."

"I hear you. I just don't want to get tangled up in something I don't understand."

"That's a fair assessment. You need to know that I could use your help."

"What does Mario think about partnering with another gringo?"

"He knows we need the help. Besides, he would rather spend his time at his ranch in the sierra than work too much. He thinks the war will end soon and is planning all our retirements."

"Is he willing to split the profit?"

"There is enough money to go around," boasted Samuel. "I guarantee that much for certain."

Daniel nodded. He leaned back against his saddle, covered himself with his bedroll, and stared at the countless stars shimmering in the coal black sky.

The men sat together for a long time without talking. Neither man required words as a measure of their friendship. The next time Samuel went to pass the bottle, he realized that Daniel was fast asleep.

Samuel took a final drink and capped the bottle. He looked to the sky and estimated the hour, calculating that if he rode through the night he could cross the Rio Grande by daylight. Leaving the bottle at his friend's side, Samuel gathered his horse and rode south toward the river and an important meeting with Pancho Villa's henchmen.

CHAPTER 9

Glenn Spring

IT WAS DARK when the lieutenant rode into the village of Glenn Spring, which was little more than a humble gathering of mud houses; hand-dug, dry-stacked rock barns; and stick corrals. He judged there to be about thirty-odd buildings comprising the town.

A snarling pack of mongrel dogs announced his arrival. Women in high-collared dresses stood in dimly lit doorways surrounded by their children. No one waved or called out a greeting.

Six metal retort towers dominated the center of the community. Beneath the towers, men fed baled brush into a furnace dug into the hard ground. Grateful for an unanticipated distraction from their work, the soot-faced laborers leaned on their pitchforks and watched the soldier approach.

"Howdy. You must be the new lieutenant. Jack Thompson, right?" called the only clean-faced man standing near the crude furnace.

The lieutenant stopped his horse, dropped to the ground, and shook the man's hand. The man introduced himself as Ellis Wallace.

"Sergeant McKinney said he was expecting you. I own the candelilla retort operation here. We make wax from the leaves of the candelilla plant. I take it you didn't have any trouble finding your way, what with the storm and all."

"No, sir." The lieutenant sighed. He had no desire to discuss that damn storm.

"I take it this is your first time in the Big Bend."

"Yes, sir, it is," answered the lieutenant, looking around for signs of the army post.

"Well, I was born in Presidio County in a time when mothers hid their children from shiftless, thieving Apaches. This has also been a dangerous place, but things were becoming quite pleasant until the damn war in Mexico ran up against the border. Now, a man needs a keen eye, a good rifle, and a pair of pistols to safely get about." Ellis stopped talking and stared at the young officer. "You must be bone tired, son. Your barracks are in the redoubt up that rise there." He pointed for emphasis.

"Thank you, sir. I'm certain we will have time to get better acquainted soon." The lieutenant waved farewell and followed a two-track path up the hill, twilight illuminated by the thinnest sliver of a new moon. Upon reaching the army redoubt, he tethered his horse on an iron hitch and walked through the heavy wooden gate. Inside, eight soldiers sat beneath the thatched veranda cleaning their rifles.

Corporal Hawkins was the first to realize that the unannounced visitor was their new commanding officer. The corporal jumped to his feet and called the men to attention.

"At ease, men," commanded the lieutenant.

The soldiers gathered around him. The men were obviously excited to know their new officer, yet the lieutenant was too tired to explain himself. "Corporal, could you have one of the men collect my gear and stable my horse?"

"Yes, sir," answered Hawkins, making quick hand signals that assigned two men to the task.

Sergeant McKinney stepped from the adobe building at the center of the redoubt. He shook hands with the lieutenant, and they exchanged names.

"In here, Lieutenant," said McKinney with a friendly wave of his right arm.

The small room held two bunks, a bookshelf, and a pair of sooty kerosene lamps. Marshal Navarro sat at a pine-board table examining a map. Hanging his hat on a hand-carved mesquite peg pounded into the thick mud wall near the door, the lieutenant sat down at the table.

Navarro looked at the lieutenant but did not offer his hand.

"What are you planning?" asked the lieutenant.

Navarro dropped his eyes back on the map, ignoring the question. Frustrated, the lieutenant glanced at McKinney.

"It's another patrol, sir."

"What are we patrolling for?"

Before McKinney could respond, two soldiers pushed their way into the room and placed the lieutenant's gear near the door.

"Tell Corporal Hawkins that we leave at dawn," said Navarro, never looking up from the map.

Private Harlow froze in the doorway. He glanced at McKinney for confirmation of the order.

McKinney made a subtle gesture with his chin toward the door and nodded.

Shaking his head in disgust, Harlow turned for the door pushing the other soldier before him. "We better go tell Hawkins."

Navarro stood. "Are you ready for an orientation, Lieutenant?"

The lieutenant looked to McKinney then back to Navarro. Questions formed in his mind, but instinct caused him to hold his tongue.

"We are after a group of filibusters from Boquillas. I will explain all that tomorrow. Be ready at daylight," said Navarro, rolling up his map before disappearing through the door and into the night.

"You look tired, sir," said McKinney. "That bunk in the corner is yours."

"Thanks." The lieutenant walked to his cot, sat down, and rubbed his eyes with the palms of his hands. The marshal's words had caused a vivid image of the one-eyed, gold-toothed Mexican to flash through the lieutenant's mind.

"Was it a difficult trip, sir?"

"Yeah, it was." The lieutenant looked up from his hands. "Have you ever been new at anything?"

"Yes, sir, I know that feeling. Granted, it has been a long time, but I understand what you're trying to say."

The lieutenant lay down on the cot without taking off his boots. He closed his eyes and asked, "Where are you from?"

"My family is from Ireland, sir. I was born and raised in New York City."

McKinney looked at the cane ceiling and talked about home for a few minutes before he realized that the lieutenant was snoring. He took a green wool blanket from a board shelf and thoughtfully covered the sleeping lieutenant.

"Get a good sleep, lieutenant. Your real education is about to begin."

PART 2:
Terlingua

Life does not consist mainly—or even largely—of facts and happenings.
It consists mainly of the storm of thoughts that is
forever blowing through one's head.
— Mark Twain

CHAPTER 10

The Chisos Mining Company

DANIEL CROSSED TERLINGUA Creek upstream of the confluence with Rough Run Creek. Beyond Terlingua Creek, he followed a well-traveled wagon road onto an eroded mesa of sun-burned rocks. Taking frequent drinks from the bottle of sotol, he rode toward the thick plume of black smoke rising over the Chisos Mining Company.

As he neared Terlingua, the first homes he encountered were hand dug from remnant layers of an ancient seabed, each building a creative collage of available materials and purpose, a unique combination of mud, rocks, and sticks. The mining community appeared skillfully carved from a barren landscape that consisted of little more than dirt, rocks, creosote bushes, lechuguilla, dog cholla, and shriveled prickly pear cactus. Although the mild breeze smelled of many things: lye, tortillas, wood smoke, goats, and burnt rock—an unfamiliar metallic stench permeated the air.

Daniel tipped his hat to a group of women hanging laundry near the road. Wide-eyed children clung to their mother's aprons and stared. None of the women returned his greeting. He dismounted at the entrance to the cemetery and hitched his horse to an iron ring mortared into the rock pillar that supported a wooden gate. Intrigued by the contorted veins of limestone bedrock, Daniel kicked at the hard ground and imagined the effort required to bury a man in this country. He studied a sarcophagus built with niches that could hold photographs, flowers, and remembrances. It pleased him that most of the graves appeared well attended.

Mexico stretched beyond the river, a panoramic vista of tortured geology: fractured limestone and volcanic chaos. Daniel admired the ribbon of green that lined Terlingua Creek as it ran through the middle of it all toward the Rio Grande, where a shadowed cleft carved the international boundary in stone. Each side of the border appeared equally massive and austere. Daniel found it difficult to believe that a place such as this actually existed.

Humbled by the view, Daniel turned and faced the Terlingua Trading Post, widely known as the largest store between San Antonio and El Paso. Beyond the store stood a two-story mansion, a row house with many doors, an adobe church, a stable, and some wood-framed cottages. A team of burros pulled a rubber-wheeled wagon loaded with large bales of brush up the hill past the trading post, where it stopped at the metal-roofed shed that housed the cinnabar furnace. The towering furnace chimney belched a steady column of thick black smoke.

Daniel mounted his horse and rode the final distance to the trading post where an Anglo man dressed in pressed linen pants and a starched-collared shirt stood in a warm splash of sunlight on the well-shaded porch.

"You must be Daniel Taylor."

"Yes, I am," said Daniel, sliding down off his horse.

"I'm the store manager and general accountant. Timothy Johnson," he said, extending his hand.

Daniel wiped his hand on his trouser leg and shook the man's hand.

"It's a pleasure to meet you," continued the man. Sit down. You must be exhausted … weary from your journey. May I offer you some lemonade?"

"That would be nice."

"Manuel!" shouted Johnson.

A teenage boy, not yet a man, appeared at the door of the trading post.

"Bring Mr. Taylor a glass of lemonade."

Manuel stared at Daniel, who judged the boy to be no more than fourteen years old.

"Go on," insisted Johnson, motioning with both of his arms for the boy to do as he was told. Then he turned to Daniel. "How was your trip?"

"Good, thank you." Daniel took off his brimmed hat and leaned against the adobe storefront.

"Did you know that the Chisos Mining Company is currently the world's most productive quicksilver mine?" Johnson asked.

"I didn't know that."

Manuel quickly returned with a glass of chilled lemonade served over cubed ice.

Daniel drank the lemonade in one continuous swallow, and then examined the ice in his glass.

"This is a strange country," declared Johnson. "What with the war threatening to spill across the border, the great distances we have to transport quicksilver to market, and the constant problems presented by the Mexican workforce, it's a wonder that we ever manage to make a profit." Johnson glanced toward Manuel, who lingered in the doorway before returning inside the store. "The Mexicans are rather indolent. They constantly try my patience, but they are the only workforce available." Johnson leaned toward Daniel and confided, "My advice is to not trust them. They are lazy, and every single one of them is a natural-born thief."

"Would you know where I'm staying?" Daniel asked.

"Of course I do. How rude of me to hold you here talking after such a long trip. Let me call the boy. Manuel!"

Manuel appeared from the store and walked part way down the porch.

"Take Mr. Taylor's belongings to the Holiday Hotel and deliver his horse to the stable. Go on, now." Johnson waved the boy to the task and then turned back to Daniel. "You should know that you will be expected to attend supper this evening."

"What time?"

"Eight o'clock at the Perry Mansion." Johnson pointed up the hill toward the two-story building. He cast a nervous glance over his right shoulder before confiding, "Mr. Perry isn't here much. He is a busy man with many commitments elsewhere, and he made a special trip in anticipation of your arrival. Mr. Perry is quite anxious about the installation of that new furnace."

"Where does the ice come from?" asked Daniel, crunching on his last piece.

"They use ice in the retort process; therefore, we have a butane-powered ice maker. Ice for drinks is one of the few amenities we enjoy in this remote country."

"That is interesting," said Daniel, setting the glass onto the bench. He returned his hat to his head and stepped off the porch. "Thanks for the hospitality, Mr. Johnson."

"The Holiday Hotel is just past the goat pens. You can't miss the place."

Daniel walked around the trading post to a stucco building with an east-facing porch and six separate doors. A sign above the porch read Holiday Hotel. Three women dressed in long black dresses came out onto the porch and collected Daniel's gear as Manuel unlashed it from the saddle.

"Gracias," said Daniel, stepping onto the porch and offering Manuel a quarter for his assistance.

The young man pocketed the coin without making eye contact.

"Manuel, could you arrange for somebody to clean my saddle and bridle?" asked Daniel as he gathered his Winchester rifle and the bottle of sotol he had slung across the pummel of his saddle in a leather pouch.

"Sí, señor," answered Manuel, leading the gelding away from the porch.

Daniel paused and watched the boy walk away. He found it difficult to determine the boy's actual temperament.

"*Venga,* señor," called the eldest woman on the porch. She carried his saddlebag as she showed him to his room. She showed him the gun rack where he could store his rifle. "*¿Quieres bañar?*"

"Sí, gracias," said Daniel.

The old woman waved Daniel into the adjacent room, where he was pleased to find a brass tub already filled with steaming hot soapy water. It seemed these women had anticipated the very moment of his arrival. Daniel did not hesitate. He undressed and slid into the tub, sinking into the hot water with a long, sad sigh.

The old woman waited with her back turned. When she heard Daniel settle in the tub, she gathered his dirty clothes and left the room.

Daniel drank sotol and soaked in the hot water for a very long time, finally emerging wrinkled and pink. Wrapping himself in a white cotton towel, he staggered to his room and collapsed onto his bed. He fell fast asleep the very moment his head hit the pillow, and dreamed of artillery.

The men take cover in a hardwood creek bottom where the air is thick with mosquitoes and small biting flies. A shell bursts overhead and wounded men cry out. Sergeant Johnston treats the wounded men, his hands covered in blood. Daniel helps the men improve their individual firing positions, digging in the soft, wet ground until they each lie as close to the earth as humanly possible. Sergeant Johnston pulls Daniel to his feet, urging him to press forward, running with the men across an open field of burnt sugar cane toward a row of blockhouses and fortified trenches. The soldiers dutifully run through withering volleys of rifle fire yelling as they charge into the Spanish trenches where the two armies fight face to face, hand to hand.

The image of that familiar knife cutting his own flesh jolted him awake.

Daniel sat up in bed and traced the long sinuous scar on his right thigh with an index finger. Reliving the guilt of having survived when so many good men had died, Daniel slid from the bed.

The tile floor felt cold on his bare feet. Daniel dressed in his work clothes—canvas overalls and a light wool shirt—pulled on socks and boots, grabbed his jacket and brimmed hat, and headed to the furnace. The pitch-black sky shimmered with too many stars to count. The night air smelled of damp creosote and burnt cinnabar. Climbing the rolling hill to the furnace, Daniel paused to marvel at the predawn view of Terlingua.

Upon entering the open-sided pavilion that housed the furnace,

Daniel saw the silhouettes of two men shouldering bales of brush into the glowing belly of the furnace; their shirts lined with rings of salt and sweat. The scene reminded him of Dante's *Inferno*—men feeding Hades's fires, forever doomed to damnation in purgatory.

When the men finished their task, they closed the furnace door and appeared to revel in what they had done. Daniel could not ascertain from their postures if the men were sincerely content with their labor, or simply relieved to have completed the immediate task. Either way, the men looked pleased. The two men walked to the west end of the shed where they settled at a warming fire and tossed corn-husked tamales onto a bed of glowing embers.

Daniel sneezed and surprised the men. They jumped to their feet, took off their round-brimmed straw hats and held them tight against their bellies, each turning his hat in his hands.

"Buenos días, señores," said Daniel.

"Buenos días, señor," answered the men.

Knowing their humility was rooted more in fear than respect, and that these men would stand with their hats in their hands until he spoke or acted, Daniel walked to their fire and squatted on his heels. "¿*Podría tener uno?*" he asked, pointing at the tamales roasting on the fire.

The two men glanced at each other with wide eyes and shared a moment of incredulous doubt before the older of the two men said, "Sí, *mi jefe.*"

Daniel took the offered tamale with exaggerated care. Tossing the tamale back and forth between his hands, he asked, "¿*Hay chili?*"

"Sí," said the older man, passing Daniel a corked, small blue glass bottle of dried *chili piquen.*

Sitting together at the fire, the men ate tamales without speaking.

Only after eating did Daniel ask the men if they would show him around the furnace. At first, the men followed the strange gringo at a respectable distance. Daniel led them in circles around the furnace asking rapid-fire questions, checking the plumbing, the temperature and pressure gages, the kiln's design, and the innovative engineering techniques.

"I heard that you use ice in the retort process," inquired Daniel. "Can you show me how that works?"

Excited by his interest, the Mexicans scampered onto a rickety scaffold and explained how they stuffed ice into a series of metal tubes to increase the amount of quicksilver that condensed from the steam that boiled off the melting rocks. The concept of Perry making ice in the desert to melt rocks into quicksilver fascinated Daniel.

The Mexicans politely excused themselves and went to stoke the furnace. Daniel rolled cigarettes and watched the men work. When they had completed their task, he offered them each a lit cigarette and asked their names.

"*Yo soy Miguel Acosta*," said the older man. "My friends call me, Gato. This is my younger brother, Francisco; he is Paco. Who are you?"

"Daniel Taylor. Perry hired me to install the new furnace." Daniel paused to gauge the men's reaction before asking specifically about chronic, recurring, or unresolved problems.

It took a considerable amount of time and conversation for the Mexicans to talk honestly about anything of significance. Gato did most of the talking, while Paco said little of importance. Ultimately, Gato informed Daniel that none of the Anglos had ever bothered to ask their opinions about anything, much less about the furnace.

"And Perry," asked Daniel, "is he a good man?"

Neither man had anything to say about Howard Perry.

"I don't know these men, and being new here, I value your opinions," explained Daniel.

Gato shook his head. "The gringos don't speak directly to us, the laborers. They only talk with the Mexican supervisors. Men like Huicho Alvarez, our supervisor here at the furnace. The mine superintendent is Tom Green. Green only speaks directly to us when he is angry. He is the big boss, who runs everything through Mexican straw bosses. Only the independent workers—the wood gatherers and water haulers—talk directly to the gringos at the mine; and they do so only when necessary."

The story Gato told made it quite apparent that the Mexicans laborers and American managers coexisted symbiotically, yet as mutually exclusive as possible. It was a familiar story, one that rarely changed with time or geography.

"What about the furnace?" Daniel asked. "Tell me about the heating cycles."

The Chisos Mining Company | 65

Gato explained that it took three weeks of constant heating for the furnace to reach operating temperature before they could muck it clean of the valuable quicksilver. The furnace should be ready for the hoppers to be loaded with ore today or tomorrow. He described how the muckers pulled the soot during the day to dredge the liquid quicksilver. This would take all day and it would cool the furnace. At night, the Acosta brothers currently had the job of getting the furnace to melting temperature. The temperature would be kept high until condensation formed and quicksilver dripped into flasks that when filled weighed about seventy-six pounds.

Daniel told the men that the weight of a quicksilver flask had been established over two millennia ago by Roman laws as the maximum a slave should carry. Both men nodded their heads as if impressed by this small fact.

"How often is the furnace allowed to cool?"

"It's shut down about every six weeks and cleaned," Gato said.

"The night shift must be good duty, no? Not as many bosses." Daniel grinned at the brothers, who smiled back and exchanged embarrassed glances.

Gato asked about the new furnace. He wanted to know how it would change his job.

"The new furnace will require less maintenance and burn hotter, but nothing else will change. It won't make your job any easier, although it will make Perry more money."

Paco elbowed Gato and pointed to the furnace door.

Standing, Gato said, "We should get back to the furnace."

Daniel thanked the men for the tamales and conversation and turned to go. As he walked down the hill to the Holiday Hotel, the rising sun crested the jagged mountains along the eastern horizon. He was very impressed with the men's knowledge of both the furnace and the smelter process.

The stench of burning rock was overwhelming, yet Daniel noticed the subtle odor of damp creosote brush. It was a most peculiar smell that he was quickly coming to appreciate.

The Acosta brothers stood in the shadow of the furnace shed and watched the new man walk away.

"I have never heard such an accent," said Paco.

"Neither have I," replied Gato. "When he spoke, I could almost smell mangos, and now I crave a good bottle of dark, sweet rum."

"Me too," laughed Paco, throwing an arm around his older brother. The men returned to their labor.

⁓～⸝⁓

Daniel discovered two Anglo men on the porch of the Holiday Hotel drinking coffee and basking in the warmth of the early morning sun. They introduced themselves as Dr. Wright, a metallurgist and professor of economic geology at the University of Texas at Austin, and Mr. Joann Udolph, a geologist.

"Perry was upset that you missed supper last night," said Dr. Wright.

"I fell asleep after my bath. Perry should understand my exhaustion."

"You obviously don't know Perry," said Udolph, a cynical grin creasing his sun-browned face, eyes sparkling like islands of Caribbean-blue. His nails were cracked and bruised. It was obvious that the man spent considerable time digging in the hard ground beneath the blistering desert sun.

A young Mexican girl brought Daniel a cup of coffee, and he thanked her in Spanish. The girl nervously refilled the carafe of coffee that sat on the table before she returned to the small kitchen at the south end of the porch.

"I hear that your Spanish is quite good," said Udolph.

Daniel nodded and smiled.

"Perry mentioned that you served in the wars with the Spanish," said Dr. Wright.

"Yes." Daniel looked past the men to a procession of Anglos walking toward the Holiday Hotel from the Perry mansion. "Do you have many problems digging mine shafts in this country?" asked Daniel, shifting the conversation from the past into the present.

"Our biggest problem is flooding," said Udolph.

"Flooding?" asked Daniel.

"Yes, flooding."

"Do you have many cave-ins?"

"Of course we do. This rock is both porous and fractured," replied Udolph. "The Mexicans are good at digging, but they rely more on the intervention of saints and superstition than timbers and engineering for preventing collapses."

"How deep are you going for quality cinnabar?"

"That depends. Most of the ore lies about two hundred feet down, yet some excavations run as deep as six hundred feet." Udolph looked over his shoulder and saw the men nearing the porch. He refilled his coffee cup, excused himself, and walked down the shaded porch to a long table covered with maps.

"Good morning, gentlemen," called Johnson, stepping onto the porch.

Daniel and Dr. Wright each answered, "Good morning."

"I would like to introduce you to Howard Perry, the owner and proprietary genius behind the success of this profitable operation." Johnson said.

Perry offered Daniel a fat-fingered hand to shake. It appeared that Perry was going to say something, yet the words never reached his lips.

Johnson introduced Tom Green, the mine superintendent.

"Glad to meet you," said Daniel.

Tom Green's hand was rough and calloused. His eyes burned with an unspoken anger.

A heavy silence settled upon the porch.

Daniel noticed the Mexican serving girl peeking through the kitchen screen door. He picked up the coffee carafe and said, "Would you gentlemen like a cup of coffee?"

"I didn't come for coffee," said Perry curtly. "I need you and Dr. Wright to accompany Green on a furnace inspection. Most everything we ordered has arrived, and I'm eager to begin the installation of the new furnace."

Daniel started to explain that he had already spent two hours at the furnace, but did not. Better to leave it alone for now. "That is a fine idea," said Daniel, drinking the last of his coffee.

"You will attend supper tonight." Perry insisted.

Looking Perry in the eye, Daniel nodded.

Dr. Wright set his brimmed hat on his head. "Shall we?"

Tom Green led the way off the porch, and the men walked to the furnace without speaking.

In his own mind, Daniel could not understand how Perry could be so upset about a new employee missing a single meal.

———

Daniel took to his work with a great deal of energy. He spent entire nights at the furnace, experimenting with different fuel combinations, taking detailed notes, and drawing sketches of ideas he had for improving the current operation. He boldly asked questions of anyone regardless of his position or social standing. His ability to speak Spanish allowed him to communicate directly with the laborers, and this became a constant source of irritation for both Green and the Mexican bosses.

It took very little time for the furnace boss to complain about the new gringo, and Daniel recognized that Huicho perceived him as a threat to his limited authority. Huicho soon nicknamed him "*El viejo pendejo.*" Daniel knew that the epithet roughly meant "old bastard," although it was not an exact translation. *Pendejo* was a word reserved for angry moments energized by raw emotions heavy with hate.

During the long hours working at the furnace, Daniel encouraged the Mexicans to talk with him about life in the Big Bend. He learned that the laborers generally came from the small villages and ranches of northern Mexico and that a person's job defined his social status; even the most humble Mexican laborer looked down on the Indians that performed the dangerous excavation jobs. The Mexicans harbored no illusions about life. A son claimed his father's job when he died, and brothers fought for their dead brother's job. The men spoke of how difficult their lives were, yet they were aware that across the river it was much worse. In Mexico, men earned less than half the pay and had limited access to the goods and services provided by the trading post. Moreover, living in Mexico required enduring the brutality of a seemingly endless civil war.

Surprisingly, the Mexicans did not differentiate between Texas and Mexico unless one spoke of places beyond Marfa, Alpine, and Marathon. From their perspective, it appeared that the United States did not exist until one traveled north of the railroad connecting San Antonio and El Paso. The country in between the railroad and the river was neither; somehow, it was both, a peculiar blend of juxtaposed cultures.

Daniel became a regular guest of the Acostas. The Acosta home, a small adobe house more appropriately called a *jacal*, provided the most basic essentials. Crudely constructed of available materials, the jacal was a place to store possessions and escape the elements. Most of the living happened outside under an expansive veranda of sotol stalks and river cane, where the women cooked on an open-hearth stove alongside an earthen *horno*, which was for baking. Shards of blue glass from Phillips Milk of Magnesia bottles lay scattered in the yard.

Gato and Paco Acosta hailed from Pedritas, a cluster of farms south of the Mariscal Mine, a two-hour ride south across the river into Mexico. They considered themselves lucky to have their jobs, which in their minds were sufficient as long as they could buy most things available for sale in the trading post. As the friendship matured, Gato spoke of the war in Mexico, although he was exceptionally careful who heard his words when he spoke his mind.

The oldest Acosta brother had died last summer in an accidental explosion at the Mariscal Mine. Gato wept when he explained how their youngest brother, Juan Carlos, had ridden off with Chico Cano in October 1913. A year later, Gato had found Juan Carlos swinging from a rope grotesquely bloated with the August heat. Gato explained how another brother had died of typhoid at the age of three, two sisters had died of measles before turning five years old, and one sister had followed her husband into Villa's Army.

Daniel learned many interesting things from their conversations—how Perry paid the miners with Mexican silver pesos at an exchange rate of half their fair-trade value, and that Paco stole quicksilver by drinking it chased with Phillips elixir, reclaiming the mercury from his stools to sell on the black market.

The last Saturday in February was unseasonably warm, and Daniel paid for a neighborhood fiesta at the Acosta home that included a burro-shaped piñata filled with penny candy. The Acosta brothers roasted two goats while their wives and daughters boiled pinto beans and grilled dozens of corn tortillas on a wood-fired brazier. After the generous meal, Gato opened a fresh bottle of sotol, and the night degenerated into a drunken argument about the Mexican pesos that Perry stamped with a large C.

"Don't you understand how Perry underpays you?" asked Daniel.

"Money is money as far as I'm concerned," growled Paco. "Who cares if that fat old bastard stamps the pesos he pays us with?"

Gato lurched forward in his chair, eyes swollen with liquor-inspired anger. "It allows Perry to track how much outside money comes into the community."

"I'm not stupid, pendejo," cursed Paco.

"Besides that," agreed Daniel, "what I cannot believe is that Perry pays you in Mexican pesos at half the current exchange rate."

"Then he robs us with inflated prices when we spend our stamped pesos in his store." Paco shook his fist and cursed Howard Perry's mother.

Daniel judged that both men held a revolutionary understanding of their situation.

Paco slammed his empty glass on the table. "But tell me, what would we have if we had remained in Mexico? There is no money, no food, and the crazy revolutionary assholes indiscriminately kill people without cause. It is better here. At least nobody wants to execute me, no?" shouted Paco, wiping the constant drool from his trembling lip with a dirty rag.

Gato grabbed his brother's shoulder. "What he is saying, asshole, is that by working Mexicans, Perry doubles his money and he doesn't have to put up with gringo laborers who would demand more than we know to ask for, you stupid ox!"

Paco made an insulting hand gesture at his brother, grabbed the almost-empty bottle and stomped off into the night.

Gato rose to challenge him.

Daniel grabbed his arm. "Sit down. Let him go."

Gato pulled his arm from Daniel's grasp. He fell into his chair and cursed his sibling. "He doesn't understand a damn thing."

"Yes, he does," replied Daniel. "He just doesn't care. In his mind, the cure is worse than the disease. What has Paco to gain in standing against his many masters?"

Gato stared at his hands. "Our lives are dictated by petty tyrants."

"Only if we allow it to be so," said Daniel.

Gato raised his eyes.

"Paco is the smart one. He will work at the old man's furnace, coughing up pieces of his lungs and drooling like a mad hatter until he dies at a young age. You will get angry and do something rash."

"You think?" argued Gato. "It is more likely that Paco will steal once too often and get caught."

The men shared a good laugh, but Daniel had indeed noticed Paco's penchant for theft.

"Are these my only choices?" Gato asked.

"That is between you and your God. What else can you do except work here in Terlingua? Go home across the river and raise goats, frijoles, and babies?"

Gato shook his head. "I take it you haven't heard of the Plan de San Diego?"

"No."

"Of course not," said Gato. "You're not from here, from the border." He straightened in his chair. "This winter, a group of patriots near Brownsville declared their independence from Yankee tyranny in our homeland. Mexicans rooted north of the Rio Grande want to reclaim the land stolen from our grandfathers. Your newspapers called these men—men like Chico Cano—bandits and revolutionaries when they are actually proud rancheros who fight for our lost heritage, our lands, and our pride."

Daniel leaned his elbows on the table and narrowed his eyes. "I'm not sure I would ride that horse into battle."

"What have we to lose? Our lives are pathetic. We live no better than our animals."

Daniel stared into his friend's eyes. "You have two choices. Stay here and work yourself to death, or join the banditry. There is no in between for men like you."

"Men like me?" shouted Gato, rising from his chair.

Daniel pulled a pewter flask from his jacket pocket and handed it to Gato. "In life, we each have our own unique set of problems; therefore, our choices are rarely the same."

Gato saluted his friend, took a long drink and sat back down.

The men talked about the most current news of the war in Mexico until they finished Daniel's flask. Paco never returned. Daylight creased the horizon when they staggered out of the veranda into the moonless night to relieve themselves.

"The nights are getting warmer," said Daniel.

"It will be hot soon," answered Gato.

They faced east toward the illuminated Chisos Mountains and swayed like men lost at sea.

"We have to be very careful what we say, even when we are drunk," whispered Gato with half-lidded bloodshot eyes.

"I understand," said Daniel, acknowledging Gato's statement as fact.

They shook hands and said good night.

Sobered by the conversation, Daniel walked up the hill to the Holiday Hotel as dawn cast orange-purple streaks across the sky, dissolving the inky darkness of the night's embrace.

Surrounded by a circle of his peers—all the Mexican supervisors at the mine—Huicho stood in the shade of a two-wheeled burro cart in front of the trading post trying to explain what he did not know. "I don't know why he asked to see me," said Huicho, wiping his forehead with a salt-stained bandana. "I just don't know."

The men argued passionately about what unknown reason could have made Tom Green send for Huicho alone until Green stepped from the shadow inside his office on the trading post porch, and shouted, "Huicho, get yourself in here!"

Huicho ran toward the office as commanded. He removed his hat, clutched it in both hands against his belly, and made his way into Green's office, flinching when he saw Marshal Navarro sitting on the edge of the large wooden desk that dominated the room.

"Sí, mi jefe?" said Huicho, his eyes cast down at the polished wood floor.

"I heard the nickname you gave to Daniel," said Green, smiling and looking to gauge Navarro's reaction.

Huicho stopped turning his hat in his hands.

"El viejo pendejo," said Green. "That's funny."

Navarro neither laughed nor smiled.

Although Huicho smiled, he did not lift his gaze from his own feet.

"I want you to keep an eye on Daniel for us. Okay?"

"Sí, mi jefe."

"I know you've got your own reasons for hating the man. Me? I am worried about the man's sympathies with the Mexicans. Strikes and labor uprisings are far too common in the mines across northern Mexico. Men like Daniel are trouble for us. I have told Perry these same words." Green paused and hardened his stare. "Look at me, son."

Huicho raised his eyes with great care.

"I want you to keep track of Daniel for us. You understand?"

"Sí, mi jefe."

"Good. Now go," commanded Green, waving Huicho out of the room with the stub of his unlit cigar. He watched Huicho leave the room before turning to face Navarro. "I don't like this new man, Marshal."

"So it seems."

"I just know he is in cahoots with that Sam Jenkins and up to no good." Green spit a thick brown splatter of tobacco juice into a brass spittoon on the floor next to his desk.

"If you feel that way about him, we should run him off."

"Perry won't let me until he gets that new furnace installed and running. Perry thinks he needs this man's expertise, and I have to admit that he has proven that he knows what he is doing. We best just do what we're told, for now."

"You know Samuel ain't working for our partners anymore?" said Navarro.

"Yeah, I heard."

"I might need Perry to quit doing business with him."

"That's not practical. Perry needs things we cannot purchase legally. You know that."

Navarro sat his hat on his head and stepped toward the door. "It might not be practical for you or Perry. That's your problem, not mine. Samuel running his own trades is becoming a problem for me personally." Navarro paused for emphasis before concluding, "It can't be tolerated much longer."

Outside, Huicho lingered on the porch hoping to hear what Navarro was saying. Although he could hear the man's words, their meaning was impossible to grasp.

"What are you doing?" hissed Manuel.

Huicho jumped, frightened at being caught eavesdropping. He turned and faced Manuel.

Manuel shook his broom at Huicho. "What are you doing, *buey*? You know that you aren't allowed to remain here after you have completed your business."

"What I'm doing is none your business. You are the storekeeper's boy; your job is to sweep floors. Don't speak to me in this fashion." Huicho squared his shoulders toward Manuel. "I know you steal things from Señor Perry."

"Screw you, pendejo!" cursed Manuel.

Huicho pulled on his hat and stepped off the porch. This was neither the time nor the place to settle things properly.

The men near the burro cart had waited for him to return. They had witnessed the confrontation on the porch and pressed Huicho with questions: What happened? What did Manuel say? What did Green want with you?

Huicho shot an angry glance over his shoulder at Manuel, who stood in the doorway of the trading post with crossed arms.

"Walk with me to the furnace and I will explain what is expected of us."

CHAPTER 11

A Wagon of Bullets

SPRING TRANSFORMED THE desert into a cornucopia of wildflowers. A tidal wave of bluebonnets accompanied by a generous splash of yellow desert marigolds decorated the eroded hills along Terlingua Creek.

Daniel needed relief from the tension he felt from both Tom Green and Huicho. He knew that Huicho constantly bitched about his friendly relations with the laborers at the furnace. No matter how he turned the problem in his mind, Daniel suspected that Huicho's attitude would ultimately ripen into a violent confrontation. He had seen this pattern before and felt trapped in a web from which he could not escape. Maybe his taking a few days off from the mine might provide a sense of relief for everyone involved.

Green became agitated when Daniel asked for a few days off. He could not understand a man's need for time off and threatened Daniel with termination. "If you don't adjust your insubordinate attitude, Perry is going to fire you before you get that damn furnace done."

Daniel bowed up but did not feel the urge to defend himself. In his mind, Green was not worthy of respect or concern.

"You mark my words, your days at this mine are numbered," threatened Green.

"Do what you must," Daniel said, pointing to the calendar above Green's desk. "Today is Tuesday. I will be back on Friday."

"You're a troublemaker, you know that?"

Daniel shook his head and left the man's office. He whistled for

Manuel who immediately stepped onto the porch from the shadow of the trading post door. "Bring me a fresh bottle of sotol before I get done packing my gear, son."

~~~

Daniel ran the gelding hard down past the cemetery and toward the creek. When he finally slowed the pace, he opened the fresh bottle of sotol and drank hard. He rode without stopping until he reached the confluence where the clear flowing Rough Run Creek entered the murky waters of Terlingua Creek.

Allowing Cabron a long, cool drink of creek water, Daniel considered the view. It was a chaotic medley of volcanic intrusions, fractured limestone, and plants with thorns. Rough Run Creek flowed from between twin peaks of sunburned mountains, and a flock of red birds with top knots like those of cardinals flitted along the braided creek. The blanket of yellow flowers lining the creek smelled of fresh-squeezed lemons. It was a beautiful day, neither hot nor cold—a near-perfect temperature.

Following the flock of songbirds foraging along Rough Run Creek, Daniel rode past the Study Butte cinnabar mine, where three sun-browned men stood along the crudely built furnace wall. The men watched him, but none of them waved.

The aroma of fresh corn tortillas arrived on a gentle wisp of wind. Daniel followed the scent of toasted corn through a tangled forest of thorn brush and stunted trees that lined the creek and arrived on an alluvial fan of scattered creosote brush.

Following a trail, he rode into a sheltered basin at the base of an igneous mountain and discovered a mud-caulked hut of sotol and ocotillo sticks dug into a graveled hillside. Nearby, five goats and a dark-gray burro napped in a small brush corral. Three children ran from the corral through the shaded porch of the jacal. The two young girls chased each other, their uncombed hair flying wildly as they ran. A little boy, barely two years old, wore only a shirt.

Dogs erupted from their napping places with an explosion of barking. Daniel cursed the charging dogs in Spanish, and they stopped just short of his horse. Growling and sniffing, the dogs tucked their tails deep between their hind legs and kept a respectable distance.

Upon seeing the rider, the younger of the two girls covered her mouth with fright. The older girl saw the gringo's reflection in her sister's eyes and screamed for her mother, "Mama, Mama!" She ran with her sister toward the jacal, gathering her brother under one arm during flight. The children ran like the wind, disappearing into their home.

Daniel could hear the excited conversation from inside the dwelling. All he could do was to sit on his horse, surrounded by groveling curs, and wait for the people to calm down. It would take them some time to conclude that he was not leaving. He considered lighting a cigar. Eventually, the dogs lost interest and returned to their shade.

After a very long time, a gray-haired woman leaning on a carved wooden cane emerged from the jacal. She stepped from the porch, shaded her eyes with the palm of her hand, and greeted the persistent stranger, "Buenas tardes."

"Buenas tardes, señora," answered Daniel, waiting a polite moment before continuing in Spanish. "Excuse me for the interruption of your privacy. I was hoping to pay you for a plate of beans and perhaps some tortillas."

The old woman considered the man. He knew she could see that he wore his pistol under his jacket, and would know that his Spanish sounded different from that of most Texans. She nodded and said, loud enough for those inside to hear, "Maria, all he wants is something to eat." Then the old woman waved Daniel onto the porch. "Sit down, please."

Daniel tethered his horse to the fence that surrounded the corral and sat down to a simple meal of beans and tortillas served with fresh jalapeños and cilantro. The entire family assembled on the porch, and he was a bit self-conscious with so many eyes turned on him. The food was both simple and delicious, with a hint of cinnamon in the beans. Maria handed Daniel fresh tortillas until he asked her to stop. The moment he finished eating, she brought a cup of hot tea steeped a dark green color. It tasted bitter and was difficult to swallow. "What is it?"

When she spoke, Maria covered her stained and poorly formed teeth with a hand. "*La hediondilla.*"

Daniel laughed and repeated the name in English, "Little stinker."

He recognized the smell but did not know which plant she meant. "Which plant is it?"

Maria pointed to one of the dried herbs suspended from the porch beam, and he immediately recognized it as the creosote plant.

The old woman rocked in her hand-hewn chair as she sewed a patch onto a pair of leather britches. Maria leaned with crossed arms in the doorway of the jacal, amused by her daughters who pretended to ignore the visitor. The girls played a game of make-believe with a pile of calcite crystals and creek pebbles; their brother chased a puppy with an ocotillo branch. He giggled each time he struck the dog, which when hit yelped for mercy.

Leaning back in his chair against the corner post of the porch, Daniel surveyed the jacal—a mud-plastered frame of juniper posts, sotol stalks, and ocotillo whips. Dried herbs hung along the inside edge of the porch where river cane had been woven to block the most direct afternoon sun. The thoughtful construction of the structure amazed him, and he briefly considered their simple life here in the desert.

"Where are you coming from?" asked the older woman.

"Terlingua," said Daniel, thinking of cigars and wanting another drink of strong liquor.

"You work at the Chisos Mine?"

"Yes."

"Your accent is different. Where were you born?" she asked.

"Tennessee."

"It's in the United States?" *Tennessee* meant nothing to her.

"Yes, back east," answered Daniel.

They sat in silence and watched the children play.

When Daniel realized that the woman had finished asking her questions, he placed two quarters on the table and stood. "Thank you for the food."

"Gracias *a usted*," replied both the women.

The little girls leapt to their feet and followed Daniel to the corral where he tightened the cinch on his saddle. Nearby, the little boy tormented the youngest goat with his ocotillo stick.

Waving good-bye, Daniel turned his gelding back to the trail. The mangy dogs followed him until they caught scent of something more promising and ran growling into the brush of the bosque along Rough Run Creek.

⌒ ⌒

Stopping his horse in the shade of the cottonwood gallery along Terlingua Creek, Daniel contemplated a solitary kingfisher perched over a large pool of slow-flowing water. The calmness of the moment soothed his seething irritation, offering a temporary respite from the tension at the mine.

The rattle of an approaching wagon caused the kingfisher to fly upstream complaining on the wing. Daniel looked up to see that a single rider accompanied the heavily loaded wagon. The wagon cautiously descended from the top of a bare mesa of broken rocks toward the creek. It was Manuel riding the floppy-eared mule alongside the wagon. The wagon driver drove the team with great skill, halting the mules in midstream to allow them a long drink of creek water. The wagon was loaded with wooden crates covered with a canvas tarp.

Daniel eyed the wagon driver, who looked familiar.

Manuel rode close to where Daniel sat on his horse. "What are you doing here? I'm surprised to find you so far from the mine."

"I'm going to Terlingua Abaja then downstream as far as the mouth of Santa Elena Canyon. I want to try my hand at catching those blue catfish." Daniel glanced at the wagon driver and said, "Do I know you?"

The driver smiled but said nothing in return.

"What are you hauling?" asked Daniel.

Manuel shot a glance at his companion before he announced. *"Estamos transportando balas."*

"Bullets?" replied Daniel. "Where are you hauling all that ammunition?"

"We are delivering a payment," explained Manuel, rising proud in the saddle.

"Payment?" asked Daniel.

"A promise of coal." Manuel laughed.

"Quiet, you fool," commanded the driver.

Hearing the driver's voice brought recognition. She was the

woman he had encountered with that one-eyed Mexican rider south of Marathon. For such an attractive woman, she had the uncanny ability to disguise herself as a man.

"Aren't you two worried about thieves or the marshal I keep hearing about?"

Manuel laughed so hard he slapped his leg. "Navarro doesn't bother Perry's business."

The woman shook her head and explained, "There are others with us you cannot see."

"And Samuel?" asked Daniel.

"He isn't with us today," said Manuel.

"We had better get going," urged the woman. "We are wasting precious time."

"Wait," said Daniel. "What is your name?"

The woman hesitated.

Manuel laughed. "Her name is Ramona. Good luck with the fishing," he called, splashing across the creek as if leading the wagon.

Daniel moved aside and watched the wagon rattle past hoping Ramona would glance over her shoulder and allow him another glimpse of her clear green eyes.

As if commanded, Ramona turned on the wagon bench and pointed at the pair of vultures circling in the pale blue sky. "*Los zopilotes han vuelven.*"

"The vultures have returned," said Daniel, repeating her words. He had heard this comment many times recently and come to accept the vultures' return from their winter migration as official verification that spring had indeed arrived.

Riding downstream past the community of Terlingua Abajo, Daniel camped in the shadow of Santa Elena Canyon at the confluence of Terlingua Creek with the Rio Grande. He stretched a tarp between two large mesquite trees, organized his camp, gathered several armloads of firewood, and enjoyed a dinner of beans, bacon, and tortillas.

That evening, Daniel baited three trotlines with balls of stale bread rubbed with bacon grease and watched the sun as it receded beyond the rugged mesa where a pair of golden eagles soared. Sunset majestically reflected the high Chisos Mountains with a shifting palette of pastels—crimson fading through orange into deep shades of darkness bruised lavender. Shadows crawled across the desert landscape. Nighthawks swooped in the sky. An elf owl called for his dinner.

The first two trotlines Daniel inspected were empty, and he baited them again. The third line felt heavy and it pleased him. He worked the line downstream and out of the river, revealing a lovely, blue-hued catfish. Daniel admired the fish before putting it on a stringer. He baited the empty hook and replaced the line in the river.

Although he was content to be alone under a blanket of stars, his mind remained restless. Night fell, accompanied by a chorus of frogs. Across the river in Mexico, a burro brayed with delight. The river gurgled and slurped as it flowed, carving its way through mud, sand, and rock. No matter where Daniel directed his attention, his mind constantly returned to the green-eyed, dark-haired woman. Her eyes pulled at him like a taut rope. Ramona had stirred his blood and warmed his heart.

Daniel considered what someone at the mine had said about the people who lived in the Big Bend. "Everything that lives out here either sticks, stings, stinks, or bites, including the people."

That most likely includes the women too, he thought, and laughed to himself.

Taking another long drink of sotol, he smiled at the star encrusted sky.

～〰️～

Easter inspired a weekend of elaborate celebrations, religious parades, dances, and general drunkenness. Perry allowed the men two one-day holidays from work each year—Easter Sunday and Christmas Day—knowing from experience that most of the men would be too drunk or debilitated on these holidays to perform any meaningful work anyway.

The entire village of Terlingua gathered for a grand fiesta that culminated with a dust-stomping fandango, with everyone dancing until long after midnight. Standing alone at the edge of the dance, Daniel indulged his most sullen thoughts and drank sotol from his flask. Troubled by the anger that stirred his gut, he felt caught between two cultures, neither of which he truly understood.

"What is wrong?" called Gato Acosta, staggering alongside Daniel. "You look troubled."

Daniel smiled. "Just thinking too much, that's all."

"Then drink more," said Gato, laughing. "You will think less." He offered Daniel a fresh bottle of sotol.

Daniel raised his pewter flask, declining the offered bottle. "I'm good, thanks."

"You're thinking about leaving Terlingua."

"No." Daniel drank from his flask then slipped it into his jacket pocket. "No, I'm just tired."

"The world is full of petty tyrants," said Gato, opening the bottle in his hand.

"And a man can choose where he works."

"He can?" Gato eyed Daniel.

Daniel nodded. "Yes, he can."

Gato took a drink from the full bottle of liquor. "I need to think about that." He swayed, holding his bottle of sotol as if it were a lover. "There is no value in thinking too much about what has to be done."

"Gato!" cried a group of approaching men anxious to share his fresh bottle of sotol. The men swarmed around Gato, before leading him across the dance floor to a larger circle of men standing around a fire that licked the darkness with undulating tongues of light.

Laughing, Daniel moved into a shadow between two houses and followed the dirt road up the hill toward the Terlingua Trading Post and his room at the Holiday Hotel. He paused at the cemetery gate and marveled at the audacity of the Big Bend night sky.

Sitting down on a rock bench, Daniel considered his situation. If he stayed too long at the mine there would inevitably be a reckoning with Green, or Huicho, or both. Although his work situation was an irritant that made him restless, the strongest knot of emotions churning his gut were his constant visions of that green-eyed Mexican woman from Boquillas. Ramona held a power beyond understanding over his imagination that he found impossible to ignore.

CHAPTER 12

Collapse

MAY BROUGHT WARM, southeast winds; soft spring rains, and an eruption of stunning cactus flowers.

Tall, dark clouds formed dynamic thunderstorms over the Chisos Mountains. Some days, the storms formed angry flotillas of electrified rain that traveled from mountain peaks to mesas, swelling the creeks and encouraging the desert to erupt in ephemeral outbursts of color.

Daniel quickly embraced afternoon siestas to escape the extreme afternoon heat. Strangely, the heat usually seemed hottest in the hours prior to sunset, not in the middle of the day when the sun stood highest in the sky. Most days, Daniel took his siesta in a hammock on the porch of the Holiday Hotel. When the weather promised a potentially electric afternoon storm display, he preferred to nap in the shade of the furnace shed, sipping sotol and smoking hand-rolled cigarettes.

Today was one of those days, hot and still. A series of massive thunderstorms had grown to maturity over the Chisos Mountains. Daniel's mind drifted across the desert with the storm clouds, lost within Cretaceous considerations. He peacefully sipped sotol and admired the geologic chaos until the piercing blast of the siren shattered his reverie.

The horn's shrill tone sent a chill down his spine that brought him to his feet. He looked to the main mine shaft on the ridge above Terlingua where a thick reddish-brown cloud of dust billowed into a faded blue sky. Daniel hurried through the furnace shed calling for the Mexicans to follow him.

Paco stopped Daniel with a tug on his sleeve. "We cannot leave the furnace."

Daniel nodded, acknowledging the statement as truth. "That is okay, but I should go help if I am able." He broke loose from the man's grasp and ran toward the rising cloud of dust.

The furnace workers helplessly watched as the dust cloud grew above the mine opening. Some prayed while others cursed. When Huicho realized that the men were not tending the furnace, he pushed them back to their labor.

It was past midnight before Daniel emerged from the mineshaft with the last of the dead bodies, his face crusted with dirt, sweat, and other men's blood. He sat on a limestone boulder, coughed violently, and spit up what felt like pieces of his lungs. Women and children gathered near the mine entrance and wept as men carried dead relatives down the hill to be prepared for burial.

Udolph emerged from the mine, leaned on a timber post, and suffered a coughing fit. He pulled a flask of sotol from his hip pocket, took a drink, and offered it to Daniel.

Daniel accepted the offer and took two drinks before returning the flask. He wiped his mouth with the back of a filthy shirtsleeve. "What happened?"

"We were lucky it didn't flood."

Daniel spit. "Those dead men didn't share in that luck."

"It doesn't matter," said Udolph between drinks of sotol. "The Mexicans have no proper choices in life. Lose your compassion. It won't serve you well in this place."

Daniel hawked a wad of thick green mucous and yanked the flask from Udolph's hand. In taking a long drink, he spied Howard Perry, Timothy Johnson, Tom Green, and Huicho Alvarez, coming up the hill. Daniel returned the flask and stood. Even at a distance, he could see the fight in Green's eye.

Green immediately confronted Daniel. "You've got no business down in that mine."

Daniel saw no reason to defend his actions with words.

"What have you got to say for yourself?" bellowed Perry, gasping from the exertion of climbing the steep hill.

"I would hope that you are upset about men dying in your mine shaft."

"Those men don't mean squat to me!" Perry struggled to settle his breathing.

Green turned to Udolph. "How bad is it?"

"Where have you been?" shouted Udolph.

"Waiting for the all-clear signal, you fool," snapped Green.

"We lost most of tunnel five and a small portion of the main tunnel at that intersection."

"It didn't flood, did it?"

Udolph spit. "I wouldn't be here talking with you if it had."

"I want men back in there before the dust settles," commanded Perry.

"Yes, sir," said Green. "Huicho, gather a cleanup crew."

Huicho flinched. It was not his job.

"I'm worried about you," said Perry.

Daniel took a half step toward Perry.

Green stepped between them, challenging Daniel. "You're asking for trouble, boy."

"For what, pulling dead bodies out of your mine?"

"For instigation," said Green. "You're a damn trouble maker."

"And you're a son-of-a-bitch!" said Daniel, turning to leave.

Green reared back and took a swing, but Daniel had seen it coming. He turned back and deflected the blow with his right arm, and then he popped Green with his left fist, landing the blow square on the man's right ear. Daniel followed this with a knee to the gut, and finally dropped Green to the ground with a double-fisted smack to the back of his head.

"Don't ever try that again," said Daniel, staring down at Green.

Pushing himself up onto his knees, Green gasped for air.

Udolph raised an eyebrow and muttered a remark that no one heard: "He is good with those hands."

Perry stood slack-jawed, as if unable to speak.

"He shouldn't have taken a swing at me." Daniel waited a few seconds for Perry to respond before he turned to go. Walking down the hill, he felt the wails of the mourners reverberate deep in his heart, stirring ancestral pain known only to the living.

~~~

The morning after the cave-in, Daniel slept until a loud knock rattled his room door. Sitting up, he yelled, "Just a minute." Then he climbed out bed, pulled on his pants and a chambray shirt, and opened the door. He was sincerely surprised to find Second Lieutenant Jack Thompson holding two steaming cups of coffee.

"Morning, Daniel."

"Good morning," Daniel replied, smiling at the unexpected visitor.

"Coffee?" asked the lieutenant.

"Thank you." Daniel took the cup and the men shook hands. "How have you been?"

"Just fine, thank you."

Daniel dragged up two chairs and the men settled on the porch. They sat in silence, adjusting to each other's company, and watched the bustle behind the trading post where men were building pine boxes.

"What happened here?"

"There was an accident last night."

"Some men died?"

"Too many," said Daniel.

"From the look of your hands, I'd assume you were there."

"I was."

"You okay?"

"Mostly, I guess." Daniel paused. "I seem to be at odds with most of the Anglos who work here, except maybe Dr. Wright. Honestly, I don't have much respect for management."

"I'm having a similar problem," said the lieutenant with a little laugh.

"What's wrong?"

The lieutenant sipped his coffee and stared at his boots. "I want to blame Marshal Navarro, although it's my fault for not realizing what he was doing."

"What happened?"

"Mexican bandits raided a ranch house near Alamo Springs. They stole some horses and killed some folks—shot a man, his wife, and their sixteen-year-old boy. Later that week, the postmaster got a good look at men riding some of the stolen horses and told Marshal Navarro. You know that the Anglos around here credit Chico Cano for most everything bad that happens that can't be blamed on someone else."

"Chico Cano seems to be some kind of Robin Hood for the local folks along the river," said Daniel.

"Honestly, I can't blame the Mexicans for mythologizing Cano," the lieutenant agreed, "although he is a man of variable allegiances. Compared to Navarro, Cano wears a white hat."

"I keep hearing things about this Marshal Navarro," said Daniel, nodding in agreement.

"That man is a piece of work all right," groaned the lieutenant, falling silent.

Daniel allowed the man some time before he asked, "So what happened?"

"Navarro demanded our assistance in trailing the suspicious riders with the stolen horses," said the lieutenant. "And I was eager to oblige him. Navarro gathered half a dozen Texas Rangers, and we rode together to a little village toward Presidio."

"Was the village in Texas or Mexico?"

"Texas," answered the lieutenant, shaking his head, "Those rangers are a foul-smelling bunch."

Daniel nodded. "I've heard that same comment about the rangers from the Mexicans here at the mine."

"It was near midnight when we arrived in the sleepy village. The rangers went to banging on doors while we secured the perimeter. They rounded up all the men and boys old enough to carry a rifle and forced them into a rock corral."

Daniel sipped his coffee and leaned back in his chair.

"Women were bawling, wailing like she-cats, and some of the men were pissing their pants. At this point, Navarro told me to take the soldiers and leave. Sergeant McKinney was upset and did not want to leave. I told him that it wasn't our business—we should allow the marshal and his rangers to settle the matter." The lieutenant raised his eyes, which had become moist with tears. "No sooner had we ridden out of the village than all hell broke loose. Sergeant McKinney ordered the men to turn around. We raced back to the village, but the shooting had ended before we arrived. The rangers were laughing and joking, holstering their pistols.

"How many did they kill?"

"We buried twenty-five men and boys."

"Dear God," said Daniel.

"Those who jumped the corral and ran toward the brush were shot in the back."

Daniel stared through the dancing heat waves that blended earth and sky. What the lieutenant had witnessed had been a common tactic in the Philippines. Many times during his career, Daniel had followed orders and had led a bayonet charge through an undefended village of women and children. He searched for words that might ease the lieutenant's conscience, knowing from personal experience that nothing would release him from his acquired nightmare. Words could not change what had occurred.

The men finished their coffee without speaking.

Sergeant McKinney approached the Holiday Hotel trailing a second horse. He acknowledged Daniel, and then said, "Lieutenant, your horse is ready."

"Thanks, Sergeant." The lieutenant stood and turned to face Daniel. "Thanks for listening."

"I wish I knew what to tell you."

The lieutenant moved to the edge of the porch. "It'll work itself out. It always does one way or another."

"Good luck," said Daniel. "Remember, rebellions are born of such oppression."

The lieutenant swung onto his horse. "War isn't very gallant, is it?"

"This isn't war."

"Navarro thinks it is."

"Don't worry yourself about what you think other men think. It will only cause you misery, and it might get you killed."

The lieutenant waved good-bye as he rode away, closely followed by Sergeant McKinney.

Daniel watched the soldiers disappear beyond the trading post. He measured the lieutenant's tragic story against his own, rediscovering the story of the world: the dominant economic class brutalizing an impoverished people. Who dared resist? Society intentionally domesticates people to be docile. A person must be incredibly desperate to choose the risk of rebellion over servitude. Sadly, history teaches that modern rebellions ultimately fail even when they have appeared to win.

Troubled by strong emotions, Daniel felt the urge for a drink. He stepped off the porch and went in search of a fresh bottle of sotol. Walking past the goat pens, he wiped his forehead with a shirtsleeve. "It's going to be a hot one today," he muttered to the goats.

In front of the trading post, he encountered a crowd of men and boys gathered around the traveling postmaster. The talkative postmaster was as thin as a *tasajillo* cactus, his skin dark brown from riding his mail route under the harsh desert sun.

"You can read all about it in the newspapers that I brought for sale. Something big is about to happen. The way I personally heard Captain Henry tell it was that Villa has General Obregón, Carranza's commanding general, surrounded at Celaya, and this could be the deciding battle of their long and protracted war."

Everyone was hungry for news of the war in Mexico. Those who could afford a newspaper crowded in close hoping to buy one. The rest of the men formed a loose semicircle around the postmaster, absorbing his proclamations as fact.

"Pancho Villa has surrounded the one-armed General Obregón in the town of Celaya, in the state of Querétaro, and there is about to occur the most decisive battle of the war. These newspapers I brought for sale claim that Carranza himself is afraid to return to Mexico City because the people in the capital city support Villa. In a desperate effort to engage Villa's army, Obregón has gotten himself surrounded. It doesn't look good for Carranza and the Constitutionalists."

Daniel found himself drawn into the growing ring of men gathered at the edge of the porch. He bought a two-penny newspaper from the kid hawking them for the postmaster, tucked the folded paper under his arm, and wandered off to sit down in the shade of the goat pens, where he could still hear the postmaster talk. He thoughtfully read the entire newspaper word by word hoping to understand what was happening at Celaya. A recruitment advertisement seeking soldiers, engineers, and explosive experts piqued his interest, and he wondered what the jobs paid.

Looking up from his paper at the men gathered around the postmaster, Daniel laughed. He had never seen so many folks in one place at the same time in Terlingua except at a fandango.

The Mexicans who did not understand English soon bored of the postmaster's loud speech and drifted back to whatever they were doing before news of the war had arrived. Daniel closed his eyes, relaxed against a cedar fence post, and speculated on the outcome of the pending battle of Celaya.

"A-hum," growled Tom Green in a false clearing of his throat.

Daniel opened his eyes. Green stood two paces away with fisted hands on his hips. Green was not alone. Huicho stood a few steps behind him, also glaring at Daniel.

"You will never again enter my mine shafts. You understand?" insisted Green.

Daniel looked the man in the eye, but did not respond.

"Mark my words. There is going to be trouble."

"I will do as I please, especially when men need help."

"You are an instigator, aren't you?"

"You need to quit making up stories in your mind about who you think I am." Daniel folded the newspaper and stood up, tucking the paper under his right arm.

"Perry has grown tired of your insubordination," threatened Green. "I won't stand for this."

"Stand for what?"

"You're causing trouble among the Mexicans."

"Do what you have to do." Daniel felt the urge for a drink grow stronger. He spied Manuel lingering inside the dark shadow of the trading post door and moved past Green toward the store.

Green spit as he turned and watched Daniel walk away.

Stepping onto the porch, Daniel called to Manuel. "Go get me a fresh bottle."

Manuel answered from the shadow inside the door. "I will bring it to your room."

CHAPTER 13

Death by Machete

THAT NIGHT AT supper, Tom Green berated Daniel for his familiarity with the Mexicans. Daniel said little in return, until Green reached across the table and waved his fist in his face. A roaring argument ensued.

Johnson joined the verbal battle, blaming Daniel for every act of petty theft ever committed at the trading post.

Udolph drank shots of sotol and grinned.

Dr. Wright stared at his plate and said nothing.

Perry furrowed his brow and rubbed his hands, nurturing his hatred of men like Daniel, although he knew that engineers were in short supply along the Mexican border. With the new furnace installation not yet completed, Perry remained silent for the moment.

Unable to endure the accusations and strong words, Daniel left the table. Green followed him to the door yelling vile threats. Retreating down the hill, Daniel grabbed the bottle of sotol from his room, and then stomped through the darkness to the limestone ledge at the rim of Long Draw. He sat on the cool white ledge rock and threw back large swallows of the fiery liquor.

Daniel stared into the inky-black, star bejeweled sky. In searching his pockets, he found the stub of a cigar but not a single match. He lifted his eyes toward the cupola of heaven, and cursed. "Dammit!"

"What's wrong?" called a familiar voice.

Startled, Daniel rose to his feet. "Samuel?"

Samuel stepped from the darkness onto the ledge rock. "So, what are you doing out here drinking all alone?"

"Don't get me started."

The men vigorously shook hands. Samuel grabbed Daniel by the upper arms with both his hands and exclaimed, "You look healthy."

"Why thank you, you old snake. You ride off in the dark without as much as a simple good-bye. Where have you been all this time?"

"Slow down, Colonel. Let me get a drink. Then I will tell you a few things about where I have been and what I'm doing." Samuel took the bottle and the men sat down on the ledge rock.

In between drinks Samuel asked, "How's your job?"

"I got into it with Tom Green at supper."

"I heard. Manuel told me you come out here whenever you get mad to the point of violence."

"Manuel told you that?" said Daniel, reclaiming the bottle.

"There are few secrets in Terlingua."

"So it would appear."

"I've been waiting for you to get tired of working for Perry. No sense coming to talk business with you if you still liked your job." Samuel grinned. "Manuel said you and Green have been going at it for weeks."

"What's with you and this Manuel kid?"

"He keeps an eye on my business interests with Perry. Watch out for that little bastard. You might think he is just a boy, but that kid has got a mean streak a mile wide."

"Interesting," mused Daniel, passing the bottle. "What kind of business are you doing with Perry?"

"Our primary arrangements involve the charcoal and brush to run your stinking furnace and mine timbers. Besides that, we arrange cattle shipments for Perry and his business associates. They typically pay in ammunition, which we swap with Villa for gold, silver, and more cattle," explained Samuel.

"You know," said Daniel laughing, "a few months back, I came across Manuel and that Mexican woman from Boquillas in Terlingua Creek with one of your wagons of ammunition."

Samuel poked Daniel with the bottle. "Still thinking about her?"

"And you don't?"

"Not like that." Samuel smiled. "She's particular that one is."

The men laughed and shared the bottle.

Daniel relaxed. Laughing with an old friend was good medicine.

"How long are you planning on working for Perry?" Samuel asked.

"I don't know. The new furnace is assembled, and we plan to test fire it soon."

The men passed the bottle back and forth in silence for a while.

"It's a beautiful night," Samuel said.

Daniel agreed. "I like the way the limestone reflects the starlight."

"It is a curious county, isn't it?"

"It grows on a man in a fashion."

The men lapsed into silence again, the bottle circling between them.

"What about your personal relationship with Perry?" Daniel asked. "He seems like a duck out of water. How did he land here in Terlingua?"

"I heard he won the mine in a card game."

"Really?" Daniel laughed at the thought.

"That's what I heard."

"I don't see how that man scrapes enough wood and charcoal out of this country to heat his furnace."

"And this is just one of several mines in the district. Did you know that Perry is excited about the idea of hauling coal out of Mexico to Terlingua?"

"Where is there any coal? Where would it come from?"

"Down below Boquillas, a bit south of Múzquiz. In reality, it will never happen. The nearest coal is too far south. There are no existing railroad tracks, and northern Mexico is far too unstable for that kind of development. Too many underemployed soldiers taking what they can when they can. Villa's brother and I are simply tapping Perry for imaginary startup capital—and other things. No one has the slightest intention of delivering a single speck of coal to these mines."

"Pancho Villa's brother?" Daniel asked.

"Yes, Pancho Villa's brother. Raul handles the money for Villa."

"So, have you met Pancho Villa?"

Samuel smiled.

"Well, I'll be damned."

Samuel shrugged, "I arrange commodity negotiations for men with money to invest, and skim as much as possible with every trade. Villa's diminishing military success has been good for my business. He is a regular customer who pays his debts with other men's money."

Daniel laughed.

"Mario Torreón thinks Villa is defeated." Samuel explained. "He believes that the weaker Villa becomes, the more money he will desperately waste to prevent his military destruction. Now that Villa was defeated at Celaya, he will be desperate for munitions and supplies."

"But I read just today that Villa had Obregón surrounded at Celaya."

Samuel laughed. "He did, but Obregón's German advisors taught Villa a bloody lesson about the lethal combination of barbed wire and machine guns. Word from Mexico is that Villa lost five thousand of his best cavalry, his famous *dorados*, in the battle," said Samuel. "Where did you hear your information about Celaya?"

"I read it in a San Antonio newspaper."

"Printed news is old news. Besides, a man can't believe half of what that bastard Hearst prints in his filthy yellow newspapers," advised Samuel. "Forget Villa. It is more fun to talk about Perry and his Chisos Mining Company. Perry has extracted an incredible amount of wealth from these mines. What other entrepreneur in North America hauls this amount of product over a hundred miles of bad road from the middle of nowhere, to a transcontinental railroad and a booming international market? Do you know how rich Perry is?"

"I can only imagine."

"They say he has mansions in Chicago and Maine and that he owns a damn yacht that he sails himself. However, rich men have a hard time understanding that everything changes. All wars end, and good deals go bad," said Samuel.

"Even your good deals?"

"Even my good deal is changing fast, especially as the war in Mexico draws to a conclusion."

"Why do you think the war is ending? How are you so certain things are changing?" Daniel asked, noticing a slight tremor in his friend's hand when the man raised the bottle for his next drink.

"I showed up in Saltillo," explained Samuel, "to collect a significant payment and arrange another munitions shipment for Villa. I had just settled in my room when a dozen armed men kicked in the door, manacled my hands and feet, and threw me in jail." Samuel looked away. "They whipped me," he whispered, holding the bottle with both hands and staring deep into the dark night.

"Whipped you?"

Samuel took a drink and paused for a moment before offering Daniel the bottle. "They hauled me to jail, whipped me, and threw me into a rat-infested cell. I sat in that stinking jail cell for three days with a stooped-over old jailer who liked to talk. The old man told me that I was in the same cell where Mexican officials had incarcerated Stephen F. Austin. He also told me that the man who had arrested me, Colonel Reyes, made a habit of executing gringos, stealing their money, and lying to Villa."

"This Colonel Reyes stole Villa's money that was intended for you? But he works for Villa?"

Samuel nodded, rubbed his neck, and then reclaimed the bottle. "It was money that Villa owed me, but it was the first time that I had encountered this man, Colonel Reyes."

"What happened? Did you get your money? How did you escape?"

Samuel spoke with his eyes cast down. "On a warm Sunday morning, soldiers dragged me from my jail cell into an open courtyard at the back of the jail." Samuel paused. He closed his eyes and exhaled a stale breath. "I can still hear the Sunday morning cathedral bells ringing the faithful to mass. It's funny what one remembers about bad experiences."

Daniel took the bottle and a drink.

"I hope I sell the gun and the bullet that kills that bastard, Colonel Reyes. Better yet, I hope I get to pull the trigger." Samuel snatched the bottle from Daniel's hand. "They dragged me to a cottonwood tree where five dead men were hanging from a thick branch, their necks stretched such that the bodies did not look human. Flies swarmed at their eyes, noses, ears, and around the cuffs of their boots where their shit dripped."

Samuel untied the scarf around his neck and pushed down his shirt collar to expose a raw, raised scar. It was lopsided, thicker on one side.

"So they hung you?" Daniel asked in disbelief. "Then what happened?"

"It was a goddamned miracle, I'm telling you. You aren't going to believe me." Samuel's eyes sparkled. "To be honest, I wouldn't believe it myself if I hadn't been there."

"Finish your story, and I will judge for myself what to believe," said Daniel, finally able to laugh a little.

"They hung me—the sixth man—on the far end of that one tree branch. Those bastards did not allow me the privilege of snapping my neck and dying quickly. Instead, they eased me down until my feet dangled about six inches off the ground. I reckon they figured it was more entertaining to watch a man hang there and choke to death real slow ..." Samuel wiped his mouth with the back of his hand before he continued. "Then a miracle occurred. A violent wind came up and brought with it hailstones the size of hens' eggs. When my executioners turned to run for the building, a bolt of lightning jumped from the heavens and exploded the hanging tree. That lightning burnt all the ropes in half, and I fell to the ground along with the dead men. The fleeing soldiers blew up as if an artillery shell had landed on them. I am telling you, Daniel, it was the wildest thing I have ever witnessed. Those Mexican soldiers lay there with their shoes exploded, clothes ripped apart at the seams, and their brains dripping out their ears. The concussion disoriented me, but I knew I had precious little time to make good an escape. In the confusion, I somehow managed to steal a horse. I galloped like hell, home to Texas."

"Damn," remarked Daniel.

The two men passed the bottle back and forth until Samuel said, "It isn't as easy to operate now that Villa's henchman have turned on him. Since my hanging, I have managed to reconnect personally with Villa through Ojinaga, and business is good, for now. I've just got fewer middlemen to rake the profits." Samuel cleared his throat and looked at his hands. "I could use your help, Daniel. That is if you're interested."

"I don't know, Samuel," said Daniel. "What about men like Reyes?"

"What about him?"

"Did Villa deal with Reyes?"

"No," said Samuel.

"No."

"No, I didn't tell him."

"Why not?" asked Daniel.

"Why? It would only complicate matters. What Reyes did was business. It wasn't personal."

"But you're eager to kill him? That isn't personal?"

"No," said Samuel, shaking his head. "Killing him is purely business."

Daniel grimaced, "I don't know. It sounds likely a deadly business."

"I could use the help. In case you haven't noticed, the Mexicans respect you."

"Let me think about it."

"I wish you would take my offer under serious consideration. I truly need your help."

Daniel grinned at his friend. "You're asking me to partner with a dead man?"

Samuel stood and offered his hand. He pulled Daniel to his feet then tossed the empty bottle into the desert. "I calculate that, the more we drink, the quicker you might accept my offer."

Daniel laughed as they walked toward the lighted porch of the trading post. "I'll drink to that, my friend."

Nearing the trading post, Daniel and Samuel realized that something terrible was happening.

A young boy ran toward them. "Please help my brother." The adolescent tugged on Daniel's sleeve. "Hurry, señor, they are going to beat him to death. Hurry, señor, they are going to hurt my brother. Don't let them whip him."

Parting the crowd, they saw Manuel lashed over a wooden barrel laid on its side, his arms and legs strapped to posts set firmly in the ground. Huicho Alvarez ripped Manuel's shirt off his back and loosened his britches.

Samuel stepped in front of Daniel and stopped him, placing his left hand firmly on his friend's chest. "Did you bring a pistol?" he whispered.

"No, I didn't."

"Take this," said Samuel, slipping Daniel his own pistol.

"Let's make sure we scout this before we do anything rash," said Daniel, tucking the pistol into the belt on his pants.

Johnson appeared at the door of the trading post holding a leather whip. Without hesitation, he reared back and struck Manuel, who screamed. The lash drew blood. When Johnson saw Samuel, his heart quickened. "This is none of your business," said Johnson, lashing the boy a second time.

Manuel screamed as the blow cut his backside, raising another bloody welt. He was dizzy with pain, and his curses softened to a whimper.

Huicho glared at Daniel, offering a challenge as a murmur of fear ran through the crowd.

Samuel moved sideways toward Johnson. "Whatever he did, two lashes is enough punishment."

Johnson's face flared. He flicked the whip and it resounded with a sharp crack. "You don't think I know how you encourage this boy to pilfer from us?"

"Hit him again and I'm going to kick your ass."

The instant Johnson squared his shoulders Samuel pounced. He knocked the man to the hard ground with a flurry of blows. Johnson did not attempt to defend himself much less fight back.

In the confusion, Huicho lunged at Daniel who was surprised but not totally caught off guard. Daniel skillfully slipped the borrowed pistol from his waistline and held the barrel square between Huicho's eyes; the hammer cocked.

Huicho froze where he stood.

Samuel kicked Johnson for good measure before ripping the whip from his hand. "Somebody cut Manuel loose, *pronto!*"

The group of men nearest the barrel loosened Manuel's bonds. Standing, Manuel straightened his clothes. He clenched both fists and stomped at the ground. Several of the men attempted to restrain him. The tension of violence had not been resolved, and the crowd pulsed with anticipation.

Johnson ran a sleeve across his bloodied nose. He touched the lower portion of his ear, where blood dripped, staining the collar of his pressed shirt.

Samuel helped Johnson to his feet and pointed him toward the trading post door. "Get yourself cleaned up." Only then did he notice that Daniel was holding a pistol against Huicho's forehead. Huicho stared defiantly at both the pistol and the man holding it.

"Well, what have we got here?" remarked Samuel, circling the two men. "Looks like the big bucks have got their antlers tangled in a knot. This must be what I once heard described as a Mexican standoff, no?"

Daniel allowed the slightest grin to crease his face.

"If you take that pistol off his forehead, he's going to try and stick you with that knife he's got hanging on his belt," said Samuel.

"He might."

"You think he understands what we're saying?"

"Nah," said Daniel. "His eyes are as cold as last week's campfire."

Samuel eased close to Huicho, whispering, "*No se mueve,* pendejo. Don't move." He carefully pulled the eight-inch steel blade knife from the leather sheath on the Mexican's belt.

That proved all the distraction Huicho needed. He swept a foot around Daniel's knee and the two men fell. Daniel dropped the pistol, and Huicho dove on top of Daniel, fists flying.

Samuel retrieved the pistol from the melee and stuffed it in his belt. He considered this fight an opportunity to measure whether or not Daniel had gone soft.

Huicho landed several hard body punches before Daniel managed to regain his feet, reorganize, and properly reconnoiter his opponent. Huicho kept rushing at him swinging wildly, trying to establish close contact where his strength could damage the gringo. Daniel landed a series of accurate blows that cut the flesh over Huicho's eyebrows and broke his nose. The more Huicho bled, the madder he got. Huicho charged, and Daniel stood the man on his heels with a well-placed right fist to the chin. Huicho rocked from his heels to his toes then back again, doing his very best to keep from falling.

"Put him down!" yelled Samuel.

Daniel glanced at his friend, who had somehow managed to find a fresh bottle of sotol. Samuel pointed at the ground with his right thumb.

Unnoticed through the dust and excitement, Manuel moved close to the fight with a machete in his right hand. The crowd gasped when the machete pierced Huicho in the back and the bloody point of the metal blade protruded from his belly. Manuel turned the blade murderously until Huicho's knees buckled and he fell to the ground.

The crowd gasped, and Daniel turned to face Huicho as he fell.

Drawn by the noise, Johnson appeared through the door. "Jesus Christ!" he screeched, rushing too late to Huicho's aid. "Who did this? Who killed him?"

Manuel looked at his bloody hands. He cursed Johnson then escaped into the dark desert.

"Stop him," screamed Johnson. "Get him."

Johnson tried to pursue Manuel, but he lacked sufficient strength to part the crowd. All he could do was shout after the boy as he disappeared into the night.

"Stop him!"

~~~~~~

After Huicho's murder, the Mexican bosses at the mine refused to work with Daniel. They openly claimed that Daniel was an agitator. Tom Green was equally tired of Daniel. He echoed the sentiment to Perry, claiming that Daniel was inciting the laborers to demand better working conditions and higher pay. Worse, he might convince the Mexicans to demand their wages in American dollars. Johnson avoided Daniel, except when he had business in the store. Dr. Wright also dodged him. Daniel tried on two occasions to speak with Dr. Wright, yet the tired old man resisted both attempts.

When Marshal Navarro arrived in Terlingua to investigate the murder, he spent an entire morning talking with Perry, Green, and Johnson. It was after noon before Navarro looked for Daniel at the furnace. Navarro politely introduced himself and explained that he needed to ask some questions. At Navarro's suggestion, the two men walked into the scattered creosote brush beyond the furnace where they could talk privately.

"I understand that you were involved in the altercation that resulted in the murder of the Mexican gentleman, Señor Alvarez." Navarro stood with his feet firmly planted and worked his hat back on his head.

Daniel nodded "Yes, sir, you could say I was involved."

"I understand you held a gun on Señor Alvarez while your companion assaulted Mr. Johnson." Navarro pulled a dark blue kerchief from his hip pocket and wiped his brow.

"Yes, sir, I did hold a gun to the man's head, but only after he came at me with malicious intent."

"Did you know why Mr. Johnson was whipping that boy?" Navarro asked, shoving the bandana into a hip pocket.

"No, sir, I didn't at the time it happened. There was no need to know why he was giving Manuel that whipping. Perry does not own these people. A man should be allowed due process regardless of the crime."

"Do you know where Manuel went?"

"No, sir, I don't know where he went."

"How well did you know the boy?" asked Navarro, hooking his thumbs in the belt loops of his trousers. He looked uncomfortably over his shoulder toward the furnace. He could see the Mexicans gathered in deepest shadows of the furnace shed, eager to eavesdrop on their conversation.

It frustrated Daniel that Navarro would not get straight to the point, whatever it was. He rocked onto his boot heels and waited for Navarro's full attention before saying, "I didn't know the young man on a personal level. Neither did I have a business relationship with him beyond his position at the trading post." Daniel ran his shirtsleeve across his forehead. The sun was direct and intense. He did not mind answering questions, but the accusatory tone riled him. "Manuel took care of my horse and tack. That was the limit of our association." Daniel thought for a moment, and then added, "I will admit to having a friendship or two with the men working at the furnace, but I wasn't friendly with Manuel. Not like I am with the men I work with every day."

"Why did you feel the need to put a gun to Señor Alvarez' forehead?" asked Navarro.

"Marshal, if you'd have seen the look in that man's eyes, you would have done the same, perhaps worse."

Navarro drew back his shoulders. "They tell me you ride with the Mexicans. Is that true?"

"They can kiss my ass. I ride with anyone I damn well please until somebody passes a law against it."

Navarro crossed his arms. "How well do you know Samuel Jenkins?"

Daniel frowned. "Why?"

"Answer the question," commanded Navarro, exposing his impatience.

"We were in the army together."

"He was your roommate at West Point, correct?"

Navarro's intimate knowledge of his personal history surprised Daniel. "Why are you asking me these questions when you already know the answers? What is your point?"

"My point, sir, is that you and your friend of many years instigated a fight that resulted in the murder of one of Perry's valuable employees at the hands of a trouble-making, no-good youngster who deserved his whipping. That boy had been caught red-handed in the act of stealing ammunition." Navarro moved closer to Daniel's face. "Now that you helped him get away, he's no doubt gone and joined an established armed group of thieves, which will further contribute to the violence and thievery that plagues my jurisdiction."

Daniel sensed that the confrontation had escalated to a dangerous threshold. There would be nothing gained in challenging the marshal. Daniel simply wanted the conversation concluded. He relaxed his posture and shifted his body weight onto his heels, a half step away from Navarro.

Navarro reacted to Daniel's retreat. His fisted hands opened and he placed them on his tired lower back. In a calm voice, he explained the crux of the matter. "I don't mind folks selling guns to Villa, or buying cattle of questionable ownership. What I don't appreciate is mercenary bastards coming in here and instigating trouble with either the Mexicans or the mines." Navarro spit tobacco juice onto the hard ground, a gesture of frustration. "For the record, I need to hear your version of what happened that night."

Daniel exhaled, and then told the story of what had occurred in complete detail, including the part where Huicho disarmed him and almost kicked his ass. Navarro did not interrupt Daniel once during the telling of his story. When Daniel finished, he asked Navarro, "Are we done?"

"For now," said Navarro. "There is one more thing you should know. Your friend Samuel has gone from helping people get things done to making too much money."

"You mean that Samuel angered your friends and business associates by starting his own business through Ojinaga?" Daniel wanted Navarro to know that he knew the real deal.

"I don't give a damn what you think you know about local business protocols. Men who once proudly did business with Samuel are offering a free rope to hang him." Navarro narrowed his eyes. "Do business with Samuel at your own risk."

"Are we done, Marshal?"

"We're done."

Walking back to the furnace, Daniel laughed when he saw the laborers scurry from their observation posts, each stumbling over the other as he hurried back to his neglected duties.

CHAPTER 14

¡Ya Basta! Enough Already!

THE SUMMER NIGHTS were unbearably hot. To cope with the heat, Daniel sprinkled water on his pillow and sheets before lying down to sleep. His nightmares had assimilated the ghosts of marauding Comanche warriors raiding deep into Mexico, stealing everything of value, the trail north lined with the bleached bones and bodies of both captives and livestock.

Unable to sleep, Daniel climbed out of bed and stepped onto the porch. He watched daylight caress the Chisos Mountains with a soft, orange light. Sunrise clarified feelings into thought, causing him to speak. "It is time to leave this place."

A terrible wail pierced the darkness announcing the ominous dust cloud that billowed above the primary mine works. Another cave-in. Daniel shook his head and leaned on a porch post.

Dr. Wright came onto the porch rubbing his face with the palms of his hands. "What happened?"

Daniel looked at the man and then nodded toward the mine works on the hill above Terlingua.

"Oh my!" exclaimed Dr. Wright. "Not again."

The housekeepers ran from their shared room, slamming the screen door. "*Date prisa, niñas!*" cried the oldest woman. She handed the younger girls blankets and strips of muslin cloth. "They will need those things." She made the sign of the cross and ran with the girls toward the mine.

Exhaling a long slow breath, Daniel went to his room.

"You aren't going up there, are you?" Dr. Wright spoke to him through the screen door. "Perry will fire you, or possibly worse. They considered having Navarro arrest you for sedition. Did you know that?"

Shouldering into his jacket, Daniel pushed his way through the screen door and returned onto the porch. "Well, they can quit worrying. I'm finished working here, Dr. Wright. Now if you will excuse me," said Daniel, stepping off the porch. "I'm going to see what I can do to help."

Daniel hustled up the hill to the mine entrance where he found Udolph bent over and gasping for air.

"What happened?"

Udolph coughed until he spit a thick wad of brown phlegm from his raw throat. "I don't know. I was taking samples from the digger's baskets when she blew out."

"Was there an explosion?"

"No, I think it simply collapsed."

"Who's down there?"

"Nobody," answered Udolph.

"You mean to tell me there weren't any Mexicans down there?"

"Yeah, there are Mexicans down there."

"Dammit, man," cursed Daniel, turning to the mine entrance where a man in the rescue basket made the sign of the cross before disappearing into the dust-choked abyss. Shaking his head, Daniel walked away from Udolph to join the men on the rope who were lowering the rescue basket into the mine. The rope went slack and they retrieved the basket. When it emerged, Daniel volunteered to go next. No one tried to stop him. An old man offered him a carbide lamp.

"Gracias," said Daniel. Tying a kerchief over his mouth and nose, he lit the headlamp with a loud pop and braced himself as the basket descended into the darkness below.

~~~

The first three men who emerged from the mine walked with minimal assistance. The next two men were strapped to pine boards. Both men were conscious. One had a bloody skull and a limp arm. The other had suffered a broken femur; the injured leg twisted in a painful angle. Grief-stricken women and children swarmed the survivors.

The sun climbed high into the dust-stained sky before rescuers lifted the last of five dead men from the mine. Daniel carried the last dead man to the surface and handed him to his family. Mournful relatives placed the crumpled body on a freshly hewn pine board and covered the corpse with a white sheet.

It was difficult to breathe. Daniel squatted on his heels and wiped his face with a filthy kerchief. His lungs burned. His eyes, nose, and throat were caked with mucus and dust. His head throbbed, and his ears rang from the din of machinery. Yet Daniel heard Tom Green yell over the noise of the grieving mob gathered at mine entrance.

"Lecho, you stupid bastard," bellowed Green, pushing his way through the crowd. "Lecho, you lazy bastard, I told you to get those timbers installed."

Green pushed the man called Lecho against a pile of mine timbers, grabbed him by the shirt collar, and slapped him across the face with his open right hand. The impact of the blow silenced the crowd.

Strangely, Daniel noticed a pair of ravens circling the cloud of dust that hung above the mine as Tom Green drew back his hand a second time and threw a long calculated punch. Lecho fell to the ground with a spray of blood and saliva. The Mexican lay on the ground not attempting a defense. The lack of response infuriated Green. "Goddamn you, Lecho, I'm going to hold you personally responsible for this."

"What are you doing?" shouted Daniel, intercepting Green's right arm in midswing.

Jerking free of his grasp, Green growled, "Stay out of this."

"Leave the man alone. If you lay one more hand on him, I will beat you myself."

The comment startled Green. "I'm telling Perry to fire you."

"You can't fire me. I quit."

Green flinched. Daniel had quit. There was nothing more to fight about, yet he continued to clench his fists and stomp at the ground.

Daniel helped Lecho to his feet, and said, "Go and do what must be done."

Lecho gathered his crumbled straw hat and began organizing the necessary work team.

"You leave that man alone," said Daniel, staring Green in the eye before turning and walking back down the hill to the Holiday Hotel.

~⁓~

That same afternoon, Daniel settled his accounts at the trading post, including the cost of his horse. He said a brief good-bye to the men at the furnace and spent the early evening drinking most of a bottle of sotol with Gato Acosta while waiting for the hot sun to set.

It was midnight when Dr. Wright found Daniel in the livery stable rigging his horse. "Where are you headed? Back east?" Dr. Wright asked, his expression a confused mixture of curiosity and concern.

"No." Daniel pulled the last loop on the cinch, tested the knot, and dropped the stirrup. "South, I imagine," he said, securing his saddlebags and bedroll onto his saddle.

"I'm not like them," explained Dr. Wright, struggling for words. "I just can't afford to say anything about the way they treat the workers."

"I know." Daniel turned to his horse and slipped his left boot in the stirrup.

"Don't be a fool. They're just Mexicans." Dr. Wright insisted.

Daniel swung onto his horse. He adjusted himself in the saddle, pushing with his legs to test the length of the stirrups. "No human beings should be treated the way these men are, Dr. Wright. You know that all Perry cares about is cheap labor and profit. I saw it in Cuba, Honduras, Nicaragua, then again in the Philippines." Daniel heeled the gelding out of the barn. He pushed back his brimmed hat and looked to the sky. It was a hot night. A distant thunderstorm flashed heat lightning. The air smelled of rain.

Dr. Wright followed him outside. "They say you are an agitator."

"They say a lot of things," said Daniel. "I only hope I was some help for you."

"You were. You did a good job. I have never seen the men as happy as when they were working with you. Green and the others work the Mexicans until they have nothing left to give, expecting their children to step in when it's their turn." Dr. Wright rubbed his face with both hands. "I just don't understand why you risk everything to defend the Mexicans."

Daniel reached for the bottle of sotol in his jacket pocket. He took two long pulls then spoke with a far away voice. "In the Philippines, I was with General Wood when we trapped a large group of Muslims on Mount Dajo. We kept them pinned down with small arms fire in a barren crater while our ships off the coast fired on them." A deep emotional ache shook his body, a tsunami of sadness flooding his soul. "Nine hundred men, women, and children died there. I had the task of executing the wounded and personally led a detail of men through the carnage to eliminate any survivors."

Daniel rubbed the back of his neck and looked to the stars. "I received a handful of medals for my actions that day. Most of the soldiers did not mind the duty. They kept any valuables they found during the killing frenzy. One man collected dozens of gold teeth."

A dogfight exploded near the trading post. Both men turned in that direction and peered through the darkness until somebody yelled at the dogs in Spanish and the noise ended.

"What happened on Mount Dajo changed me." Daniel nodded at the doctor. "Although my closest friends still claim that my Cuban wife changed me the most."

"You are married?" asked Dr. Wright.

"I was. She died years ago."

"I'm sorry."

"It was a long time ago. After the massacre on Mount Dajo, we cornered a small group of militants in the village of Bud Bagsak, and I received orders to turn our machine guns on the entire village, prior to allowing the noncombatants to clear the area. I refused the order, and General Wood had me arrested. Ultimately, I resigned my commission in Manila and drifted back to Tennessee on my own dime. It took me two years to find my way home." Daniel fell silent. He felt that he had shared too much.

"What has a soldier murdering civilians got to do with a man like Perry paying folks to honestly perform dangerous work?"

Sitting on his horse, Daniel stared at the sky and said nothing in response.

"So be it," said Dr. Wright, shaking his head. "I have to confess that none of the gossip I have heard about you includes anything similar to what you just shared."

"Such is life."

The men shook hands, and Daniel turned his horse south toward Mexico.

CHAPTER 15

To the River

DANIEL SPENT HIS first night away from the Chisos Mining Company camped in a grove of cottonwood trees along Terlingua Creek. The next morning, he followed the rain-swollen creek south toward Mexico. The viscous mud-hued water cut through cobbled strata of ancient creek beds, carving tree roots from the bank and carrying them downstream.

The sun was burning hot in the afternoon sky when he rode into the humble gathering of mud and rock houses that formed the community of Terlingua Abaja. His arrival brought the entire village into the street. Men and boys crowded around his horse. The news of his confrontation with Tom Green had traveled Terlingua Creek faster than his horse had carried him, and the Mexicans hailed him as a hero.

Inspired by the excitement, Daniel sat in the shade of the dirt-floor *tienda*—the only store in town—and bought crudely bottled, homemade beers for everyone who wanted them. A gallon jug of sotol appeared, and a pack of young boys killed a pair of goats under the supervision of a single old man.

The men drank while the women cooked.

At sunset, five men with an accordion, a tattered drum, and two guitars, including one they called a *guitarrón*, appeared in the plaza, and a rowdy dance commenced that lasted well beyond midnight. The fandango ended without a single fistfight, although the town drunks continued to drink until daylight before they wandered home to sleep.

Nursing a hangover, Daniel stayed on a few days. He passed the time helping a small group of old men gather corn stalks, tie them into bundles, and stack them in a small cave along Terlingua Creek. The men also used the cool, damp cave to store crocks of beans, corn, and canned meats. After a daily siesta, the men played cards, smoked tobacco, and talked about their field crops—mostly corn, beans, squash, tomatoes, chilies, onions, and melons. They also talked about chickens, goats, stalking deer, fishing, and women. Often, they simply gossiped, as grown men are prone to do.

Inevitably, the discussion would shift to the war in Mexico. Each man had lost someone in the war—an uncle, a cousin, brother, or son. They agreed that the war was much like rain. It was something they could not influence. It was necessary. It was not about land reform. It was about control. It was about power.

Daniel stayed in Terlingua Abaja until the last stalk of sweet corn was cut and field-stacked. He left the old men asleep in their cave at daylight, riding west over the mesa of eagles following an old trail across the flat-topped mesa, where he discovered a side trail leading south. The steep trail wound down into a canyon of wind-and-water-polished pinnacles as the setting sun streaked the sky with delicate rays of failing light.

At first, Daniel mistook the roar of the river for the wind. Not until he saw the tumbling water entering Santa Elena Canyon did he truly understand what he heard. He actually felt the river rattling his bones; the constant roar dominated everything, even his thoughts.

Daniel rode upstream across sculpted sand dunes that drifted from the river's edge onto marble-like ledge rock shelves. Crossing the river into Mexico above the confluence of San Carlos Creek, he encountered an old man camped in a grove of *palo verde* trees.

Strangely, Rosalio Gonzalez-Luna did not seem surprised to have a gringo ride into his camp. His eyes twinkled with mischief, and he was both talkative and generous. Nicknamed Chalio, he claimed to be eighty-four years old, although he moved like a man half his age. Chalio welcomed Daniel into his humble camp and actively mentored Daniel's growing passion for catching, cooking, and eating the little blue catfish that swam in the deepest river eddies.

The men fished separately, only coming together to share a smoke and discuss tactics before returning to their lines. For bait, Daniel used stale bread rubbed with bacon fat, alternating with little pieces of pink-colored lye soap. Chalio, on the other hand, preferred the insects he found under rocks along the riverbank. No matter how hard he tried, Chalio could not communicate something obviously very important about the bait he used. Daniel understood it changed forms during its life, but into what he did not know.

In the hour before dawn, the river suddenly changed colors from green to brown, and San Carlos Creek exploded with a flood of debris, mud, rocks, and water. The creek swelled into a tangle of brush and rock-red water until it almost filled the narrow side canyon that led into the river. The Rio Grande quickly rose to the edge of the bluff beneath their camp, which was well situated on a rock ledge. Daniel marveled at how the river pulsed, swollen with rainwater from unseen storms miles and miles upstream.

With the river running so high, the men were unable to fish. Confident that the river was not going to clear any time soon, Chalio decided to go home to Los Alamos, Chihuahua. He quickly packed, said good-bye, and then rode toward home, south along San Carlos Creek.

Daniel stayed in the camp and watched the Rio Grande recede, leaving its banks lined with mud and a random collection of debris. He found a bloated cow carcass deposited high in the branches of a cottonwood tree. On a whim, Daniel climbed the rimrock on the south side of Santa Elena Canyon and walked a few miles downstream. Whenever the canyon allowed, he leaned over the edge and peered down at the river below.

Upon returning to his camp, Daniel spied what appeared to be a body floating face down in the river. Hustling down the last embankment toward the river, he saw the dead man's gloved hand pointing at him. Daniel squatted on his boot heels, lit a cigar, and thought about what he could realistically do for the dead man.

Cicadas made a deafening noise. Shimmering heat waves danced from the limestone cliffs that constantly swallowed the mighty river. Cumulus clouds formed over distant mountain peaks in Mexico, promising more rain. The damp odor of creosote brush and drying river mud scented the warm, upriver breeze.

The dead man swirled in the eddy, his arms extended as if crucified, his hair forming an ebony halo. The corpse rolled onto its back, exposing its bloated face to the hot sun. A school of silvery minnows swam through the man's long black hair. Big blue bottle flies buzzed around his eyes, which were swollen shut by death's embrace.

"That decides it," declared Daniel, accepting that he was not obliged to haul the man onto dry ground for a proper Christian burial. "I don't know why I need to explain myself to a dead man. I am not dragging you out of the river. The river killed you, now let the river bury you."

Standing, Daniel removed his hat and clutched it tight against his belly with both hands. "I'm sorry for the loved ones you left behind, you poor fellow." He looked up at the hot blue sky and said, "Go with God."

Settling his brimmed hat back onto his head, Daniel turned away from the river and went to break camp.

CHAPTER 16

Peyote Dance

EAST BEYOND THE foothills of the Sierra Ponce de Leon in Mexico, Daniel bought a few provisions from the only store in the sleepy village of Santa Elena: coffee, tobacco, stick matches, bacon, corn tortillas, and four cans of beans. He continued downstream along the rain-swollen Rio Grande, crossing the river into Texas at Woodson's Camp.

The day was hot. As he rode beyond the shelter of trees growing near the river, he encountered little shade along the trail that contoured through the rolling desert hills. The geology of the Chisos Mountains fascinated Daniel—igneous peaks and ridges that pierced contorted layers of tortured limestone; an endless ocean of desert crowned by gorgeous, sky-island mountains of yellow pines, douglas-firs, and Pleistocene remnants of quaking aspen trees.

Daniel made camp near an abandoned brick-making camp on the north end of Mariscal Mountain. Restless, he rose before dawn and made a breakfast of beans, bacon fat, and tortillas on a small warming fire. Breaking camp, he rode through a barren landscape of fractured limestone hills, scattered herds of semi-feral cattle, and herds of goats attended only by dogs.

Late in the day, Daniel crossed the Rio Grande into Mexico near the village of San Vicente. He admired the Rio Grande at this location—a ribbon of green flowing toward the Sierra del Carmen, swallowed by the shadowed cleft marking Boquillas Canyon. The patient, powerful river had literally parted the massive limestone cliffs of a most spectacular mountain.

A covey of quail exploded from the thicket of brush inside an adobe ruin, and the idea of fresh quail for supper pleased Daniel. While gathering firewood, he discovered a Spanish silver peso, some square nails, several discarded wooden boxes, and a few pieces of wire—everything he required to construct a proper box trap. Daniel arranged his camp, cared for his horse, and set to hunting quail.

Sitting beneath countless stars, Daniel ate a delicious supper of roasted quail stuffed with fresh green chilies, wild oregano, and stale corn tortillas. As he ate, he recalled the stories he had heard told in Terlingua about the Spanish forts near the Mexican villages of San Vincente and San Carlos. The Spanish had built the forts in the eighteenth century as a defense against the murderous Comanche raids that had essentially depopulated most of northern Mexico.

Mounted Comanche warriors were ferocious soldiers. Had the Spaniards actively challenged the marauding Comanche warriors, or were they merely opportunists seeking undiscovered mineral wealth who hid in the dark? Daniel assumed that these Spaniards had cowered in fear during the season of the Comanche moons.

"History is a nothing but a conglomerate of lies," mused Daniel, wrapping himself in his bedroll. Lying beneath a blanket of stars, he exhaled a long stale breath and congratulated himself for breaking away from the Chisos Mining Company. "One man's dream is another man's misery." Daniel sighed as he surrendered to sleep, come what may.

Startled from his sleep, Daniel woke before daylight to find a man hunkered at the edge of the fire's diminished glow. The old man's presence did not threaten him; neither did it cause him to reach for his pistol. Rather, the man's eyes reflected a sense of belonging. The old man smiled, added wood to the fire, and then squatted back onto his heels.

The old man's hair was silver gray and cropped at his shoulders. His face was chocolate brown and wrinkled with many years. He wore a richly colored red scarf tied around his head, its tails trailing partway down his back. His loose-fitting shirt was neatly tucked into worn gray pants that were tied at the waist with a multicolored woven belt, and leather sandals were fastened with a cord around his ankles and a single loop between his first and second toes. The edges of his feet were cracked and calloused.

The men tended the fire without speaking, each searching for clues to the other man's world. Daniel made coffee, and they shared the remaining two quail from last night's supper warmed on coals raked from the fire.

While eating, Daniel discovered that the man's Spanish was rather incomplete. Romero Orranteño hailed from a mountainous country near the headwaters of the Conchos River. He claimed to be Raramuri and explained that the Mexicans called his people Tarahumara. Romero spoke Spanish with his tongue close to his teeth. He explained that he was on a peyote quest, the result of a story his grandfather had told him a very long time ago.

Daniel was unfamiliar with peyote and asked about it. He had a difficult time understanding the complicated answer. Romero talked about peyote, corn, and deer with great reverence. He spoke of peyote as medicine that eases the inescapable suffering of the human condition. Daniel understood the man to be pursuing visions produced by this spineless cactus that looked like a green rock, and that, when eaten, allowed men to speak with the gods.

Romero filled the coffee pot with creek water and sat it on the fire to boil. He pulled a large leather pouch from under his shirt and removed a square cloth of periwinkle-blue-and-cornflower-yellow printed material, which he carefully spread at his feet. He took a small wooden cross from the pouch and placed it on the center of the cloth. The he emptied the remaining contents of the pouch onto the cloth around the cross. He prayed over the peyote before putting it into the pot of boiling water. Romero allowed the peyote to boil before he filled Daniel's coffee cup and gestured for him to drink.

Having seen his share of human suffering, Daniel believed in the man's sensibilities. He drank the tea and choked down many pieces of the cactus. Romero packed a bone pipe, and they smoked a sweet-tasting combination of herbs.

As he watched Romero tamp out the pipe, Daniel felt a warmth move from his intestines into his blood. A pulsating, luminous awareness took possession of his conscious mind while his belly churned peyote-angry. Daniel scurried on his hands and knees into the brush and retched, sentience slipping from his grasp.

When the nausea passed, Daniel lay on his bedroll and listened to Romero sing a low, monotone song, while the cactus exploded inside his brain. His mind chased his soul, traveling without movement. Colored patterns swirled and danced, joyful little thieves stealing his humanity. Inside the darkness, a point of light drew him through shoals of nonhuman awareness, tossing him indifferently into a cactus-induced trance of insanity.

PART 3:
Mexico

The first half of the Toltec Mastery of Transformation is the destruction of an old dream or belief system. The second half of the Mastery of Transformation is the re-creation of the dream.
— Don Miguel Ruiz (http://joydancer.com/
notebook/transformation.html)

CHAPTER 17

Transformation

DANIEL SHIELDS HIS eyes from the sun, his vision blurred by the burning yellow orb. He hears a voice but can see no one. He can see only light.

"Hush, mi amor."

The disembodied voice soothes his pain. Tears cool his sunburnt face. For reasons he cannot comprehend, the air smells of clean sheets, lavender, and freshly washed hair. A cold washcloth placed on his forehead seduces his mind with fragrance.

"Rosa?"

"Shush, hombre," whispers a soft, sweet voice in lyrical Spanish.

"Why?" cries Daniel.

"Let go of your anger. Release the hurt. That is your only hope, hombre."

The comfort of an unseen Angel of Light eases his mind as Daniel drifts to sleep.

～ᵕ～

When Daniel woke, he found himself flat on his back between clean sheets in a small room illuminated by a single candle. Leaning on his elbows, he pushed himself up slightly and surveyed the room from the metal-spring bed. He took in a pine dresser, some crudely built shelves covered with fabric and folded linens, and a large picture of the Virgin of Guadalupe. A bleeding crucifix floated above the closed door.

Daniel pushed his pillows into a pile at the head of the bed and dragged his body into a sitting position. As he leaned against the whitewashed stucco wall, he realized he was wearing an oversized white cotton blouse. The familiar scars were still there on his leg and the backs of his hands, yet he could not determine where he was. His entire body ached, his head hurt something fierce, and he was hungry to the point of nausea. "I can't be dead," he said, laughing quietly. "I hurt too damn much to be dead."

Crawling out of bed, Daniel shuffled to the only door. He raised the wooden latch and pulled the door open. Greeted by sunlight and hot summer air, he shielded his eyes and tried to recognize his surroundings. His knees buckled and he collapsed onto the patio floor.

Carmelina stepped into the courtyard to see what had fallen and found Daniel lying on the patio. The eight-year old girl screamed, *"Mamá, date prisa. El hombre ha caído. ¡Prisa!"*

The next time Daniel woke, he discovered an old man asleep in a wooden chair at the foot of the bed. The man snored with his head slumped forward. He recognized the man as the one-eyed Mexican he had encountered when riding with Lieutenant Thompson.

No matter how hard he tried, he remembered nothing about how he had arrived in this room. Daniel searched his mind for memories. Thirsty, he reached for the cup of water he found sitting on the table next to the bed and drank it in a single swallow. His throat hurt, and he was disgusted to discover something thick and oily on his parched lips.

Daniel wiped his lips with the backs of his hands.

"It is balm," answered the man in the chair. "Welcome back from the dead."

Daniel stared at the man who had come awake in the chair. He was much older than he had appeared at first glance. His jet-black hair was tinged with gray at the temples, and he was clean-shaven except for a drooping mustache. His left eyelid was sewn shut. A thick scar curved from where the tear duct should have been out along his cheekbone.

The white of his one good eye was yellow with age, and his calloused hands trembled as he refilled Daniel's glass.

Smiling, the old man said, "Drink as much as you can. You were quite dehydrated. We were worried about you."

Daniel drank the second glass of water and held the glass out for the old man to pour a third. He judged that he was not in danger. "How did I happen to arrive here in this condition?"

The old man smiled. "Good. I can see your mind has survived its ordeal intact. That is a good thing. My name is Mario Torreón." Mario stood and opened window shutters, creating a flood of light in the room. He allowed his eye to adjust to the afternoon sunlight and heat before yelling, "Rafael! Tell Samuel that Daniel is awake. Run!" Mario watched the boy run to his errand before returning to the chair at the foot of the bed.

The two men sat in silence until Samuel entered the room reeking of mules and leather, his shirtsleeves rolled up past his elbows and britches tucked in the tops of his boots. "I'm glad to see that you've decided to rejoin the living," he said, laughing.

Daniel shook his head and smiled.

"Ramona, bring me a chair," called Samuel.

The familiar green-eyed woman appeared at the door with a wooden chair.

Samuel took it from her, set it down backwards, and sat down, leaning his muscled arms forward over the high chair back.

Ramona lingered in the doorway.

Samuel winked. "Your nurse is happy to see that you have recovered. She was concerned that you would sleep for fifty years like the old man in the child's fable."

"What do you mean, my nurse?" Daniel frowned.

"Ramona nursed you back to life, you lucky bastard. I wanted to shoot you like a broken horse and put you out of your misery. Only Ramona suspected that you intended to live."

Daniel turned to the woman. "Gracias, Señora."

Ramona acknowledged his gratitude with a smile. "Do you want anything?"

"Something to eat, perhaps?" asked Daniel. "But only if it isn't too much trouble."

"Is everybody hungry?" Ramona asked Mario and Samuel.

Mario said, "Yes, thank you."

Samuel acknowledged her question with an affirmative nod of his head.

Ramona left the room with a twirl of her cotton skirt.

Samuel scooted his chair toward the bed. "She needs a husband."

"She isn't married?" asked Daniel, not hiding his surprise.

"Ramona lost her husband at the mine." Samuel leaned toward the bed. "I think she liked nursing you, you lucky bastard."

Mario shook his head, rolling his one good eye.

"Where did you find me?" asked Daniel, anxious to learn what had happened.

"Mario found you passed out in the desert. You were missing a boot. How you came to be like that, we don't rightly know," explained Samuel.

"Missing a boot?"

"Sock-footed," smiled Mario.

Daniel exhaled and briefly looked to the ceiling as if for answers. "Where am I?"

"You are in Boquillas, in my house," Mario said.

"Boquillas, Mexico?"

"Yes," answered Mario.

"What happened to me?"

"Who knows?" said Samuel.

"A Tarahumara man rescued you and brought us to you," said Mario.

"Tell me about this man," Daniel asked.

"He didn't say much," said Mario. "His Spanish wasn't too good."

"When did you find me?"

"Two days ago," said Samuel.

"And how long have I been in this bed, asleep?"

"Almost thirty hours," Mario estimated.

"What about my horse?"

Mario looked to Samuel.

"Either it's lost or the Indian took it, we think." Samuel said.

"You think?"

"Mario told the Indian that if he found your horse to bring it," explained Samuel.

"If he finds it, he will bring it," Mario agreed.

"Where did you find me?"

"North of La Unión on the road to San Vicente," Mario said.

"You were sunburned, cut, bruised, and missing one boot," interjected Samuel. "You were a mess. You had pissed and crapped all in your pants."

Daniel frowned.

Mario's face softened. "We weren't sure if you'd been beaten or gone crazy. You don't remember us finding you?"

Daniel shook his head. "No. I don't remember anything about that, except ..."

"Except what?" Samuel asked.

"I vaguely remember an old man wandering into my camp."

"He remembers the *nagual*," said Mario.

"It would appear so." Samuel grinned.

"Nagual?" Daniel asked.

"Mario thinks the Tarahumara is a shaman of sorts ... a sorcerer," explained Samuel.

Mario walked to the open window. "It's another nice sunset."

Daniel looked at the wall opposite the window where the setting sun cast soft shades of yellow and orange light.

"You remember the old man?" asked Mario.

"All I remember is that he appeared in my camp."

"What do you mean he just appeared?" asked Mario.

"I was camped at the Spanish ruins near San Vicente and woke before daylight to find this strange fellow tending my fire."

Mario turned to face Daniel and asked, "Did you offer him food? Did he eat?"

"What does that have to do with anything?"

"If the nagual refused food then he was most likely an apparition," Mario explained.

"A ghost, you say? You expect me to believe that a ghost stole my horse!"

"Forget the damn horse," groaned Mario. "That *brujo* was capable of stealing things far more important than your horse."

Daniel laughed. "Brujo!"

"Our world is different than yours," said Mario.

"What makes you think he was a witch?"

"When an unknown man wanders into your camp in the middle of the night, and if this man refuses food," Mario explained.

"But he didn't refuse food, he ate quite well as a matter of fact," said Daniel.

"One can't be too careful," insisted Mario.

"Mario worries that the Indian's touch might have cursed the rest of us with the same dark spell that stole your mind," said Samuel.

Ramona called from the kitchen, "*Ya!*"

Mario waggled his right index finger. "This nagual is a powerful shaman. He is very capable of stealing valuable parts of your soul."

"If you are lucky, he took something you don't need," joked Samuel.

"Maybe he just took my horse," grumbled Daniel.

Mario scowled. "Let the horse go. It will be returned in time."

"You want to eat in that nightshirt or get dressed?" asked Samuel.

"I want to get dressed." Daniel moved to the edge of the bed and tested his balance.

Samuel retrieved a pair of pants from the shelf and placed them on the bed. "Ramona had to throw out your clothes. She altered these to fit."

Daniel slipped on the canvas pants, pleasantly surprised about how well they fit.

～〰～〰〰

Ramona served steaming bowls of chicken soup with cabbage slaw, refried beans, beefsteak, and dozens of steaming hot, corn tortillas.

Daniel inhaled the aromatic steam rising from the rich broth. He smiled at Ramona and sipped a spoonful of soup. The men ate without speaking, allowing Daniel to enjoy the curative effects of the meal. He ate deliberately, relishing every bite. When the men finished eating, Ramona cleared the table, and Mario rolled four cigarettes.

Samuel wiped his chin with a cloth napkin and belched. He got up from the table and returned with a bottle of sotol and four glasses.

Daniel placed a hand over one of the glasses. "No, thank you. I don't need any right now."

Samuel poured three glasses and sat down. He drank his glass of sotol in one swallow and poured himself another.

Mario lit all four cigarettes with a single match and gave one each to Daniel and Samuel.

Ramona brought Daniel a cup of coffee and took her cigarette from Mario. She claimed a glass of sotol as her own.

"Did you recover any of my gear?" asked Daniel.

"Ramona's son-in-law Sergio found it at the presidio near San Vicente," answered Samuel.

"What do I owe you?"

"What do you mean?" Mario asked.

"For any trouble or inconvenience I might have caused for you."

"You owe us nothing except your friendship," Mario said.

"Thank you for your hospitality," said Daniel with a deferential nod.

"It's nothing," said Mario, waving his hand for emphasis. "Let us return to your story. Why did you leave Terlingua?"

"I left for a thousand reasons. Honestly, I couldn't contribute to men living in conditions that approached indentured servitude."

"To Perry and that Tom Green you were an agitator," sneered Samuel.

"I didn't go there to cause trouble. I went to make money, only I discovered that distilling quicksilver kills men. It's no different than gutting them with a machete. Perry's attitude toward his laborers is bullshit, Green treats the Mexicans like feudal serfs, Johnson robs them of their wages at the trading post, and Udolph kills far too many men as they dig ore."

Mario tapped Samuel's knee and asked, "Who is Udolph?"

"Udolph is the geologist, the one digging the cinnabar."

"Ah," exclaimed Mario. "He is the German bastard."

"Austrian, actually," commented Daniel, "but you got the bastard part right. Terlingua is sufficiently isolated from the rest of America that the workers at the mine have no idea how bad they have it. Their only comparison is Mexico."

"We know that Perry lives in fear of the Mexicans organizing and striking, and that he depends upon Navarro and the US Army to protect his production," Mario said.

"Both the Mexican and American governments need his quicksilver for the detonators on all those bombs they're building for their bloody little wars," added Samuel.

"It's true," Mario said. "The wars in Mexico, Europe, and elsewhere are good for business."

"Except for those who do the killing and dying," argued Daniel.

Samuel leaned forward. "Everyone thinks you quit because Navarro discovered you were plotting with the laborers to dynamite the furnace, or possibly the mine shafts."

"That is ridiculous!" insisted Daniel.

"That is simply what we heard," said Samuel.

"What you heard? From whom?"

Mario sipped his sotol and smiled. "You have to understand that our news doesn't arrive on printed pages. The wagon drivers, wood cutters, and water haulers bring us our news. These men gather stories and bring us our news. We heard you fought with Green over Perry's treatment of the Mexicans. Your act of compassion was influential. You see, my friend, Mexico is at war with itself. We are suffering a cultural metamorphosis much like a caterpillar transforming into a moth."

"Didn't you know that Gato Acosta got caught with dynamite?" Samuel asked.

"What?" Daniel sat forward in his chair, leaning on the table with both his elbows. "What would he do with dynamite besides sell it on the black market? Tom Green is a fool."

"Green claimed that Gato intended to blow up the furnace," said Samuel.

"Gato loved that machine," said Daniel, shaking his head in disbelief.

"He was angry because Perry ran you off," explained Samuel.

"Perry didn't run me off."

"Regardless," said Samuel, "Navarro found boxes of dynamite at the Acosta house."

"Where is Gato, in jail?"

"No, he slipped away before they could arrest him."

"What about Paco?"

"Navarro hauled that poor boy to Marfa. They intend to hang him for espionage."

"Christ!" exclaimed Daniel.

Carmelina came from the kitchen and lit the oil lamp on the table. The girl leaned into her mother's shoulder and watched a moth circle the warm soft light.

"On the border, we have learned to live between the hammer and the anvil and have been taught that when you are the anvil, you bear what life demands. But when you are the hammer?"

"You strike," said Ramona, raising her glass. She took a long drink, set her glass down, and said, "We live with the worst of both worlds, crushed by the weight of conflicting cultures. If we fail to fight enough, we starve. When we fight too hard, we are repressed. Both the Anglo and Mexican aristocracy perpetually demand that we maintain our proper economic, social, and political station in this life. We have to take what we can, when we can."

"An honest man works for his wages," Daniel said.

"Only a gringo with a pocketful of money believes those things," replied Ramona. "Your acts of confrontation inspired desperate men to be brave."

Daniel felt the fire that burned in Ramona's heart. It showed in her eyes. He relaxed in his chair and respectfully said, "It is true that I didn't like the way Perry and Green treated the Mexicans. I did get involved in some things I should have left alone, but I didn't encourage anyone to sabotage the furnace."

Ramona smiled and her face softened. "Acts of compassion often serve to inspire desperate men."

"Nobody should give so much for so little in return," said Daniel.

"That doesn't matter," said Mario. "It simply doesn't matter."

A sudden surge of weariness swept Daniel's emotions. He realized that, for the first time in a very long time, he was where he belonged. "I appreciate your hospitality, but I need to lie down."

Ramona moved to his side and offered her body as a crutch, and Daniel walked to his room with the assistance of the kind-hearted woman.

CHAPTER 18

Vengeance

"CARRIAGE!" SHOUTED PRIVATE Owen from his lookout above the arroyo.

Second Lieutenant Thompson waved acknowledgement and turned to Marshal Navarro where he rested in the shade of a mesquite tree. He could not tell if Navarro was awake, so he repeated the message. "Somebody is coming!"

Navarro spit and wiped his chin with the back of a gloved hand. "I'm not deaf, Lieutenant." He glanced toward the soldiers gathered in the dry wash and said, "Tell the sergeant to stop that car."

The lieutenant turned without speaking and walked to his soldiers.

"What is he expecting?" asked Sergeant McKinney.

"A carload of liquor," said the lieutenant. "Did you ever wonder what that man does with all the confiscated sotol?"

"I try not to think about it much," said McKinney, laughing. His words became hard to hear against the clatter of the Ford Model A car that came into sight, rumbling up the arroyo, and he waved the soldiers to their duty. The lieutenant stood firm in the arroyo and called for the driver to stop.

When the driver saw the soldiers in the road, he slammed on the brakes, and the car skidded to a halt. The passenger hit the driver with his straw hat and yelled for him to turn around.

The lieutenant could hear the two men arguing although he could

129

not decipher their words, as they spoke in Spanish. He saw the passenger look over his shoulder and wave for the driver to turn around. The lieutenant reached for his pistol and hurried toward the car. Cursing their predicament and desperate to escape, the driver shoved the car in reverse, the rear tires churning up a cloud of dust and sand.

A gunshot pierced the afternoon heat. The windshield shattered, and the car careened into an embankment. The passenger jumped from the car and fell to his knees, his shirt and pants covered with blood. The driver lay slumped against the steering wheel.

To a man, the soldiers flinched and looked toward the marshal.

Navarro sheathed his rifle and relit his stub of a cigar.

"Jesus Christ," cursed the lieutenant, holstering his pistol. "Did you have to go and kill the boy?"

"He tried to escape," said Navarro, pushing his way past the lieutenant toward the car.

McKinney secured the passenger, pulling him to his feet and tying his wrists with a length of rawhide. "That other one is dead, Lieutenant. What should we do with this feller?"

"Leave him," commanded Navarro, opening a crate in the backseat of the car. Extracting a bottle, he took several long drinks, and then said, "Ya'll head back to Glenn Spring. I will take this boy and his dead brother to Marfa."

The lieutenant knew what might happen to the boy, and he knew that it did not matter what he thought. There was nothing to do except leave. "Get them saddled, Sergeant."

McKinney whistled and signaled the soldiers to their horses.

Checking to confirm that the driver was truly dead, the lieutenant asked Navarro, "Do you know these boys?"

"That dead boy there is Julio Martinez," replied Navarro. "The one pissing his pants is Pedro, Julio's younger brother. They have been a thorn in my ass for a number of years."

McKinney brought the lieutenant his horse.

"You boys want any of this sotol?" asked Navarro.

"No," said the lieutenant, throwing himself into the saddle and spurring his horse west toward Glenn Spring.

The soldiers followed the lieutenant up the two-track road to where it rose out of the arroyo onto a flat-topped mesa covered in short bunch grass. None of the soldiers looked back when a single shot echoed along the lonely desert hills.

Sergeant McKinney and Corporal Hawkins rode alongside the lieutenant. McKinney wiped his forehead with a gloved hand. "There was nothing we could have done for that boy, Lieutenant."

Looking at McKinney, the lieutenant asked, "What do you think makes that man so damn mean?"

"No one told you?" McKinney asked.

"Told me what?"

"Marshal Navarro inherited that tin star from his brother after he was murdered."

"Murdered! By whom?"

"He was bushwhacked, so nobody rightly knows," said McKinney.

"Where did it happen?"

"I heard it happened along the river, upstream from San Vicente, below the Solis Farm," claimed McKinney.

"Ellis Wallace told me that it happened closer to Boquillas," said Corporal Hawkins.

"Regardless of where it happened," explained McKinney, "they found Navarro's brother floating face down in the Rio Grande."

"Can a man avenge his brother's murder?" the lieutenant asked them. "Can any man avenge a murder?"

McKinney spat and wiped his mouth with the back of his gloved right hand. "Well, Lieutenant, in my mind, revenge only poisons the man who carries it. What I do know is that revenge has poisoned that marshal to the point of making him more dangerous than a cornered rattlesnake."

"So it seems, Sergeant," said the lieutenant.

"You know what scares me about that man?" asked Hawkins, looking from McKinney to the lieutenant. When neither man objected, he concluded, "That man doesn't have an ounce of empathy or remorse in him, sir."

CHAPTER 19

Ramona

DANIEL ENJOYED ALMOST two weeks' convalescence before Samuel approached him about the business of smuggling. It was a warm, humid Sunday morning, and the air smelled of rain. Samuel found him in Mario's kitchen, drinking coffee with Ramona.

"Buenos días," said Samuel, entering the kitchen and joining them at the table.

Daniel nodded and smiled. "Good morning."

Ramona stood, poured a third cup of coffee, and sat it on the table in front of Samuel.

Samuel wrapped his hands around the cup and smiled. "It's time to go to work."

Daniel nodded. "Okay."

Ramona turned away from the table and returned to the task of cleaning a large pile of onions and garlic.

"What needs to be done?" asked Daniel.

"We need to ride the countryside and get you oriented," explained Samuel.

Mario entered the kitchen from the front room carrying his traveling gear. "Ramona can manage without us for a few days." Mario placed his saddlebag on a metal chair and poured himself a cup of coffee. "Get packed, Daniel. We can talk while we ride."

The men rode the primary trails across the Big Bend, confirming windmills, springs, and ephemeral, slickrock waterholes called *tinajas*. They rode through the high Chisos, up Terlingua Creek, and then back to Boquillas along Tornillo Creek. The men talked at length about the business and Daniel's role in it. Samuel wanted Daniel to transport deposits to the bank in Marfa. Mario wanted him to watch over merchandise when it had to be stored in Boquillas, and to manage the livestock required to operate the business. It seemed simple enough.

Riding suited Daniel. He enjoyed traveling with little purpose beyond learning trails and watering holes, but his heart soared when they returned to Boquillas, as he yearned for the quiet mornings with Ramona in the kitchen.

With Daniel established in Boquillas and comfortable with his responsibilities, Samuel rode upstream to Ojinaga to arrange another deal. The same day, Mario disappeared into the high sierra to his remote mountain cabin.

Daniel savored his mornings in the kitchen with Ramona, drinking coffee, eating freshly toasted corn tortillas rubbed with butter, and listening to her stories of Boquillas. Evenings, Daniel fished for blue catfish in the Rio Grande.

Ramona soon joined Daniel most evenings at the river. Sitting together on the bank of the Rio Grande, they shared stories of their lives and dreams. Ramona talked about the people in her life explaining how Mario's wife had died last winter from tuberculosis, and that Mario was much older than he looked. She talked about her life in Boquillas, about the physical things that she could touch, smell, cook, and eat; how the town had doubled in size with the arrival of the cable tram that transported lead ore directly across the river to La Noria, over in Texas. She shared the names of plants and landmarks and told funny stories as she provided Daniel with her unwritten version of the history of Boquillas. Through Ramona, Daniel came to know Boquillas as a humble town of mud huts and dry-stacked rock houses, burros, hungry chickens, and simple dreams. Ultimately, Ramona expressed few expectations from life beyond kindness.

Her story of Mario's missing left eye fascinated Daniel. Ramona told the story several times, always telling it from Mario's perspective. When he was a young boy, a witch had stolen his eye. Mario perceived his stolen eye as retribution for an unknown sin. When Daniel questioned her belief in the old man's story, Ramona refused to deny Mario's opinion about what had happened.

In return, Daniel spoke of faraway places and things he had seen, although it took time for him to ask Ramona the most intimate of questions. They were alone in the kitchen when he found his nerve. "May I ask what happened with your husband?"

Ramona was rolling masa for corn tortillas. Her knees buckled; she sat down and held her stomach with crossed arms.

"I'm sorry," mumbled Daniel, wishing he could retract the question.

She dismissed his concern with a wave of her right arm. "No, it's okay to ask." Ramona crossed herself and glanced at the ceiling. "We were very much in love, but not at first. I was fourteen. Like my oldest daughter Ofelia and her husband Sergio, we never had a proper wedding. When I began to show, I moved into the house of Pablo's parents. Pablo had no choice in the matter." Ramona wiped her moist eyes with her apron and smiled. "My husband, God rest his soul, was very good at digging tunnels in the Puerta Rica Mine. Most of the workers at the mine were indios: Kickapoo, Hechisero, Apache, Tarahumara, and Yaqui. Pablo began working there when he was twelve years old. Not many of the Mexicans enjoyed going so deep beneath the ground, yet my Pablo lived to dig those tunnels."

Standing, Ramona took a masa ball, flattened it in a metal press, and dropped it onto the hot griddle. She repeated the process until a dozen sizzling tortillas lined the comal. The room soon smelled of toasted corn. Ramona turned from the stove and leaned against a counter.

"Pablo had been sick with a fever and had stayed home from work. He was delirious and suffered violent nightmares. That night, the gringo jefe came by our house and complained about his absence, demanding he not miss another day. Pablo went to work the next day and died inside the mountain."

"There was a cave-in?" asked Daniel.

"Yes." Her voice was far away.

"When did this happen?"

"It was three years ago this April."

"I'm sorry," said Daniel, reliving his own memories of dead men pulled from the dust and darkness of a collapsed mine shaft.

She wiped her damp eyes, and then turned the tortillas on the stove. "When my family left to fight with Carranza, Mario provided for us."

Daniel moved close to Ramona. A spark flashed between them. He gently placed his hands on her shoulders, laid his cheek on the crown of her head, smelled her hair, and whispered a heart-felt, "I'm sorry."

Ramona turned into his arms. She locked her hands in the small of his back and kissed him softly on the lips. They embraced for an eternity before Daniel looked deep into Ramona's clear, green eyes.

The pounding, vibrating sound of horses nearing the house shattered the intimacy of the moment.

Ramona pulled from his embrace seeming both frustrated and relieved.

Daniel grabbed a warm tortilla and went outside, where Samuel sat on his horse, accompanied by four riders. Samuel's uncut stallion fought against its bit, turning agitated half circles. Two of the riders were Mario's grandsons, Chato and Tomás. Manuel, the boy who had killed the mine supervisor in Terlingua, was also with them. The fourth rider wore a full beard, and Daniel failed to recognize him. The man seemed familiar, yet the rarity of seeing a bearded Mexican confused his memory.

"You boys coming in?" asked Daniel, speaking directly to Mario's grandsons.

"Not now, thanks," answered Samuel. He pointed at the bearded rider and said, "This one wanted to stop by and say hello."

The bearded Mexican laughed. "You don't remember me, amigo?"

Hearing the man's voice brought recognition. "Gato, you bearded bastard!"

Gato slid off his horse, and the men vigorously shook hands. He held the gringo by the shoulders and asked, "How are you?"

"Fine," answered Daniel. "What happened in Terlingua after I left?"

"After you quit and rode off into Mexico, Paco and I had the opportunity to steal some dynamite and we got caught. Neither Perry nor Green was smart enough to understand that we did not intend to sabotage anything. We were simply hoping to supplement our incomes. Marshal Navarro took Paco to Marfa." Gato looked at his boots. "I managed to slip across the river before they arrested me."

"I'm sorry about Paco." Daniel said.

Gato frowned. "Such things are best left unspoken."

"And now you work with Samuel?"

"It pays better than feeding that furnace. And I work less."

"He is a damn good hand." Samuel said.

"I know," Daniel agreed. "Where are you headed in such a hurry?"

"We have some cattle to exchange for ammunition."

"Where'd you get the cattle this time?"

Samuel grinned. "Here and there."

"You need my help?" asked Daniel.

Samuel tossed Daniel a leather bag heavy with gold coins. "For now, just keep banking the money." Samuel waved Gato to his horse. "Get ready though, we're fixing to make us all enough to retire," boasted Samuel.

Without further explanation, Samuel spurred his horse and led the mounted men toward the Rio Grande. Daniel watched the riders disappear into the bosque at the river's edge before he turned back to the house.

~ ~ ~

Daniel was disappointed when Ramona did not turn up at the river that evening. He waited until midnight before riding upstream to his favorite hot spring, where he soaked until his fingers wrinkled. Sitting naked on the limestone bluff above the hot spring, Daniel smoked a rolled cigarette and watched the waning moon sink from the sky. Emotions clouded his mind, and he felt things in his heart that had been dormant for many years.

Chilled by a down-river breeze, Daniel climbed back into the spring. The warm water that rushed into the natural rock tub from deep in the earth soothed both his body and mind. He did not hear Ramona walk onto the ledge above the hot springs and shed her clothes, yet he sensed her presence. Upon seeing her uncovered breasts in the pale moonlight, he thought he was dreaming.

Ramona stood naked in the warm night air, the fine hairs on her thighs reflecting the delicate moonlight. As she reached for his hand, he sensed her nervousness as well as her yearning. He held her hand and guided her down into the pool. Ramona curled into his arms. The warm embrace of the cascading water melded their spirits. They lay together in the hot water without speaking until lustful curiosity set them to exploring each other's bodies. Only then did Daniel accept that this was not a dream.

"It has been a very long time since I have enjoyed such affection," Daniel confessed.

Ramona smiled as she absorbed his words. She laid her head against his chest and closed her eyes.

"What do you want to know?" Daniel asked.

"Tell me about Rosa," said Ramona, looking deep into his eyes.

Daniel flinched. "How did you know her name?"

"You talked of her when you were unconscious. When Mario brought you to Boquillas."

Daniel opened his life to Ramona. He told her how he had fallen in love and married Rosa in Cuba. How the Cuban government had arrested Rosa for sedition, for helping her family and country, and how she had died with a fever during childbirth. Daniel spoke of his passionate love for his first wife and the transformative experience of her patriotic fervor. He spoke of the horrible acts he had committed and witnessed in the Philippines and other places.

Ramona listened with a compassionate heart as the night turned to day. She allowed Daniel his moment of confession. When he finished talking, Ramona pulled Daniel to her breasts offering the curative power of a woman's desire.

⌒◡◡◠

They rode double from the hot springs back to Boquillas. Ramona rode with her arms tightly wrapped around his body, her hands folded across his belly. A moisture-scented breeze caressed the trees along the river: willows, mesquites and *huisache* trees. Boquillas appeared asleep, except for an old man sitting alone on his porch drinking coffee.

Ofelia stepped from the house onto the porch holding her baby-swollen stomach, her hands sticky with masa. "Where were you, Mama?" Ofelia made no pretense about her disapproval of her mother's behavior.

"Young lady, don't you question me. Get back to your masa," demanded Ramona, slipping from the horse to the ground. She followed her daughter into the house where an argument erupted.

Daniel sat on his horse, uncertain what to do or say.

Sergio, the father of Ofelia's baby, approached Daniel from the side of the house and whispered, "There is a soldier waiting to speak with you down at the river."

"A soldier?" asked Daniel. "Where is he?"

"Down by the river," said Sergio, waving him to follow.

Sergio led Daniel to the river where he discovered the lieutenant slouched in the saddle, a bottle in his right hand.

"Are you okay?" Daniel helped the lieutenant off his horse. "Damn, son, you're quite drunk."

The lieutenant leaned on Daniel.

"We should get you up to the house. Get some food into you. How did you happen to find me?" Daniel asked.

"Mr. Langford, the man who owns the developed hot springs on the American side of the river, told me first," replied the lieutenant, throwing back a long drink from a fresh bottle. "But it sure seems that everyone along this stretch of the Rio Grande knows about you."

"Haven't you had enough?"

"Not yet," said the lieutenant.

"Let's get you something to eat."

The men walked the trail from the river back to Boquillas. Sergio followed them, leading the soldier's horse. As they neared the house, Daniel told Sergio, "Take care of his horse, and mine, and then come eat."

Sergio led the lieutenant's horse toward the corral as Ramona stepped onto the porch.

"This is Ramona."

"Ma'am," said the lieutenant, tipping his hat.

Ramona leaned into Daniel's shoulder and asked, "Do you need anything?"

"A glass for the lieutenant," replied Daniel, kissing Ramona on the cheek, "and maybe some food?"

Ramona brought two glasses and sat them on a small table on the porch.

The lieutenant filled both glasses, and Ramona took a glass for herself, leaving none for Daniel.

"You aren't drinking, but she is?" asked the lieutenant.

Daniel ignored the question. "How is life at Glenn Spring?"

"We stay busy."

"Sit down," said Daniel.

"I have to tell you, I hate that marshal," confessed the lieutenant, sitting down in the offered chair.

"Navarro?" said Daniel, taking a chair.

"Yeah," muttered the lieutenant. "The man's got a penchant for violence."

"I heard about the Martinez boys," said Daniel. "Did he really shoot them in cold blood?"

The lieutenant looked up from his hands with wet eyes. "They did try to run."

"I guess that justifies murder."

Ramona did not understand the words, but the instant she heard Navarro's name used in connection with the dead Martinez brothers, she seemed to take a chill. She refilled her glass and disappeared into the house.

The lieutenant half stood. "Did I offend her?"

"That would be hard to do."

"Let's not talk about that. Why did you leave Terlingua?"

"I was done," answered Daniel.

"I heard what happened to that Mexican foreman. We have been looking for his murderer ever since."

"You have heard Navarro's version of what happened. Enough about that," said Daniel. "Tell me about Glenn Spring. How are things going for you? Is it an adventure?"

"Oh, it sure doesn't seem like much of an adventure. Honestly, I follow Navarro around and perform his dirty work. We chase shadows, mostly, but what troubles me is how ruthless Navarro can be. Most of the men we detain, he interrogates with violence bordering on sadism, and more than a few have been summarily executed. The lucky ones we haul to Marfa where they face long sentences of hard labor in the Texas penal system. Others have died at the end of a short rope." The lieutenant lifted his glass and took another drink. "This isn't how I pictured it was going to be out here. I thought there would be battles and skirmishes … honest combat between willing armies," lamented the lieutenant.

"Well, it sounds to me as if you're seeing your fair share of action."

The lieutenant said nothing in response.

After a long pause, Daniel asked, "What's this I hear about you and that Hernandez girl?"

The lieutenant blushed. "How is it that you know about Irma?"

Daniel laughed. "The Big Bend is big country, but it is very a small community. There isn't anything secret about you courting a local girl, especially one as young as Irma Hernandez."

"My how people love to gossip around here," whined the lieutenant, coming to his feet. He walked to the edge of the porch and stared into the rising sun as it climbed high into the sky, warming the desert. "When did you quit drinking?"

"About the time I landed here."

Ramona suddenly returned from the house onto the porch shouting, "The baby is coming."

"What?" Daniel said.

"The baby!" cried Ramona, spinning a full circle before dashing back into the house.

"Looks like you're going to be a grandpa," said the lieutenant, laughing.

"Well I'll be damned." Daniel grinned. "Let's go see what we can do to help."

CHAPTER 20

Comanche Moon

THE MONSOON-INSPIRED RAINS lingered into October, and the nights turned cool.

Returning from a trip to the Marfa bank, Daniel indulged his curiosity and went exploring farther afield. He rode south from Marfa through Pinto Canyon to a remote hot spring located a few miles north of the ranching community of Ruidosa. Daniel soaked in the hot water and lounged in the deepest shade of the largest cottonwood tree. Vermilion flycatchers caught insects on the wing while the ancient rhythm of cicadas accompanied the heat waves rising from the desert into a soft blue sky.

Rested, Daniel broke camp, rode downstream along the Rio Grande to Ojinaga, and rented a room at a boarding house on the town's central plaza. The sun fell from the sky, and Daniel enjoyed a nap before finding a restaurant where he ate an extravagant meal of oysters and roasted pork served with white cheese, pinto beans, and corn tortillas.

Taking pleasure in Ojinaga, Daniel examined the statuary and artwork in the Catholic church as he walked a slow circle around the plaza. He sat down at an outdoor café, drank warm beer, and listened to barefoot musicians play fanciful corridos of war.

The sound of horseshoes on cobblestones echoed from the crumbled façade of the adobe church and government buildings. *"Viva Mexico!"* shouted the six well-armed Villistas riding into the center of the plaza. Each man held a bottle in one hand and a gun in the other hand.

One of the riders fired his pistol into the air shouting praise to his commanding general. "Viva Villa! Viva Mexico!" Too tired to risk a drunken interaction with Villista revolutionaries, Daniel settled his bill and returned to his room.

Departing Ojinaga before dawn, Daniel rode through several farming communities, including the village of Mulato. In 1910, Villa's soldiers had defeated Carranza's Federales in a decisive battle in Mulato that reportedly turned the streets red with blood. Staying south of the river, he rode to the mouth of Santa Elena Canyon and the confluence of San Carlos Creek. He fished for blue catfish and paid respect to the memory of the dead man he had found floating in the river after leaving Terlingua back in June. Remembering the dead caused him to suffer a complex tangle of emotions.

From the confluence of San Carlos Creek and the Rio Grande, Daniel rode east over the mesa of eagles and across Terlingua Creek into the broken volcanic peaks of the lower Chisos Mountains. The incomplete memory of what had happened after the Tarahumara man had dosed him with peyote no longer angered him. None of what he remembered about his break from ordinary consciousness made sense. Inexplicably, he had noticed a measureable change in his general disposition after his encounter with the shaman. Undeniably, both his anger and his craving for alcohol had recently diminished. Ramona claimed that the peyote had caressed his broken heart, allowing him to choose love over fear.

The smell of goats arrived on the wind. Daniel sat on his horse and watched a herd of goats spill from the bosque onto the graveled floodplain on the Mexican side of the river as a pair of mongrel dogs steered the meandering goats downstream where they paused for a drink of river water. The dogs noticed Daniel. They watched him while the goats drank, unconcerned about his presence. For reasons known only to the dogs, they started barking at the goats. Nipping at hooves, the dogs herded the goats back into the ribbon of forest that separated the river from the desert.

Looking over his shoulder at the setting sun, Daniel reconsidered his earlier decision to ride the final miles home to Boquillas in the dark. He sat on his horse and watched the last of the goats disappear into the arroyo beyond the floodplain. As he listened to the animals recede into the desert, he decided it best to find a suitable place to camp. He could leave at first light, have sufficient time to soak in the hot springs along the way, and be home before noon.

Following the goats beyond the river, Daniel discovered a ramshackle jacal with a small brush corral. A giant beehive stained the limestone cliffs above the jacal, and the air reverberated with the buzz of bees. Daniel surveyed the goatherder's camp. It was simple and well designed. An old man closed a brush gate behind the last goat to enter the improvised corral. He limped as he walked to the wood-fired stove under a canvas tarp. The old man kindled the fire in the stove and began chopping dried goat meat on a carved mesquite root table.

Hungry, Daniel nudged his horse forward. Not wanting to surprise the man, he whistled a popular corrido that he had heard on the plaza in Ojinaga.

The old man looked up from his work. He pushed the chopped goat meat into a skillet with the dull edge of the knife and said, "Buenas tardes."

"Buenas tardes," said Daniel, tipping the brim of his hat. "Could I trade you money or tobacco for a plate of food? That is if you have enough to share."

The old man smiled. "Around here there is always enough goat meat and rarely enough tobacco. What is your destination?"

"Boquillas, Mexico."

"Boquillas?" asked the old man.

"Yes, sir, Boquillas," said Daniel.

"You are welcome to camp here tonight. One never knows what might happen to a man alone in the bosque after dark."

"Thank you. Would you mind if I put my horse in the corral with yours?"

"Please. There is plenty of cut green river cane if your horse is hungry."

Daniel nodded with appreciation and attended to his horse.

The old man cooked the goat meat and served up a delicious meal of *carne picada* with toasted stale corn tortillas. They ate at an unlevel table of rough-cut boards.

After supper, they exchanged names and Daniel shared his tobacco with Don Génaro Luna-Brito. The men sat under a canopy of stars, smoked hand-rolled cigarettes, and listened to the sounds of the night. The night air was thick with nighthawks on the wing. The men shared few words beyond imagined explanations of unfamiliar sounds. Don Génaro pointed out the clacking sound of a roadrunner hunting his prey. A chorus of red-spotted toads celebrated the waxing yellow-tinged moon that rose beyond the silhouette of rugged mountains beyond the Rio Grande.

Long after moonrise, Daniel asked the old man about his life along the river, and Don Génaro spoke at length about his life with the goats. When pressed about current events in Mexico, Don Génaro expressed little concern or empathy for the war.

"What about the Spaniards who built the presidio near here?" Daniel asked.

Don Génaro grinned, and his eyes sparkled with delight. "My ancestors came to this land with the first people chasing the large game animals across the American savanna. My grandfather claimed that our ancestors have lived in their place for hundreds of generations, maybe longer."

Daniel whistled and nodded his head. It was difficult to imagine a lineage of people rooted in one geographic location for that length of time. It troubled his sense of history.

"My ancestors lived in peace and were only occasionally harassed by wandering Apache, Kiowa, Tonkawa, Kickapoo, or other nomadic tribes. Most folks came in search of peyote and trade goods. La Junta, the town where the Rio Conchos and the Rio Grande join that we call Ojinaga, has been a thriving trade center for thousands of years. Everything changed when the Comanche acquired horses from the Spanish."

Don Génaro paused to allow Daniel time to assimilate his unique concept of time.

"When the Spanish came, they came for conquest and precious metals. They were holy warriors ... crusaders in search of a perverted dream of material wealth. The Spanish enslaved my ancestors and condemned them to labor in their damn mines extracting silver, gold, and copper. It was several generations before my ancestors managed to rise up and expel the bastards. I do not pretend to know what is true for other nations, but here in Mexico there are far too many petty tyrants all waiting their chance to torment the unfortunate. Dispose of one and another appears in his place."

Don Génaro stood and walked to his jacal. The old man returned with a hempen bag that held a Spanish helmet and breastplate. He handed both items to Daniel.

Engraved on the helmet was the Christ child crowned with a full nimbus of light rays. The breastplate held a faded engraved image of the Virgin. There was a dent in the helmet, which Don Génaro believed to have been a fatal blow. He claimed that his ancestors had murdered the last Spanish soldiers, burned their fort, and buried the remaining silver and gold in the desert.

"Has anyone found the buried treasure?" Daniel asked.

Don Génaro laughed. "Not that I know of, though many fools have wasted far too many years looking for it."

Daniel returned the armor to the old man; he remembered that Gato had also spoken of the petty tyrants in his life. "It seems that men are always chasing something."

"And you? What are you chasing?"

Daniel nodded. Smiling, he said, "Those elusive blue catfish in the Rio Grande."

Don Génaro laughed.

"And you?" Daniel asked. "What are you chasing?"

"Another sunrise is all that I ask of life."

"Then we should fish tonight, no?" said Daniel.

"We should, while there is still time and the desire to fish."

Ramona met Daniel at the outer gate to the yard.

"Where have you been? We have been worried sick about you."

"We?" asked Daniel, sliding down off his horses and into Ramona's arms.

"I was worried, okay?"

They walked to the corral holding hands. Daniel kissed her nose and then tended his horse.

"It never takes the others so many days to ride to Marfa and back. Where have you been?"

"Ojinaga," said Daniel.

"Ojinaga!" shouted Ramona.

Daniel allowed her an angry moment before changing the subject. "Do you know an old man named Don Génaro?"

"Don Brito?" asked Ramona.

"Yes."

"I know of him. They say he is touched."

"Really?" Daniel smiled.

"Yes," said Ramona.

"In what way?" Daniel asked taking his gear into the rock barn.

"He doesn't see life the same as others," explained Ramona, her fisted hands on her hips.

"That is a silly reason to think a man daft."

"How much time did you waste with Don Brito?"

"Enough time to catch a few fish."

"Did you bring some home?" asked Ramona, standing in the door to the barn.

"They've been gutted," said Daniel, pulling a string of freshly caught fish from a damp burlap bag.

"You might get Carmelina to finish cleaning them for you, but it will likely cost you a nickel's worth of candy," Ramona said, laughing. "You know, there is much to be done to prepare for the fiesta tonight."

"Fiesta?" asked Daniel.

"It is the Day of the Dead."

"Oh."

Ramona laughed. "Why should you care, really? You have no relatives or love ones buried at our cemetery, do you?"

"No, I don't," said Daniel with a shake of his head. "Not yet."

"If you stay home, you will babysit," said Ramona, turning toward the house with a full sweep of her gingham skirt. "I'm going to get dressed. Talk to Ofelia, please?"

***

Bottle rockets exploded above the cemetery and gunshots flashed, celebratory lightning in honor of the dead. Daniel sat down in his favorite porch chair and propped up his feet.

Ofelia came from the house carrying a beer. "You want this?" she asked.

"Yes, thank you," said Daniel, accepting the open bottle of beer. "Did you get Pablito to sleep?"

"Yes, he is asleep," said Ofelia, wrapping a shawl around her shoulders. "Are you sure it's okay for me to go to the dance?"

"I'm certain, my child. Go dance with your mother for me."

"Thank you." Ofelia smiled. She turned and walked into the night.

Daniel sipped his beer, rolled a cigarette, and rocked in his chair. Beyond Boquillas, he could see a procession of candles entering the cemetery at the edge of town. Music and laughter drifted across the desert, and the warm night air smelled of grilled *carne* and roasted corn. A towering thunderstorm flashed heat lightning above San Vicente anticline. Stars wheeled a determined path across the moonless sky. In the distance, a burro brayed, complaining about things only burros would understand.

Daniel fell asleep in his chair and dreamed of numinous electric storms illuminating shadow-shrouded serpentine geologic waves.

~~~

Lavender-scented hair lifted his dreaming toward consciousness.

"Daniel," whispered Ramona. "You will sleep better in our bed, mi amor. It's more comfortable than this stiff-backed, rocking chair."

Daniel opened his eyes and smiled. "How was the party?"

Ramona raised her arms over her head and laughed. "The damn priest got drunk, and one of the boys shot his own foot ..."

"Who shot his foot?"

"It doesn't matter who, does it? It was a good dance, and everyone asked about you."

"What did they ask?"

Ramona smiled and offered her lover her hand. "They wanted to know if I have fallen in love with the babysitter."

Daniel took her hand.

Ramona leaned forward and kissed him as he stood. "How did the baby sleep?"

"Just fine," said Daniel. He patted Ramona on her ass.

She smiled and looked him in the eyes. "Thank you for being so kind to my daughter."

Daniel smiled. "You are welcome. She is kind to me. That makes it easy to be kind in return."

"It's nice that we are able to provide her and Sergio with a proper wedding," said Ramona. "Thank you for helping make that a possibility."

"My pleasure." Daniel nodded at her. "I need to lie down before I wake up."

"As you command, my love," said Ramona, laughing and leading him by the hand into the house.

CHAPTER 21

The Wedding

THE DEEMERS WERE an older couple who owned the store across the river in Boquillas, Texas. They were old friends of the Torreón family and had insisted on hosting the fiesta for Ofelia and Sergio in celebration of the birth of their son, Pablo. The party also served as a semiformal wedding for the young couple. The Deemers were incredibly generous people who knew everyone who lived along this stretch of the river, and they loved to host parties.

Many women labored in the crowded kitchen, each with a specific task. One woman pressed damp, yellow dough balls into corn tortillas. Another arranged them on a comal on the wood-fired stove where pinto beans boiled in a large pot and red rice sizzled in two large skillets. Three women stood at a square table chopping ingredients for potato salad. At another table, women prepared green chili salsa. Mrs. Deemer leaned on her cane and supervised a group of young girls making tamales, their nimble fingers spreading masa onto cornhusks.

Little Carmelina, Ramona's youngest daughter, stood on an apple crate to reach the tortillas on the back of the stove. She was cute as an angel in her knee-length white dress, a bow in her hair, new shoes, and a white lace apron tied at the waist.

Out in the yard, Deemer smoked a hand-rolled cigarette and offered encouragement while his grandsons and nephews excavated the cooked pig buried beneath a mound of glowing hot coals. It took six boys to lift the steaming *barbacoa* from the pit. After accomplishing the task, the boys compared biceps and congratulated each other on a job well done.

Beneath the filtered shade of the mature cottonwood trees, four women covered long wooden tables with blue gingham tablecloths. People soon gathered at the tables to enjoy heaping plates of barbacoa, beans, potato salad, cabbage slaw, red rice, tamales, and fresh corn tortillas. To drink, there were coffee, mint tea, and a crock of cool spring water.

The lieutenant arrived with Irma Hernandez on his arm. It was obvious that young Irma was enamored with the attractive gringo.

Ramona quietly fussed to Daniel about soldiers taking advantage of young girls. Daniel listened patiently for a few minutes before offering Ramona his flask of sotol. The flask often served as an effective antidote for Ramona's irritations. Ramona took a long drink. She rose onto her toes, kissed Daniel's cheek, and snuggled against his shoulder. "I'm glad you no longer drink so much. It leaves more for me."

As the bride, Ofelia shared her first dance with Mario, who served as the family's *patrón*, Mario pinned an American twenty-dollar bill to her satin dress. Others stood in an informal line with either pesos or dollars in their hands for the privilege of dancing with the bride. Only when the line of guests waiting to dance with the bride had subsided did Mario allow Ofelia to dance with her husband.

The band played a few polkas before striking up a lively *cumbia* promenade. Carmelina grabbed Daniel and Ramona by the hands and they joined the dancers circling the large fire blazing in the center of the dance area. The fire threw swarms of sparks spiraling high into the moonless night.

As he danced, Daniel considered what a fine wedding party it was. Samuel and his crew had managed to stay at the periphery without causing trouble. Everyone was well fed, and the fandango had begun. In that very moment of happiness, Daniel noticed a band of riders. It was Marshal Navarro and a posse of Texas Rangers.

Awareness of the rangers crept unevenly through the crowd. The dancers edged almost imperceptibly away from the rangers in a futile attempt to disappear into the shadows beyond the fire's glow. The guitarrón player was the first musician to hoist his instrument onto his shoulder and run for the house.

The mounted rangers herded the wedding guests into an ever-tightening circle. Marshal Navarro whistled, gesturing for his men to secure the houses. Two men dismounted, pulled their pistols, and hurried to the main house, where they gathered everyone on the porch. Mrs. Deemer turned and threatened a ranger with her cane as he pushed her from behind with his gun.

Daniel held Ramona and Carmelina and tried to calm those near them as best he could.

The lieutenant softly assured Irma it was going to be okay and stepped to Daniel's side.

Navarro spit, and said, "Jackson, I'm confident that we can control that lieutenant, but I'm less certain how Daniel will react."

"Yes, sir," said Jackson.

Agitated, Deemer pushed his way toward Navarro. "What is the meaning of this? You are interrupting our celebration."

"I can see that and I want to apologize for the unfortunate disturbance." Navarro crossed his right leg over the saddle horn and grinned, obviously enjoying himself. "We are looking for two things, Mr. Deemer. We are looking for a murderer who we have reason to suspect is here at this fiesta. Second, we have orders from the federal government to intercept and arrest anyone trading arms or munitions with the Villistas." Navarro spit a thick stream of brown tobacco juice and looked Daniel in the eye. "Does anyone have a problem with this?"

"Do you have warrants authorizing a search of private property?" asked Deemer. "Or are you and your men acting as common thugs? Which is it this time?"

Jackson heeled his horse forward and cursed. "Why you disrespecting son-of-a–bitch!" The Texas Ranger struck Deemer across the right cheek with a slashing blow from his quirt. The old man fell to the ground.

Carmelina disappeared into the folds of her mother's flowing dress. Mother and daughter hugged each other, their green eyes sharing a common fear.

Daniel locked eyes with Navarro and made his way through the crowd. Ramona held his hand until he slipped away. Daniel stopped just beyond the reach of the ranger's quirt. His fists opened and closed, exposing his willingness to attack despite the odds stacked against him. "You okay, Mr. Deemer?" Daniel asked without looking at the man.

Deemer rediscovered his courage and rose to his knees. "I'm okay." He wiped the bloody crescent forming on his cheek.

Navarro spit. "Daniel, you need to know that the law has changed. It isn't legal to sell munitions to Villa anymore, and I'm planning on putting that friend of yours out of business."

The lieutenant moved forward, and Daniel reached to restrain him.

"Hold it right there, Lieutenant," said Navarro, raising his right hand. "Do not try to impress your girl friend by being a hero. Jackson, take the lieutenant to his horse."

Jackson dropped to the ground with his pistol drawn.

Daniel could see the lieutenant struggle with his conscience. He knew the lieutenant had seen what Navarro was capable of unleashing on the Mexican people.

Finding his voice, the lieutenant said, "Not tonight." When violence happened to strangers, it had not mattered as much. However, here, tonight, with people he knew … it was personal. The sound of his own voice strengthened his nerve, and he repeated himself. "Not tonight."

"Jackson," commanded Navarro.

"Yes, sir," answered the pimple-faced Jackson.

"Escort the lieutenant to his horse."

Jackson waved his gun at the lieutenant. "Come on, Lieutenant, sir."

"Call off your boy, Marshal," shouted the lieutenant, lunging toward Navarro.

Jackson slammed his pistol against the lieutenant's skull, and he fell to the ground unconscious.

Navarro ran the back of his gloved hand across his unshaven face. "Jackson, secure that man! Charlie," shouted Navarro across the crowd, "round up the menfolk into the corral and let Carson take a good look at them."

Charlie repeated the command for all the rangers to hear. "Get the men into that corral, boys."

After the rangers had secured all the menfolk inside the corral, Carson searched each man's face for clues of criminality as if he were a mystic divining palms. He questioned each man, weighing the answers against an unknown standard of truth. If he was satisfied, he pushed the man back through the gate. The dismissed men gathered at the edge of the corral.

The continued presence of these freed Mexicans irritated Charlie. "Damn you, men. Gather your women and go home!" shouted Charlie. When nobody moved, he fired his pistol into the air. "Don't you stupid bastards understand English? Take your kin and go home!"

The single shot scattered the men who were loitering at the edge of the corral.

"Tie the lieutenant onto his horse, Jackson," commanded Navarro. "He's coming with us, whether he wants to or not."

"Yes, sir," grumbled Jackson.

Navarro watched Jackson drag the semiconscious lieutenant to his horse. "Daniel, I'm thinking it would be best for both of us if you would get your sorry, Mexican-loving self across the river before something happens we might both regret."

"It isn't over," said Daniel.

"Don't threaten me," growled Navarro. He looked beyond Daniel toward the corral. "How many you got, Charlie?"

"One's a keeper."

"Sack him, tie him, and put him on a horse with somebody."

"Are we done?" Daniel asked.

"For now," snarled Navarro.

Daniel walked to the house where he found all his girls huddled in the kitchen. Ofelia sobbed in her mother's arms; little Carmelina held her sister's baby. Daniel hugged them and counted heads. "Where's Sergio?"

"They've got him in the corral," cried Ofelia.

"Dammit," cursed Daniel. "Where's Mario?"

"I don't know," said Ramona. "I think he left when the dance began."

"Get our wagon and take the family home. I need to find Samuel."

"What are you going to do?" Ramona asked, clinging to Daniel.

"I don't know." He looked through a window to the corral where he saw Navarro kicking the hooded prisoner.

Ramona placed her hands on Daniel's face and forced him to look in her eyes. "You be careful, my love."

"I will be very careful," said Daniel. "But I won't allow Navarro to lynch Sergio."

"What are you going to do?"

"I don't know, but our hand is strong. Samuel and his crew are waiting for me."

Daniel held Ramona's face between both his hands and kissed her fully on the lips. Then he disappeared through the bedroom window at the back of the house. He slipped unseen into the nearest thicket of mesquite, ducked through a tangle of thorns, and followed an irrigation ditch to the river. He listened to the night. Over the sound of the river, he heard his name. "Daniel!"

"Samuel?"

"Over here." Samuel appeared at the edge of the river cane and offered him a hand up onto the bank. "I figured you'd come this way once you went into the house."

"Where are the men?" Daniel asked.

"I sent them to gather the horses."

"You think Navarro will harm Sergio?" asked Daniel.

"I don't think so." Samuel thought about it. "At least not right here, not in front of all these witnesses. He'd start a shooting war that wouldn't be easy to stop."

"I hope you're right. Did you hear what he said about the law changing?" Daniel asked.

"Yeah, I heard. It was bound to happen, sooner than later. You don't have a gun, do you?" Samuel smiled knowingly.

"I didn't see a need to bring a gun to Ramona's daughter's wedding."

Samuel pulled a Colt revolver from his belt and said, "For most weddings, you'd be right, but not in Boquillas, hombre! Navarro is trying to make the fight personal."

"It would appear that way," said Daniel.

The sound of horses rose from the darkness—pounding hooves splashing and clattering as the horses ran upstream.

"Here they come," said Samuel. "Go get a couple of horses from

Deemer and meet me along the cutoff road to Boquillas Crossing. I will take these men and liberate Sergio."

"Okay," exhaled Daniel, scrambling up the riverbank.

Samuel turned to meet his men, taking the reins to his horse. Throwing himself into the saddle, he waved adios and spurred his horse upstream. The heavily armed riders prepared for a fight; guns ready, pockets stuffed with cartridges.

Daniel watched the riders splash away, knowing there was nothing he could do to change the inevitable. Muttering a curse, he ran hard across the gallery forest of irrigated cottonwood trees to the Deemer's house.

Mr. Deemer stood on his porch. Seeing Daniel confused him. "I thought you went home."

"Not yet," said Daniel. "I need to borrow a horse or two."

"Take what you need."

"Thank you. Are you okay?" asked Daniel, pointing at the wound on the man's cheek.

"Yeah," whispered Deemer. "It'll heal just fine."

"How is Mrs. Deemer?" Daniel looked over his shoulder, eager to get going.

"By morning, she will be okay."

"I'm sorry for the trouble," said Daniel.

"Don't be. It was a beautiful wedding. We cannot prevent men like Navarro from doing what they do. Don't you go and do anything stupid."

Daniel nodded, impressed by the man's patience. "Navarro lit this fuse."

"It never matters who lights the fuse. What matters is who gets hurt when things explode," said Deemer. "Do what needs to be done … just be careful."

"I will try, Mr. Deemer. I promise you that much." Daniel nodded good-bye, stepped off the porch, and ran toward the corral.

───∼∽───

Charlie led the posse through a pasture of closely cropped grass into a field of brown corn stubble and broken melons. Jackson followed Charlie with the lieutenant's horse in tow. They had bound the lieutenant's wrists and lashed them to the horn of his saddle. Carson rode double with Sergio, the boy's hands tied behind his back and the feed sack still cinched over his head.

The posse rode single file from the cultivated fields of the floodplain through a dense forest of bent mesquite trees, up a rocky two-track road lined with white thorn acacia, creosote brush, and tasajillo cactus. The men rode in silence toward the low mountain pass that led to Tornillo Creek.

A single shot lit the night. A man slumped in his saddle, and then fell onto the neck of his horse. There was a brief pause after the first shot before the bushwhackers attacked in force. Shots flashed and men screamed. The man riding double with Sergio grabbed his right thigh and fell from his horse, knocking Sergio to the ground. The ranger's severed femoral artery filled his boot with blood. One man lost control of his horse, which skittered sideways off the trail tossing him ass over elbows down a twenty-foot ledge of jagged rock, lechuguilla, and dog cholla.

Marshal Navarro reached for his rifle as a bullet tore through his right shoulder. He reeled in the saddle and struggled to stay mounted. His right hand refused to take hold of the rifle. Navarro slid off his horse and took cover behind a rock best he could. The remaining posse of Texas Rangers broke and galloped down the trail.

Manuel ran forward and beat the nearest man on the head with a rock. He grabbed Sergio, loosened his bound hands, and removed the feed sack from his head.

Navarro held his pistol with his left hand, took aim, and fired. Dirt flew near Manuel's feet.

Manuel pushed Sergio toward safety before turning to face Navarro. "*Chinga madre,* pendejo!" yelled Manuel, firing his rifle without aiming.

The posse regrouped and charged up the trail to rescue Navarro.

Hearing horses, Manuel turned and escaped back down the arroyo toward safety.

Daniel saw the muzzle flash of rifles. The individual shots echoed across the valley floor. He heard shouts, more shots, and then silence. He resisted a strong desire to go investigate. Instead, he sat cross-legged on the low, bald knob of a hill in the pale light of the waning moon and waited, two horses tethered at his side.

Orion sank toward the horizon before Daniel heard footsteps. His horses turned toward the noise, their ears piqued forward. Moving to the far side of the horses for cover, Daniel watched the arroyo.

Soon, Samuel appeared from the darkness.

"Samuel," called Daniel.

Samuel waved Daniel into the wash.

"What happened?" asked Daniel.

"We rescued Sergio."

"Where is he?"

"He rode off with the others. It appears they hauled ass straight for the river." Samuel spit. "Don't worry. Sergio is okay."

Daniel narrowed his eyes and repeated his original question. "What happened?"

Samuel shook his head. "Manuel started it. Somebody got hit badly though, because Sergio was covered with blood, none of which was his."

"Do you know what happened to the lieutenant?

"I don't know."

"Marshal Navarro?"

Samuel shrugged, indifferent to Navarro's fate.

Daniel reached for Samuel's rifle, pulled it from the sheath, and smelled the hammer. "Who fired first?"

"I told you. Manuel fired first." Samuel reclaimed his rifle and turned to go. "It never matters who fired second or third does it? We need to quit jawing and get our asses across the river."

Daniel rose to the saddle and followed Samuel back to the safety of Mexico.

CHAPTER 22

A Cold Wind

DANIEL SAT AT the river's edge in an improvised burlap chair suspended from the cropped arms of an ancient mesquite tree. Fat gray clouds obscured the sky. The New Year had brought freezing temperatures, and a frigid breeze rattled the willows lining the riverbank.

Dawn painted the east-facing mountains across the river in Texas, where limestone cliffs reflected the changing light creating dark, ephemeral shadows. Daniel saw the shadows as ghosts … personal demons he believed already exorcised. Hoping to dispel his foul mood, Daniel attended the trotline suspended in the current that separated the swift flowing river from the lazy eddy running upstream along the bank. A fat carp rolled in the eddy, its open lips sucking foam.

The whispered rumors from the communities along the river kept Daniel on edge. The fear of retribution was a constant worry. No one doubted Marshal Navarro's ability or willingness to seek revenge.

Daniel sat in his chair, rolled a cigarette, and pushed aside his most troubling thoughts. Waiting for retaliation had been especially difficult for Ramona; love had arrived in her life a mere half step in front of the devil. Samuel had liberated Sergio, gunning down Marshal Navarro and three Texas Rangers in the process. There was no denying it. Daniel had been involved. Revenge was inevitable. Navarro was too proud not to strike back, no matter how long it took.

Ramona had repeatedly told Daniel that he should accept Mario's offer and spend more time at the ranch house in the high sierra. Part of him knew she was right. Although he had personally done nothing wrong, it might be best for everyone involved if he would head for the mountains until the worst of the fear had passed.

A lone rider appeared from the bosque across the river. Daniel tensed and touched his pistol. The rider leaned in the saddle as he guided his horse down the steep embankment onto the gravel bar on the Texas riverbank. The horse paused for a drink at the river's edge before crossing the river. Daniel relaxed only after he realized that the rider was the lieutenant. He had not seen the lieutenant since the night of the wedding dance. Even at a distance, it was apparent that the lieutenant was quite drunk.

"What are you doing so damn drunk at this hour?" called Daniel, as the lieutenant rode out of the Rio Grande into Mexico.

Sliding off his horse, the lieutenant wobbled so much he leaned against his saddle. "How's the fishing?"

"Not good." Daniel frowned. "What are you doing?"

"I'm on my way back to Glenn Spring from Marfa."

"You know that Boquillas isn't on the way to Glenn Spring from Marfa?"

The lieutenant smiled.

"How's your head?" asked Daniel. "That ranger hit you pretty hard."

"It bought me a couple of days in the field hospital at Marfa." The lieutenant laughed and took a drink from the bottle of liquor in his right hand. "At first, I actually thought that the army was sincerely concerned about my health, although it turned out they were more interested in chewing my ass." The lieutenant waved the bottle at Daniel. "You want some of this?"

"No thanks."

"Suit yourself." The lieutenant took a long drink.

Daniel rolled a smoke and offered it to the lieutenant, who declined the offer with a wave of the bottle. Nodding, Daniel struck a match and lit the cigarette for himself.

"Things are changing. Changing quicker than one can imagine," said the lieutenant. "There are some things you need to know." Swaying, he stared at the mouth of Boquillas Canyon.

Daniel followed the lieutenant's gaze to the shadowed cleft where the Rio Grande churned its way through massive limestone cliffs. Two ravens surfed on the wind where it flowed over the mountain.

"It's true what Navarro said about the law changing. Not only did they make it illegal to sell weapons or ammunition to Villa, Captain Henry ordered me to arrest anyone that I suspect of delivering weapons to the Villistas. It doesn't matter if it's a dirt-poor Mexican or ex-soldiers." The lieutenant looked at Daniel and frowned. "And, I was ordered to disassociate myself from Irma."

Daniel nodded. "Somehow that doesn't surprise me." Daniel noticed one of his trotlines sink with the weight of a caught fish. "What about Navarro?"

The lieutenant took another drink before saying, "He's madder than a wet cat. They winged him good, and because of it, he's a little bound up on the one side."

"What about those other men who got hurt?"

"Fat Charlie was gut shot, but the bullet went clean through him missing everything. The other two did not have the same luck. One bled to death, and the other man broke his neck when he fell into that arroyo. Navarro says he saw Manuel break open that man's head with a rock. Navarro is still angry that his posse turned tail and ran under fire. Every one of those boys has a score to settle. It is personal, now. You know that, don't you?"

"Yes," said Daniel, acknowledging that he understood. "How are you faring through all this?"

"I asked for a transfer. It will be slow in coming," said the lieutenant, again offering the bottle.

Daniel refused the bottle with a raised right hand. "I take it you came to warn me?"

Throwing back a drink, the lieutenant swayed but said nothing in response.

"And, I'm guessing the captain told you that arresting Samuel was the best way to save your career?"

The lieutenant kicked at river-polished rock with the heel of his boot and took another drink.

"And me?" asked Daniel.

"Captain Henry thinks you've gone Mexican."

"Stupid bastard," said Daniel, standing. "I need to check those lines. Wait here until I call for your help."

"Sure," answered the lieutenant.

Daniel walked across the mudflat to a narrow limestone ledge on the downstream side of the swirling river eddy. He carefully made his way across the ledge to the spike driven into the rock anchoring his trotline. Grabbing the line with a gloved hand, Daniel dragged it toward the bank, shouting, "Untie the line there and bring it this way a bit."

The lieutenant loosened the trotline from the mesquite tree, raised it over his shoulder, and walked toward the river.

The men worked the line across the eddy onto the limestone ledge. Daniel retrieved the hooked fish: two blue catfish and a large yellow catfish. He slid the fish onto the stringer tied to a nail driven into the limestone ledge, re-baited the empty treble hooks, and reset the line.

Suddenly, Ramona appeared from the brush along the riverbank riding her jenny burro.

"Hello, Lieutenant," said Ramona.

"Hello," answered the lieutenant, slurring his words.

"It's early to be drunk, no?" asked Ramona, sitting on her burro.

Daniel handed Ramona the fish. "Leave him alone."

"What a shame." Ramona tied the fish to her saddle, leaned down and kissed Daniel, and turned for home. She looked over her shoulder and waved good-bye.

"What's with her?" asked the lieutenant.

"What do you mean?"

"She seemed upset." The lieutenant took a drink from his bottle and wiped his mouth with a gloved hand.

"Think about it. Navarro likely blames me for what happened the night of the wedding and because of that, soldiers make her nervous right now. It does not matter what uniform a soldier wears or who is in the uniform. Soldiers act on their orders, not their true feelings. That is what scares her." Daniel shook his head. "She doesn't dislike you. Don't take it personally."

The lieutenant took another drink. "That is pretty much the same thing Langford told me last night when I tried to see Irma."

"What do you mean, when you tried to see Irma?"

"Her father met me at the gate to their yard with a shotgun—again.

When I pressed the old man he fired both barrels into the dirt at my feet, and his boys threatened me with shovels and picks. Langford came to my aid just as I was about to take on five or six full-grown Mexicans to get at my Irma. Fortunately for all of us, Langford dragged me out of there before something bad happened."

Daniel nodded, but said nothing.

"I'd better get going. I'm already late, and almost drunk enough to try my luck with Irma's kinfolk again." The lieutenant grinned.

Daniel did not attempt to detain him.

Rising into the saddle, the lieutenant spurred his horse into the Rio Grande. When he made it across the river, he turned in the saddle and faced south.

"*Vaya con Dios*," whispered Daniel, waving good-bye.

The lieutenant swallowed the last drops from his bottle, and then smashed it on the ground before disappearing back into Texas.

Back at home, Daniel was morose in the immediate wake of the lieutenant's brief visit. Ramona sensed his dark mood and tried her best to cheer him up with food. She offered him tamales, yet his attitude did not improve. By midday, Daniel found an excuse to make a trip to the village store. He lingered in the doorway of the kitchen expecting an argument. When none came, he kissed Ramona and left.

Ramona followed him outside and watched him ride away. Wiping her hands on her apron, she said, "Take your time, my love. I know that you will resolve your worries in your own fashion."

Daniel passed the afternoon at La Norteña, where he drank warm beer and played checkers with Toribio, the storekeeper. It fascinated Daniel that this was the only store on the Mexican side of the river, but it was not located in the actual village of Boquillas, Mexico. Rather, it stood on a limestone bluff overlooking the preferred river crossing.

The men played checkers and talked about many things, the rhythm of their conversation interrupted by the distant rumble of cable cars hauling lead from Mexico to Texas. Whenever their conversation faltered, Toribio asked about the war in Europe, yet Daniel did not say anything that Toribio did not already know.

Toribio's wife brought them two plates of beans and a basket of warm corn tortillas. After they ate, the men resumed their checker game.

"What happened? Did you have a fight with Ramona?" Toribio asked. Being a storekeeper and part-time bartender, Toribio liked to talk. He enjoyed asking people questions about their lives.

"Is my foul mood that obvious?" Daniel searched the checkerboard before moving a red checker one square closer to king's row.

Toribio jumped two red checkers and landed his black checker on the back row. He was about to win another nickel from Daniel, as he had three black kings prowling the board mopping up the remnants of the kingless red checkers.

"Damn," exclaimed Daniel, adding a black checker to the newly crowned king.

The men drank beer, smoked cigarettes, and played checkers until the sun fell toward the massive anticline of San Vicente. Daniel had lost over two dollars, but the game was not about the money. It was a simple distraction for his troubled mind.

Carmelina appeared from the trees along the river riding her mother's burro. She halted the burro alongside the store, slid to the ground, and ran straight to Daniel's side. She stared at him with her beautiful green eyes.

"What do you want, my child."

"Would you buy me a *dulce*?" she asked with a pleading expression both exaggerated and effective.

"You came all the way here this time of evening for candy?"

"Nooooo." She elongated the word with a sense of impatience.

"Here is a nickel for you. Get whatever you want."

Beaming with happiness, Carmelina followed Toribio into the store. She traded her shiny nickel for a handful of stick candy.

Guarding her treasure, she ran from the store, leapt onto the burro and yelled, "Mama said for you to come home, right now!" Carmelina hit the burro with a thorn-covered ocotillo switch and disappeared down the hill.

"You had better do as she says."

"Yeah, I should go," agreed Daniel, laughing as he stood. "Give me six beers to go. I don't think I'm done drinking today."

Toribio went into the store, got six beers, and put them in a burlap bag. "No charge," said Toribio. "I still owe you for fixing my stove."

"And the money you won playing checkers?"

Toribio waved his right hand and laughed. "You were distracted, my friend. It wouldn't be right to take your money today."

"Thanks," said Daniel, taking the beer and shaking Toribio's hand. He climbed on his horse, turned his collar against the wind, and headed home.

Nearing the house, Daniel spied lathered horses and a group of men gathered in the corral. The men stood in a half circle around Sergio and Manuel who appeared to be arguing. He did not see Samuel among them. Daniel tied his horse at the front gate and entered the yard. He sensed trouble and wanted to check with Ramona before going to the corral.

Sergio broke from the corral and ran toward the house with Manuel in pursuit. The two boys converged on Daniel before he could enter the house, and they both started talking at the same time.

They talked so loud and fast that Daniel could not understand what either of them was trying to say. "Shut up," commanded Daniel, holding up his hands. "Would the both of you please shut up?"

Ramona appeared at the front door. "Does the entire village have to hear the arrival of bad news to our house?"

"Sit down, boys," said Daniel, taking a beer from the burlap sack before passing it to Ramona. "Okay, one of you boys had better explain what is so damn important, in a fashion that I can understand."

Ofelia watched through the window of the house. Her presence distracted Sergio.

Daniel waited for the boys to speak. He looked from Sergio to Manuel. "One of you had better start talking."

Sergio spoke first. "We were riding to Ojinaga with a large payment."

"José's boys weren't with you?"

"Chato was," Sergio said.

"Where is Samuel?" interrupted Daniel.

"This is what he is trying to tell you!" hissed Manuel.

Daniel took a long drink of his beer and stared at Manuel, silencing him.

"An army patrol cut our trail," said Sergio.

"Where were you?" Daniel asked with impatience. "Was Navarro with them?"

"I don't know," said Sergio.

"Where did this happen?"

"Near Solis. We had just started for Ojinaga when the soldiers jumped us. We tried to lose them but failed. Before we could reach safety in crossing the river, Samuel sent Manuel and I downriver with the money and instructed everyone to rendezvous at Langford's Hot Springs at daylight. Samuel took the others and looped back on the soldiers. Manuel and I rode to the hot springs as instructed and waited for Samuel and the others to arrive."

Daniel glanced at Ramona where she sat in a dark shadow inside the door to the house. She was drinking a beer, and they shared a knowing smile. He noticed Ofelia perched in the open window, with her back turned to the porch nursing the baby. The juxtaposition of the nursing mother, her baby, and the insanity of violence puzzled him. He shook his head and attempted to refocus on Sergio's story. "When did this happen?" asked Daniel.

"We arrived at the hot springs at midnight, last night. The others arrived hours after daylight but without Samuel. Gato had a bullet wound in his forearm, and Chato had taken a bad fall and split his upper lip. They both needed attention, so we rode upstream to the Hernandez house." Sergio edged forward in his chair. "After we got those that were hurt to the *curandera*, Gato and Chato rode to look for Samuel. Manuel and the others thought it best for us to bring the money here, back to the safety of Mexico. That is when we encountered the lieutenant in Tornillo Creek, and he challenged us. I turned my horse and ran."

Ramona brought Daniel another beer and stood at his side.

Sergio concluded his story, "Manuel pulled his pistol and shot the lieutenant."

Taking a deep breath, Daniel asked Manuel, "Is the lieutenant dead?"

"I don't know," shouted Manuel.

Daniel touched Ramona's hand and they exchanged another knowing glance.

"He fell off his horse, and I escaped," boasted Manuel.

"How many times did you fire your gun?"

"Three," admitted Manuel.

"How close were you?"

"Close … no more than six feet away."

"Dammit!" shouted Daniel, coming to his feet. "Okay, I'm only going to ask one time. Did you kill the lieutenant?"

Manuel cursed and sprang to his feet threatening Daniel with a long-bladed knife. "So what if I shot the pendejo? He would have done the same to me given the opportunity."

"Put the knife down."

"Take it from me, viejo."

Daniel turned to Ramona and said, "Go in the house."

Ramona examined her lover. He showed her no fear, and she returned into the house.

The instant Ramona closed the door; Daniel spun and kicked Manuel in the gut. Daniel charged the boy, forcing the blade across his body, and then hit him in the nose with his right fist. He grabbed Manuel's wrist and beat his arm against a juniper porch post until the boy dropped the knife, which Sergio immediately secured.

Jerking Manuel's right wrist behind his back, Daniel ran the boy out into the yard, smacked his forehead against a rock post, and clobbered him with a full roundhouse punch. Manuel tumbled ass over elbows into the dirt. As they continued to fight, they moved through the yard back toward the corral, where Daniel finally stood over Manuel trying to see if he had any fight left in him. A small crowd of onlookers had gathered.

Without warning, Manuel's cousin, Gabriel, pulled a pistol and raised it, pointing it at Daniel's head. Just as Gabriel attempted to cock the pistol, Ramona quickly fired both barrels of her sawed-off shotgun at the boy's feet. The air reverberated with the blast. "Put it down, Gabriel, or I will kill you," commanded Ramona as she reloaded. She held the shotgun level and ready, both hammers cocked to fire.

Gabriel dropped the pistol.

Manuel pulled himself onto his knees and wiped his bloody mouth with the back of his hand.

Daniel hunkered down on his boot heels near Manuel's right ear and asked, "What is it going to be, Manuel?"

"What do you mean?" Manuel asked, spitting blood and pieces of broken tooth.

"Are we done?"

Manuel stared at the ground and said nothing.

"I take it that is your answer," said Daniel, pulling his own knife from his right boot and laying the blade against Manuel's neck.

Manuel flinched, yet his eyes remained clouded with hate.

Daniel knew what to do, but hesitated.

Footsteps sounded from beyond the yard as the nearest neighbors tentatively approached the house. The men arrived armed with shotguns, pistols, pitchforks, and clubs.

"Put it away," said Ramona to Daniel. "The opportunity has passed."

Daniel looked up. He acknowledged Ramona's warning and slipped the knife back into his boot.

Ramona turned to Sergio. "Get into the house with the girls and lock the door!" Eyes burning with determination, Ramona picked up Gabriel's pistol and tucked it into the waist of her skirt. Then, using the short-barreled shotgun to good effect, she herded Manuel and the others to the horse corral. "Leave now," she commanded.

"The pistol," said Gabriel, pointing at the weapon even as he walked in obedience to her command.

"I will consider it a gift in exchange for your life. Go home, boys."

Ramona leaned into Daniel's arms as the neighbors swarmed around them demanding to know what had occurred.

Before either Ramona or Daniel could adequately explain anything to the gathering crowd, shouts rose from the corral. Everyone turned to see Manuel run Sergio to the ground with his horse. Manuel galloped away leading a pair of loaded pack mules, followed closely by his cousin.

Daniel pulled the pistol from Ramona's skirt and pointed the gun at the fleeing rider.

Touching his right arm, Ramona said, "Let him go."

Lowering the pistol, he handed it to Ramona. "Here, this is your pistol now."

~ ⌣ ⌢

Daniel and Ramona rose before dawn and soaked in the hot springs until daylight. Upon returning home, they discovered Samuel in their kitchen making coffee.

"What happened here?" Samuel laughed as he poured a cup of coffee. "Sergio has got a white-knuckled grip on that scattergun."

Regaining control of her kitchen, Ramona took the coffee pot from Samuel and called for Ofelia to help her with breakfast. The women donned gingham aprons and set to cooking. The two men carried their coffee into the front room where Carmelina had built a fire in the potbellied stove.

"Sit down, Samuel. We need to talk."

Samuel settled in a pine chair and blew the steam off his coffee. "Sergio tells me that Ramona pulled her shotgun on Gabriel."

"Gabriel came at me with a pistol."

Samuel shook his head. "And Manuel stole the money?"

"Yes." Daniel nodded. "And you? I heard that you were likely captured by soldiers?"

"Well, that's part of what happened ..." Samuel frowned.

"Dammit, your story precedes mine," insisted Daniel. "First, tell me what happened after the soldiers jumped you."

Samuel sipped his coffee and smiled. "We were carrying a payment for Perry to Ojinaga, and soldiers from Glenn Spring cut our trail."

"Was Tomás with you?" asked Daniel.

"No," replied Samuel. "He isn't here?"

"Not since the wedding. Ramona thinks he went south to join the war."

"Probably," said Samuel. "I only pray that he found his father."

Sergio came through the room headed for the front door.

"Sit down, son," commanded Daniel.

Sergio did as instructed.

Samuel chuckled and continued his story. "I sent Manuel and

Sergio to safeguard the money, while the rest of us went to distract the soldiers."

It took all of Daniel's patience to keep from screaming at his old friend. He was offended at Samuel's casual attitude as he described setting an ambush for the Ninth Cavalry. Daniel swallowed his anger and tried to listen.

"A group of soldiers jumped us, and the crew scattered."

"What did you expect?" asked Daniel. "They're just boys."

Samuel frowned. "Those boys are no strangers to killing."

Daniel shook his head. "And you were captured?"

"I was. My horse went down with a broken leg with soldiers in hot pursuit," explained Samuel. "They bound my wrists, put me on a pack mule, and we went looking for the lieutenant at Langford's Hot Springs."

"Did you see the lieutenant?" asked Sergio.

Samuel looked at Sergio, who lowered his eyes.

"Answer his question," said Daniel. "Did you see the lieutenant?"

"Yeah, I saw the lieutenant."

"Were you with him when he got shot? Were you?"

Samuel laughed. "Which time?"

"Are you enjoying this?" asked Daniel.

"Maybe, I am," said Samuel with a wicked grin. "No, I was not with the lieutenant when Manuel shot at him, but he told me about it. Manuel shot his horse."

"Manuel shot his horse?"

"Yes, he shot his horse."

Daniel sat up in his chair and shook his head. "Wait a minute!" Daniel began to laugh. "If you were captured by the soldiers this morning, what are you doing here now?"

"That's what I've been trying to explain, dammit! Yes, I know that Manuel shot *at* the lieutenant this morning. He missed! That boy fired three times at pointblank range and only managed to kill the lieutenant's horse."

Daniel visibly relaxed in his chair. "Why aren't you in jail? Did you escape?"

Samuel smiled. "We encountered the lieutenant in Tornillo Creek. He was afoot. With me being at the back of the column, I couldn't hear the conversation between the lieutenant and McKinney. It took the two men a few minutes to sort everything out. When they quit talking, the lieutenant sent McKinney with most of the soldiers to look for my accomplices. Next, he sent his corporal with a couple of men to inform the marshal about my arrest. After stopping at Langford's to borrow a horse, we turned north with only two soldiers as an escort." Samuel smiled and shook his head. "All the lieutenant could talk about was arresting me for sedition. He sincerely believed that my arrest would return him to good standing with Captain Henry and the entire US Army."

"I don't need to hear what you think he thought. How did you escape?"

"We were riding along Tornillo Creek, and the lieutenant got nervous about a column of dust rising from our back trail. He ordered the soldiers to investigate, although to their credit they did express a strong concern about him being alone with such a dangerous and valuable prisoner." Samuel paused as his eyes brightened. "Have you ever been to Banta Shut-In?"

When Daniel did not answer, Samuel kept talking. "Banta Shut-In is an amazing place, even for the Big Bend! All of Tornillo Creek, which is a mile wide or bigger in places, squeezes into a narrow slot of black, slick rock about six feet wide."

Daniel was amazed at Samuel's ability to find beauty in moments of chaos and crisis, yet he desperately needed to hear what had happened. "Get back to what happened, would you?"

Grinning, Samuel sat back in his chair. "As we rode through the narrowest portion of the notch at Banta Shut-In, the lieutenant had me go first, and I ... well, I managed to fall."

"What do you mean you managed to fall?" asked Daniel.

"I mean just that. I managed to fall and land such that it looked like I was hurt. That greenhorn lieutenant jumped down off his horse and ran to see if I was okay. When he tried to help me, I pulled his pistol on him. The lieutenant said I was going to have to kill him. I pulled the trigger. I didn't intend to kill him. I just wanted to frighten him into letting me go."

A strong wave of emotions cascaded through Daniel's body and mind, knowing that he could not be angry with Samuel for doing what he had done to escape. Ramona had almost killed a boy, and he himself had nearly slit Manuel's throat.

"The gun didn't discharge," said Samuel. "When the pistol failed to fire, the lieutenant fell over backwards trying to get away, and I didn't have the heart to try to shoot him a second time. In the confusion, I freed my hands, which was a good thing because we ended up fighting for a spell. Ultimately, I managed to get the best of the boy, stole his horse so he couldn't follow me, and rode straight through the night to arrive here this morning."

Ofelia came into the room with the blue enamel coffee pot and refilled their cups.

"That's my story," said Samuel. "Now let's hear what you have to say about losing our money."

"Fair enough," said Daniel, visibly relieved to know that Samuel had not harmed the lieutenant. "Your crew rode in this morning all excited, and it took some doing to get them settled down enough to telling a coherent story. They told me about the soldiers, your disappearance, and Manuel shooting at the lieutenant."

"So you knew that Manuel had shot at the lieutenant, but you had no idea that he was okay?"

"Yes, that is correct." Daniel nodded. "Then, for reasons unknown, Manuel got angry, pulled a knife on me, and I took it away from him. Gabriel Acosta tried to shoot me, and Ramona dusted his boots with her shotgun."

"You let Manuel get away with our money?" Samuel asked.

"Yeah," Daniel said, and exhaled.

"Come eat," called Ramona.

"You too, Sergio," said Daniel.

Plates of food were waiting on the table in the kitchen—tamales, beans, and a heaping pile of corn tortillas.

Ramona sat down at the table and spoke her mind. "Sergio had nothing to do with what Manuel did, you know that?"

Ofelia dropped a blue enamel bowl to the floor. Her enlarged eyes betrayed her fear. Ramona turned to Ofelia. "Take Carmelina and the baby and go into the front room so we can discuss these matters in private." Looking at Samuel, she said, "I don't want you assuming things from Ofelia's reactions that are not true."

Watching the girls leave the room, Daniel said, "She's scared."

"Of what?" Samuel asked.

"Ofelia is scared of all us damn gringos," replied Daniel, "but she is especially worried that you will blame Sergio for allowing Manuel to steal the money." Ramona touched Daniel's shoulder. The gesture had a calming effect. Daniel took a deep breath and removed the cornhusks from one of his tamales.

"Sergio is terrified that you will blame him for what happened," said Ramona. "He cried in my arms, but the saddest moment was dear, sweet little Carmelina boldly volunteering to tell you what she had seen occur." Ramona shook her head and sighed. "And now the youngest is involved in our affairs."

Samuel leaned forward in his chair. "I will get the money, and Manuel will be punished. Given time, I will settle things with Manuel. My immediate and only concern is the danger of arriving empty-handed before our creditors. That money was not ours to lose. This is potentially a fatal situation. The men anticipating that payment will not take kindly to receiving explanations in lieu of money."

"What can I do to help make it right?" Daniel asked.

"I don't know. I need to think this through." He pushed away his empty plate.

"When were you supposed to make the payment?"

"Yesterday, and there isn't time to arrange a transfer from Marfa."

"How much do you need?"

"Five thousand, minimum …"

"I can pay it for you," said Daniel.

Ramona touched Daniel's arm. Her eyes shone with love.

"How can you do that?" Samuel exclaimed. "Haven't you been putting your earnings in the bank?"

"No!" Daniel laughed. "I never did trust banks that much."

Samuel grinned, "So you buried your share of the money here in Boquillas? Are you a damn pirate?"

"Thanks to you, I have more money than I care to haul to the bank. I trust the ground more than I trust that damn Marfa Bank." Daniel stood and kissed Ramona on the crown of her head. Turning to the door, he said, "Come with us, Sergio. We're going to need your help digging."

CHAPTER 23

The Vultures Return

José Torreón arrived at his father's house in Boquillas on a sun-drenched, late-winter day.

The instant Ramona spied José riding toward the house, she ran to pull her cousin from his horse with a deep-felt embrace. They walked wrapped in each other's arms to the house where Ramona introduced José to Daniel.

The two men shook hands and said hello.

Ramona hit José in the upper arm. "Where have you been?"

"To the mouth of purgatory and home again," said José with a deep sigh.

"Did Tomás find you?" asked Ramona.

"Yes," whispered José. He stared at his boots.

Ramona touched José's arm. "Are you okay?"

José wiped his moist, bloodshot eyes with the palms of his hands. "It was a choice that he made himself."

Ramona shivered.

José sighed again. "Tomás disappeared near Durango in the midst of the heaviest fighting I have ever witnessed. I knew he was dead but needed to know where. Miraculously, I encountered an American who knew of a stone corral where Villa had reportedly executed hundreds of prisoners."

"Was the American a mercenary?" Daniel asked.

"No. He was a newspaperman."

"A newspaperman you say."

"I have seen many things in this war," said José. "And now, even the news of war is a commodity to be bought and sold to an international market."

"How peculiar." Daniel frowned.

"The American led me to a riverbed littered with dead men, their hands tied behind their backs." José looked to the ceiling as if offering a silent prayer. "I walked through the bloated corpses until I recognized his belt—the one his mother made for him last Christmas."

"I'm so sorry," said Ramona.

"Damn," cursed Daniel.

José wiped a tear from his eye. "That pendejo American wanted to know about our personal history—mine and Tomás's. That nosey bastard followed me for days trying to make some kind of story out of my misery."

"Why do you still fight?" Ramona asked.

"Now, it is personal."

"And before it became personal?" said Ramona, shaking her head.

José pursed his lips. Thinking made nothing better. Exhaling, he said, "At first when I joined Carranza, we were united with Villa, Zapata, and the others against Diaz and his henchmen. In those days, we fought against tyranny. Now, Villa refuses to acknowledge the inevitable conclusion. Our war is decided, yet we still fight with our paisanos, our compatriots? Now, I fight to end the war."

"Why one fights matters not to a dead man." Ramona said. "This war has become insane. You fight for Carranza against Villa, at the same time that your father does business with Villa?" Ramona laughed.

"Life is a terrible tragedy of circumstances, is it not?" José sighed and wiped another tear from his eye with a shirtsleeve.

"I agree," said Ramona, echoing his sigh. Touching her cousin's shoulder, she said, "I am sorry for your loss."

"We are either the predator or the prey," said José. "Are there other choices in life?"

"Are you hungry?" Ramona asked.

"No, gracias," he said.

"Come to the kitchen and sit down. I will make us some fresh coffee."

José offered Daniel a cigar, and Ramona took it. She walked into the kitchen sporting a mischievous grin.

"I see who wears the pants around here," said José with a laugh, handing Daniel his own cigar. Sitting down at the kitchen table, he said, "So, I hear that Ramona definitely knows how to handle her grandfather's shotgun."

Ramona glanced over her shoulder at José, and then kindled the fire in the cookstove and readied a pot of coffee.

"You heard what happened?" Daniel asked, sensing that Ramona had been elevated in social status from a widow to a proud *Mexicana* and defender of her home.

"Yes, I heard what happened here. In the end, Manuel will get what he has earned. These things will be settled soon," said José, calmly. "I saw Samuel in Ocampo."

"So you know he was captured by the lieutenant?"

"We had the opportunity to talk."

"Samuel being a fugitive changes things, doesn't it?"

"Nothing ever remains the same," said José.

"I must admit that I'm pleased that he did not harm the lieutenant."

"Don't fret over the lieutenant. After all his calamities, he will soon have a grand opportunity to redeem himself."

Ramona poured three cups of coffee, placed them on the table, and sat down.

"What do you mean, the opportunity to redeem himself? I don't understand," said Daniel.

José sipped his coffee and smiled at Ramona. "Thank you."

Ramona returned his smile, pushing a shell ashtray toward the center of the table for their cigar ashes.

"Daniel, when are you leaving for my father's ranch house?" José asked.

"You're going hunting with us also?"

José laughed. "Yes, I'm going hunting too."

Sensing something hidden, Daniel said, "I had planned to leave tomorrow morning at daylight."

"Good. We will ride together, okay?" José took a long drink of his coffee.

"Tomorrow at daylight," replied Daniel.

José stood, touching Ramona on the crown of the head. "Thank you for the coffee." He shook Daniel's right hand and said, "I will arrive for you *mañana* at first light."

"Won't you stay?" asked Ramona, standing.

"No. I have little time here at home, and there is much to be done." José hugged Ramona, waved good-bye to Daniel, and disappeared through the door.

〜〜

Soft, heavenly rays of bruised orange light streaked the darkness when Daniel kissed Ramona good-bye and walked to his horse. Ramona stood on the porch and watched the two men ride away. She knew they would kill Manuel just as she knew there was much that she did not want to know about their business.

〜〜

Daniel and José rode south beyond the Rio Grande following a wind-scarified arroyo to the Terminal Canyon trail. Riding past the lead-ore, cable tram terminal, they crossed grasslands thick with yucca and sotol. As they gained elevation, the rolling foothills of towering yuccas gave way to a montane forest of pinion, junipers, oaks, and maples. Majestic madrone trees, scarred by the claws of hungry black bears, were scattered throughout the forest. A flock of raucous blue jays greeted them as they entered a decadent expanse of gnarled, old oaks.

José pointed at a pair of turkey vultures circling the cloudless sky and said, "The vultures returned late this year. Some say it is because of the carnage in Mexico."

Daniel nodded. "I've heard that said."

The men rode until they arrived at Mario's remote mountain ranch house. The rock-walled cabin appeared from the forest alongside a flowing creek.

"Papa, we're here," called José as they approached the house. Obviously annoyed by the lack of response, José joked, "The deaf old bastard is probably sleeping, no?"

Mario appeared at the door rubbing his one good eye with the palm of his hand. "Come inside. The beans are cooked."

Daniel and José led their horses into the crude dry-stack rock corral adjacent to the house. They carried their gear to the house, where Mario offered a supper of skillet-warmed beans, goat meat, and day-old tortillas. As they sat down to eat, they heard a rider approaching.

"Samuel," said José, going to open the door. "That man misses few meals." He stepped outside and yelled at Samuel with a loud voice. "Did you recover our money?"

"Most of it," answered Samuel, sliding to the ground. He saw Daniel and Mario standing behind José. "Did you tell him, yet?"

"No," replied José.

"Tell me what?" asked Daniel, stepping outside.

"Did they talk with you about the plan?"

"What plan?"

"We should eat first," said Mario, turning back toward the kitchen. "I'm hungry."

"Did you find Manuel?" Daniel asked.

"Yes," Samuel said, loosening the saddle on his horse.

"And he gave you the money?"

"Yes, but that is old business," said Samuel.

"He is dead?" José asked.

"He is," said Samuel.

Daniel nodded. "That boy seemed bound and determined to get himself killed."

"Does how he died matter?" asked José.

"No," said Daniel. "Not one bit."

"What matters though," said Samuel, throwing his saddle over his shoulder and moving toward the door of the house, "is eating."

"What matters," said José, moving to one side, "is robbing Villa."

"My son, the patriot!" Mario laughed and placed a fourth plate on the metal table. "Let's eat. I'm famished."

"So," asked Daniel, "what are we planning?"

"We are planning to rob Pancho Villa," said José, sitting down at the table.

"One last deal before Villa is defeated or possibly assassinated," added Samuel, settling into a chair.

"The war is ending. It is time to cash in our hand before the game ends," said José. "Mario is right though, we should discuss this in detail after we eat."

Daniel joined the men at the table. "Why do I suspect that my part in this deal involves the lieutenant?"

"Because you're a damn clairvoyant!" Samuel laughed and slapped Daniel on the back square between the shoulders.

After supper, Mario poured four cups of coffee and spread a large piece of butcher paper across the kitchen table. He took up his chewed stub of a pencil and led them through his well-planned conspiracy to separate Pancho Villa from his money. The old man drew maps and wrote outlines as he described various phases of the operation, including each man's responsibility.

Mario talked uninterrupted for almost an hour before he looked up from his plan directly at Daniel, and asked, "What do you think?"

Daniel stared at the maps and checklists and considered Mario's tactics and strategy. It was a good plan. "And you honestly don't think Villa will seek vengeance against us?"

"How could he?" asked José. "Villa won't know I was involved. He will think my father is a peyote-crazed Indian, and your role is invisible."

"I'm the only person at risk," said Samuel. "And it's a risk I'm willing to take."

"What about the lieutenant?"

"He is a soldier in search of redemption. If you were in his situation, what would you choose?" Samuel asked.

"And if we are lucky, Villa might be killed or arrested by either José or the young lieutenant," said Mario with a grin.

"And then we're done?" Daniel asked.

"Is it ever done?" Samuel laughed. "Besides, we will be rich."

"Regardless of what we decide tonight, Villa has been defeated," said José. "Sadly, the general still fields a remnant of his army, but soon he will either accept the truth, or die. It is only a matter of time."

"Things are changing," interjected Mario. "In reality, the game never remains the same—the rules are constantly changing. Soon, the rules that have allowed us to grow rich will radically change; however, until the end of days, Mexicans will forever be providing illicit commodities for Americans and the richest of Mexicans. We simply need to adapt."

"Well," asked Samuel, looking to Daniel, "are you in?"

Daniel nodded and smiled. "Let's get it done."

PART 4:
Robbing Pancho Villa

Don't let it end like this. Tell them I said something.
— Pancho Villa's last words

Chapter 24

Ramona's Concern

RAMONA WOKE TO find Daniel gathering his gear and loading his traveling saddlebag. She climbed out of bed without speaking and went to the kitchen where she built a fire and put a blue enamel pot of coffee on to boil. Standing in the bedroom doorway twirling a curl in her long black hair, Ramona watched her lover pack the last of his things until the aroma of coffee drew her from her reverie. She returned to the kitchen, poured Daniel a cup of coffee, and brought it to him in the bedroom.

"Thank you," said Daniel, trading a kiss for the coffee.

Ramona sat on the edge of the bed.

Daniel sipped his coffee and looked at Ramona. He had not told her about Mario's plan to rob Pancho Villa, yet he sensed her unspoken concern.

"Where are you going?" Ramona asked.

"Fishing," said Daniel, sitting next to her on the bed.

"No, you're not," replied Ramona. "Why do you lie to me? We agreed to have no secrets between us, didn't we?"

"Yes, but ..." Daniel put his arm around her shoulder. There was no reason to lie. Then again, there was too much danger in telling her the whole truth.

"I wish you would not go."

"I have to," said Daniel, kissing her on the cheek. "There is too much at stake not to help."

Tears flowed down her face. "Why is Sergio involved?"

Daniel started to ask how she had learned about Sergio, but did not. How she knew these things did not matter. "He isn't going with me. Sergio is riding with Mario and Samuel. He will be okay. Don't focus too much on worrying."

Ramona's eyes darkened.

Before she could speak, Daniel touched her cheek with a soft right hand. "I should be gone about ten days." He kissed her full on the mouth and wiped the tears from her face. "I will be back as quick as I can." He stood to go.

"I know what you are doing. It's very dangerous."

Daniel nodded. "That's why it is best that you remain here, at home."

Ramona raised her eyes to the cane ceiling. "When you return, we should go somewhere."

Daniel hesitated in the doorway. "What do you mean?"

"We should find somewhere else to live. Please?"

"I would consider that."

She waved him to the door with a trembling hand. "Do what needs to be done. And then hurry home."

"I promise," said Daniel, turning to go.

Ramona fell onto the bed into an uncombed pool of ebony hair and white sheets and listened to Daniel ride away.

CHAPTER 25

Langford's Hot Spring

DANIEL FOLLOWED THE Rio Grande upstream through Hot Springs Canyon. He crossed the river several times, and all the graveled fords were low enough that his saddle remained dry.

At the dry arroyo below Langford's Hot Springs, Daniel encountered Mr. Langford, the man who owned and operated the dusty resort at the confluence of the Rio Grande and Tornillo Creek. He was a happy man with a talkative disposition. Daniel always enjoyed the man's company.

"What brings you this direction?" asked Langford.

"Hot water, mostly," said Daniel. "And you?"

"Oh, I had business with old man Deemer." Langford pushed back the brim of his hat and smiled. "What about this weather? Springtime in the Big Bend is something to behold, don't you agree?"

"That it is," said Daniel.

"I love the weather this time of the year, if the damn wind isn't constantly blowing."

Daniel laughed. "No doubt. The hot, dry spring wind sure irritates folks."

"That it does," agreed Langford.

"Have you seen Lieutenant Thompson?" asked Daniel. "I was thinking of paying him a visit."

"Jack?"

"Yeah." Daniel nodded. "Jack Thompson."

"Why, you're in luck. He rode past me a while ago headed to the Hernandez house. He won't be long," said Langford with a chuckle. "Old man Hernandez will run him off quicker than he can slide down off his horse."

Daniel could actually imagine Señor Hernandez brandishing a shotgun and chasing after the lieutenant.

"He won't be long," Langford said again. "You want a cup of coffee while you wait?"

"No. Not right now, but thank you for the offer. What I need is a good soak," said Daniel.

"Suit yourself. Come up to the house when you're done, and I will make sure you get fed," offered Langford. "You've got the bathhouse to yourself. We don't get many folks these days what with all the violence along the river."

"I heard that your family has gone to live in El Paso."

"Yes, sir. It just seems the safest place for those girls of mine."

"If you don't mind me asking, what happened that made you send them away?"

Langford shook his head. "We woke one morning to find three men hanging from that mesquite across the river." Langford pointed upstream with his right index finger.

"What a horrific sight that must have been. Who were they?"

"Who was who?"

"The boys they hung there," said Daniel, pointing at the tree.

"They were all local boys, including Irma's brother, Juan Hernandez." Langford shook his head. "He was barely thirteen."

"Who hung them?"

"Who knows?"

"Damn."

"I'd better get back to the house. Make yourself comfortable," said Langford.

Daniel waved good-bye, and then rode to the bathhouse. Sliding to the ground, he tethered his horse. The bathhouse was a work of art. A German stonemason had built the magnificent structure from the limestone ledge rock that was so common in Tornillo Creek.

All the tubs were empty, and Daniel picked his favorite southeast corner tub where the narrow window allowed a striking view of the

Sierra del Carmen across the river in Mexico. He hung his brimmed hat and clothes on a pair of iron hooks, and then eased into the hot spring water.

Groaning with pleasure, he closed his eyes. While his body soaked, his mind raced with the audaciousness of Mario's plan. "Release the worry," whispered Daniel as he exhaled, stretching his body into the hot embrace of the soothing water. He knew from experience that there was nothing gained in worry. The hot water purged his body of physical stress, yet it failed to ease his worried mind.

Daniel soaked until he wrinkled, then he dragged himself from the tub and air-dried before dressing. Carrying his boots, he stepped out of the bathhouse and discovered the lieutenant sitting in the shade near the door.

"You come for a bath?"

"No, I did not. Langford said you were looking for me."

Daniel nodded, "Yes, I am." He sat on the bench next to the young man. "Is there something wrong?"

"Señor Hernandez won't even let me talk with Irma."

"I thought Captain Henry ordered you to stay away from Irma?"

"To hell with Captain Henry!" exclaimed the lieutenant, looking to the ground.

"That attitude isn't good for your career." Knowing that the plan called for him to drag the lieutenant into their scheme and possibly deeper into trouble, Daniel felt a momentary pang of guilt.

"Nothing seems to go my way," groaned the lieutenant, dropping his head into his hands. "None of it makes any sense."

"I'm sorry you're having a rough time."

The lieutenant looked up. "Don't be, it isn't your problem."

"I might have something of interest for you," said Daniel, more nervous than he had anticipated.

"What do you mean?"

"Would you be interested in knowing where to find Pancho Villa?"

"Why are you doing this?"

"Because I feel that I owe you something." Daniel paused. "My friendship has caused you nothing but problems."

"Don't you and that bastard Samuel do business with Villa?"

"We did. Villa is about to pass into the pages of history. It's only a matter of time before he surrenders or is assassinated."

"What's in this for you?"

"Can't I just do you a favor?"

"Is it ever really that simple?"

Daniel grinned. Shaking his head, he said, "No, it isn't." The lieutenant's instinct impressed him. Some resistance on his part was a sign of good character.

"Now that sounds more like the truth," the lieutenant said with a smile.

"I need to know one thing before we continue," said Daniel.

"And that is?"

"Are you madder at Navarro or Samuel? Samuel may be a man with questionable business practices, but he isn't an assassin."

"Samuel tried to kill me! If that gun hadn't misfired …," moaned the lieutenant.

"I've heard Samuel's version of that story. He did not intend to kill you. He just wanted to put the fear of God in you so he could get away."

The lieutenant pushed back his brimmed hat and wiped his forehead with a red bandana. "I can't do anything about Navarro, but I can arrest or even kill Samuel and probably get a medal for it. Which trophy would you choose?"

"They aren't my choices. You know that what happened between you and Samuel was just business, nothing personal. Someday you might be standing in his boots."

"Not me," said the lieutenant. "It's my job to arrest smugglers."

"Your job is to protect the people who live here on the border. Look, I can offer you the opportunity to arrest Pancho Villa. You decide."

"Son-of-a-bitch," cursed the lieutenant, sitting upright on the bench.

"If it works, you are golden. And you know it."

"And if I don't catch Villa?"

"In reality, your situation won't be any different. Still no Irma and no career, but you might have one interesting story to tell your grandchildren." Daniel grinned at the soldier.

"Without a spectacular shift of fortune, my career is ruined," exhaled the lieutenant. "The opportunity to capture Villa is exciting, but are you crazy?"

Daniel laughed.

Leaning forward, the lieutenant spoke in a soft whisper as if someone might be listening. "What are you suggesting?"

"We are planning to rob Pancho Villa," said Daniel.

"Holy shit!" exclaimed the lieutenant. "You want me to help you rob Pancho Villa?"

"No, Samuel will take care of that detail."

"Then what do you want from me?"

"Can we talk as we ride?" Daniel asked.

"Wait," said the lieutenant. "Seriously, what do you want from me?"

"Samuel has already set in motion a plan to rob Pancho Villa. If the plan plays properly, he will have a very short head start on Villa and be running hard for the river. Since we have a real good idea exactly where Villa is going to be in a few days, we thought you and your soldiers might want the opportunity to arrest him."

Standing, the lieutenant paced with his hat in hand. He stared at the clear blue sky. "This is against my best judgment, but I want to know everything before I decide."

Daniel nodded. "How soon can we muster your soldiers?"

"Are you listening to me? I have to hear this crazy idea before I agree to a damn thing, okay?"

"I understand, but time is a factor," said Daniel. "Can we ride to Glenn Spring while I explain? You can always say no along the way."

The lieutenant looked to his horse. "How come my stomach just rolled over?"

"That always happens the moment a man decides to look death in the face."

"Now that makes me feel better." The lieutenant laughed. "Let's go."

As they rode north to Glenn Spring, Daniel explained the plan in detail—at least the parts he thought the lieutenant needed to know.

Asking few questions, the lieutenant listened.

The sun burned a fierce hole in the clear blue sky as undulating waves of heat danced upon the eroded badlands, blending earth and sky. A single vulture twirled long lazy circles.

Somewhere unseen, a red-tailed hawk whistled.

CHAPTER 26

Chilicote, Chihuahua, Mexico

SAMUEL, MARIO, GATO, and Sergio crossed the Rio Grande at Las Hitas with malicious intent. Mario remained alone at the abandoned Spanish presidio on San Carlos Creek with ten unburdened pack mules. The others, leading a separate string of pack mules, continued south into Mexico toward a rendezvous with Pancho Villa.

The further south the men rode, the more Sergio talked. Samuel allowed him his nerves as a necessary distraction in dispelling the boy's fear. Gato did his best to ignore Sergio's idle chatter, keeping his focus on the string of pack mules and the task for which they rode. They stopped only to water the horses and mules. Day turned to night as they rode south. They arrived in the village of Chilicote, Chihuahua, at midnight.

Chilicote appeared as Mario had described it. The humble community consisted of a few widely spaced adobe houses, a small store alongside a large corral for holding animals, and an ill-repaired water tower for refilling the trains that ran between Ojinaga and Chihuahua City. Samuel stopped his horse at the edge of town and faced his companions. "Do we need to review the plan?"

"Why? All our planning will completely break down the moment Villa arrives," said Gato.

"Then that's the plan, no?" said Samuel.

"How much money is Villa going to give us?" Sergio asked.

Samuel smiled. "There will be enough money for all of us to live without working for a very long time, son."

Sergio laughed. "It's impossible to imagine that much money!"

"We have until one o'clock. About an hour from now," explained Samuel. "That's when José should arrive with the trainload of soldiers. At that point, everything hinges on Villa. If José and his soldiers can keep Villa engaged for twenty minutes, we should be able to outrun Villa to the river."

"What if Villa runs with us?" asked Sergio.

"Villa will want to fight, not run," claimed Samuel.

"What if Villa catches us?" asked Sergio.

"Sergio, it's time for you to quit asking questions. Let's get it done," commanded Samuel, spurring his horse forward.

Not a single lamp flickered in the houses of the quiet little village. Snarling dogs appeared from the shadows and nipped at the horses' feet. Clicking the twin barrels on his shotgun, Gato cursed the dogs, halting the attack. The dogs slinked back into the shadows with their tails curled between their legs.

The riders crossed the single railroad track, and then sat on their horses in front of a long adobe building that stood alongside a wooden corral. A moon shadow darkened the front of the store where the word *Tienda*, written in whitewash, glowed in the dark. An unseen man called from the darkest shadow. *"Bienvenida."*

Samuel recognized the voice as Colonel Reyes, the bastard who had hung him in Saltillo. He swallowed the lump in his throat and slid from his horse, hoping that the man's memory of the event was lacking. "And you are?" asked Samuel.

The two men stood paces apart.

"Reyes," replied the man, pushing his brown fedora back on his head. "Colonel Reyes."

Neither man offered his hand.

"And you?" asked Reyes.

"Where is the general?" asked Samuel, ignoring his question.

"He will be along soon." Reyes stared at the gringo standing before him. "Have we met before?"

"I believe not. Shall we get this done?"

Reyes pointed toward the shuttered store. "In there."

Samuel resisted the urge to rub the scar on his neck. He turned to his men and said, "Gato, bring the scale."

Reyes led them into the dimly lit store where three armed men sat drinking tequila and smoking cigarettes at an old pine table that stood in the middle of the room. Along one side of the one-room, dirt floor store stood a waist-high wooden counter lined with jars of penny candy, canned goods, sugar, and coffee. Behind the counter lay bags of flour and sacks of pinto beans next to a crate of oranges and a barrel of mealy-looking apples. A stack of bulging, leather-reinforced hempen bags lay piled on the table where the men sat.

As soon as Samuel entered the store, the Mexicans stood as they reached for their pistols.

Reyes ordered his henchmen to holster their weapons and move away from the table. The men took their bottle of tequila and squatted against the far wall. Reyes watched them carefully and issued a command: "One of you needs to stand guard outside."

The men looked at each other. Without any discussion, the youngest henchman stood, pulled on his round sombrero, and went out to stand watch.

Gato and Sergio entered the room carrying a metal scale and a length of chain. Sergio suspended the scale from a twenty-penny nail that had been hammered into a rough-hewn pine roof beam, while Gato opened the first bag of money and emptied its contents. Indian head gold coins spilled on the table.

"Damn!" said Samuel. "Where'd Villa get those American golden eagle ten-dollar coins, Colonel?"

Reyes smiled. "We procured them from the gringo Hearst."

Samuel nodded, mesmerized by the glitter of so much gold. A subtle grin creased his whiskered face, and he settled against the counter. He enjoyed the idea of stealing stolen money.

The only sound in the room was the click-click of ten-dollar coins as Gato assembled them into neat stacks of ten coins each. "Two hundred gold Indians," announced Gato, sealing the first bag with a leather tie.

"Weigh that bag as a measure. All we need is a rough count," instructed Samuel.

Every man in the room stared at the money, each imaging what he could do with all those gold coins.

"Riders are coming!" shouted the guard stationed outside.

Pointing toward his remaining henchmen, Reyes commanded, "Get up on the roof." He turned to Samuel and said, "Come with me."

Samuel followed Reyes into the dark night, his stomach churning with anticipation. The reality of confronting Pancho Villa was not as easy as he had pretended. Beads of sweat formed on his neck, and he felt several individual drops rolling down his spine. Samuel took a deep breath hoping to calm his pounding heart. He could not show fear. His life depended on it.

Reyes stood with his back to Samuel, a rifle cradled in the crook of his arm. The ground shook with the beating of hooves as the riders appeared from the arroyo beyond the edge of town. The front rider wore a brown felt fedora, and there was no doubt it was Villa. His silhouette, even in the moonlight, was unmistakable.

Samuel recalled his first encounter with Villa. They had met at Villa's house in Chihuahua City. He vividly remembered the crates of ammunition stacked between fragrant gardens of pink and purple bougainvilleas and the sound of Villa's spurs. Those magnificent spurs had sung when the infamous general crossed the shadowy marble patio floor outside his brightly lit kitchen.

Tonight, Villa rode with some thirty-odd heavily armed men. Most of the men carried military carbines and stolen American rifles. Some carried shotguns. They almost all carried pistols stuffed in their pants and bandoliers of cartridges crisscrossed on their chests.

Samuel watched Villa slow his stallion to a halt and remembered the last time he had crossed paths with Villa in Ojinaga. Samuel had sold Villa a pair of sorely needed machine guns along with ten thousand rounds of ammunition. In celebration of the sale, the general had gifted him a bottle of the finest tequila. Yet those heady days were long gone. Samuel knew the truth—although Villa's army remained in the field, his war was lost.

None of the riders appeared to notice the gringo. Rather, they leapt from their horses. A small contingent of the men moved into defensive positions around the store. The rest gathered the horses inside the nearby corral and set to building fires and boiling water for coffee. Villa's men looked tired; they had fought for too long in an endless war.

Still mounted, Villa watched his men establish themselves before he turned his full attention to Samuel. Then he slid down from his horse and walked toward Samuel. "Buenas *noches*."

"Good evening, General Villa," replied Samuel, hesitating when he realized that Villa did not intend to shake hands.

"Is the money in order?"

"So it appears, General."

"How do you like those gold Indians?"

"They are impressive, sir."

"We procured them from that bastard Hearst."

Samuel said nothing in response.

Villa turned to Reyes. "Go see if the damned storekeeper's wife has any food for us. I'm famished."

The order woke Reyes from his daydream. He acknowledged the command and went in search of food.

Villa pulled a bottle from the inside pocket of his jacket and sat down on the bench. "Explain to me your intentions."

"My men have counted one bag of the money and weighed it."

Villa waved his bottle in the air and spit. "That portion of the deal is of no interest to me as it's already done."

Samuel flushed. He had misunderstood the question.

"You have bribed the proper authorities in Texas?" Villa asked.

"Yes."

"Tell me how the money will be exchanged for the weapons. What about the American soldiers in Presidio?"

"The colonel at Presidio is an old friend. We have arranged for a fiesta. Even if something should go wrong, the soldiers will be too drunk to muster. Your appointed representative may accompany me across the river, as we previously agreed. Afterwards, we will meet you at Candelaria with the shipment as planned."

Gato stepped from the store. "We are done counting."

"Get it loaded," said Samuel.

Gato glanced from Samuel to the general before disappearing back into the store.

"Who owns the weapons?" asked Villa.

"It's my deal, General."

Villa narrowed his eyes. "If you cross me, I will burn down your house with you in it."

"I understand your concern, General, but if I may speak honestly, do you trust your man Reyes?"

Villa laughed and looked away. "I have known Reyes since I was a starving highwayman in the mountains of Durango. I trust him with my life."

"Like you trusted Tomás Urbina? What happens when the price of your assassination pays more than keeping you alive?"

Villa's face reddened and his eyes bulged. Samuel had struck a nerve. Tomás Urbina had been a trusted associate who had disappeared the previous fall with the remains of the general's treasury. Urbina had paid for his treachery with his life.

"After Urbina, I have little money left to risk with thieves." Villa waved the now empty tequila bottle. "I need this shipment of weapons and ammunition to carry the fight to that one-armed bastard Obregón." Dark emotions flashed across the general's face. Villa discarded the bottle, breaking it against the hard ground.

"A train is coming!" shouted a man from the store roof.

"From which direction?" Villa shouted.

"It's coming from the south, General—from Chihuahua City."

Colonel Reyes returned from his errand with a burrito in his hand. He handed Villa the burrito and said, "Our train is coming."

Samuel's heart pounded in his chest. "What train?"

Villa took a bite of his burrito, grinned, and said, "Our train, Samuel. We appropriated a train so that we could travel together to Ojinaga. It is a long ride!" Villa laughed.

"That wasn't part of our agreement."

"Just as there are some details that I don't care to hear, there are things that you will never know," growled Villa. The general walked to the corral behind the store and watched the train pull to a stop under a water tower.

Gato waved Samuel to the front of the store. "Did I hear Villa say that was his train?"

"Is the money loaded?" asked Samuel.

"It's done," said Gato. "Do you think the train belongs to Villa or José?"

"We are about to find out. Finish with the mules and mount up before the bones are cast," said Samuel. From where he stood with the loaded pack mules, he could easily see the train as it approached.

The train came to a halt beneath the wooden water tower. It hissed steam. Villa's men moved toward the train. They were confident it was Villa's train, until the moment when rifles appeared from the fortified boxcars.

The first volley cut through the men closest to the track. Men fell, some wounded, some dead. The stench of gunpowder filled the air as the rest of Villa's men scrambled behind corrals and returned fire. The firing was intense; the two sides separated by just a few yards.

"Stay with the money," Villa told Reyes.

Reyes did as instructed, while Villa ran to join the fight. Hurrying back to the store, Reyes confronted Samuel. "I hung you in Saltillo, didn't I?"

"You hung me all right, but you failed to kill me, pendejo."

Reyes pulled his pistol and pointed it at Samuel. Only the metallic click of Gato's short-barreled shotgun stopped Colonel Reyes from pulling the trigger.

Samuel stared at Reyes. "Kill me and you're dead too, Colonel. Put the pistol away and let's do the deal as agreed before we get killed or captured—or worse."

Reyes lowered the pistol and said, "Go!"

Gato needed no further instructions. He mounted swiftly, kicked his horse into a hard run, and led the loaded string of pack mules away. Samuel slapped Sergio's horse with his hat sending the boy galloping after Gato. Samuel leapt into the saddle and spurred his horse north toward the arroyo at the edge of town.

Reyes opened the corral, gathered his horse, and mounted. He hesitated in looking over his shoulder to consider the battle before honoring his responsibility to remain with the money. Flailing his horse with a leather quirt, Reyes rode alone up the arroyo.

Samuel skidded to a halt in the arroyo beyond town, turned, and shouldered his rifle. He waited for Reyes, and then squeezed the trigger. Reyes fell backwards off his horse, landing in a cloud of dust. Samuel sheathed his rifle, pulled a pistol from his belt, and rode cautiously to where the man lay. It was easy to see that Reyes was dead.

Rubbing the scar on his neck, Samuel said, "It's best to kill a man once you have decided to hang him, Colonel." Samuel took a moment to drag the dead man's body into the brush but made little attempt to conceal it. He took the reins of the dead man's horse and galloped toward Texas.

CHAPTER 27

San Carlos Creek

MARIO SAT WITH his back against an eroded adobe wall. He was tending a small campfire and enjoying the moments of soft and shifting light in the hour between daylight and sunrise. The uniquely delicious smell of *huisache* flowers perfumed the fine spring day; he strung slices of fresh-cut peyote onto a length of fishing line.

A growing cloud of dust rose above the road leading south into Mexico. Riders were coming. Mario soon recognized Pancho Villa leading his band of henchmen. Their horses lathered, the men appeared to be asleep in the saddle. Mario knew that both the men and their horses would need water from San Carlos Creek.

Stopping his horse in the creek that flowed just below Mario's camp, Villa dropped to the ground, rinsed out his mouth with a handful of water, and washed his face. Visibly annoyed that the one-eyed old man had not risen to greet them, he called out, "Good morning, viejo."

Mario looked up and smiled.

Villa walked up the creek bank to the edge of Mario's fire and hunkered down on his boot heels. "Are you just collecting the peyote or are you off on another planet?"

Mario spit a thick stream of tobacco juice at the ground. "I'm just collecting, my esteemed General. It's medicine for a friend."

Something about this one-eyed man disturbed Villa. "How long have you been camped here?"

"Two days," replied Mario.

"I'm looking for my *compañeros*," explained Villa. "Four men: a gringo riding with three Mexicans and a string of loaded pack mules."

Mario did not respond. He continued stringing the green peyote buttons.

"Well, old man?"

"Yes, I saw them," said Mario.

Villa's temper was rising. A twitch appeared in his right eye. "Did they ride toward Ojinaga or not?"

"No, they rode north toward Las Hitas."

That information infuriated Villa. "Chinga madre!" cursed Villa, standing and kicking at the hard ground with his right boot heel. He hurried down the embankment to his horse and shouted, "Mount up!"

Mario put down his string of peyote and called to Villa, "General!"

"What!" Villa turned his horse to face the one-eyed old man.

"There are other things you might wish to know."

"What, viejo? Tell me quickly. I'm in a hurry."

"There were only two Mexicans riding with the gringo. The men were leading a string of mules and trailing an empty saddle horse."

"They weren't riding with an older Mexican wearing a fedora like mine?"

"No," answered Mario.

"Son-of-a-bitch!" Villa cursed, and then spurred his horse down the creek.

Mario kept stringing peyote, but he was pleased by the anger and confusion he had caused Villa. When he was certain that Villa and his armed riders were gone, he leapt to his feet and whistled. He quickly gathered the unstrung peyote buttons and stuffed them into a burlap sack. Then he saddled his mule with a sense of urgency.

Sergio came down the creek on his jet-black mare leading a string of pack mules. The mules were heavily loaded with bulging canvas bags. "You are sure that he is gone?"

"I'm certain of it," insisted Mario, kicking his floppy-eared mule east toward the village of Santa Elena.

"Run, you bastards," shouted Sergio, tugging hard on the pack mules' lead line. "We need to get this money across the Rio Grande before Villa springs the next trap!"

CHAPTER 28

The Lieutenant and Villa

DANIEL AND THE lieutenant lay on their bellies on a graveled ridge of scattered creosote brush and isolated clumps of low-growing dog cholla.

"You see that?" Daniel asked, pointing.

The lieutenant focused his field glasses. "It looks like two riders leading ten mules and a horse. One of them is Samuel."

"You believe me now?"

"Okay," said the lieutenant.

"Bring your horse. We should meet them on the road," said Daniel, moving down the hill to the road and his horse.

Samuel started talking the moment he rode within earshot. "Lieutenant, I'm awful sorry about what happened between us. It wasn't personal."

Wanting to hear the conversation, Sergeant McKinney rode his horse alongside the lieutenant.

The lieutenant stared at Samuel in disbelief. "There is nothing to talk about." He wiped his forehead with the back of his gloved hand. "But someday, Samuel—"

"Now isn't time to settle imagined scores." Daniel shook his head and glared at Samuel. "Are we good?"

"Oh, we're definitely good, my friend. Things went extremely well."

"Sergio is okay?"

"Yes, he is."

"What's on those mules?" asked the lieutenant. "I didn't think you were bringing the money our direction."

"Mario has the money—some twenty thousand gold eagles. We are only stringing these loaded mules along to keep the bait fresh," explained Samuel.

McKinney whistled and grinned.

"Villa is coming?" asked the lieutenant.

"Right behind us," replied Samuel.

"How many men does he have?" Daniel asked.

"Villa rode into Chilicote with about thirty armed men—maybe more. After the skirmish José and his boys started when they arrived in that train, those who aren't wounded or dead are shook up and bone tired." Samuel hooted and slapped his thigh. "I wish you had been there, Daniel. For some reason known only to Villa, he thought the train was his. Dammit, that José orchestrated a spectacular ambush."

"Who is José and why did Villa think it was his train?" asked the lieutenant.

"Who José is," said Daniel, shaking his head, "is not important now."

Samuel shook his head. "Villa thought his men had stolen the train. That bastard actually thought we were going to take a train ride to Ojinaga to exchange his money for our weapons. It never occurred to Villa that his train was our train with José Torreón and two boxcars full of Carranza's soldiers ready for a fight. Villa got his ass kicked!"

"I'm beginning to think that this crazy idea might just work, Lieutenant," said Sergeant McKinney. "It sounds like sport, sir."

Samuel smiled. "Listen to McKinney."

Gato shaded his eyes and stared down the road. "Here he comes."

The men all turned to face the cloud of dust that was forming over the road where it disappeared behind a low, black mesa.

"The time for thinking is over." Daniel faced the lieutenant and held him by both shoulders. "Do what needs to be done, or run. The devil himself is about to arrive among us."

The lieutenant broke away from Daniel's grasp and spoke the necessary command, albeit with a tentative voice. "Get them saddled, Sergeant."

"Which way are we riding, Lieutenant?" asked McKinney.

"That way," mumbled the lieutenant, pointing his chin toward the approaching riders.

McKinney let loose a loud whoop and ran to gather the troop.

The lieutenant tightened the cinch on his saddle and climbed onto his horse.

"When you meet Villa on the road," instructed Daniel, "it could play two ways. He will either charge straight into you or scatter into those low hills along the road. If he charges within a hundred yards, dismount and form a firing line. Do not fight him in the saddle. He will butcher your green boys that way. Two volleys will break his charge." Daniel watched the lieutenant carefully. "You understand?" he asked.

The lieutenant looked Daniel in the eye. "I understand. And if he runs?"

"Like I said, he will turn into those low hills on the west side of the road. Anticipate that," said Daniel. "Keep your eye on Villa at all times. Do not chase after his soldiers. Pursue only Villa."

"What if I don't catch him?" asked the lieutenant.

Daniel exhaled. "Odds are you won't catch him."

The lieutenant frowned, and then checked his pistol.

"Excuse me, fellers," said Samuel. "Our general is about a mile out and getting closer."

"Good luck," said Daniel.

"Thanks." The lieutenant shook Daniel's hand and asked, "When will I see you?"

"I will be in Boquillas."

The lieutenant looked to his soldiers, each man stuffing cartridges into jacket pockets and doing the last-minute things a man does before combat. He mounted his horse, turned in the saddle, and waved his right arm.

Sergeant McKinney verbalized the command. "Forward, quarter time."

Daniel sat on his horse and watched the soldiers ride into battle. There was nothing left to do here. It was best to get as far down the road as possible before the hammer struck the anvil.

Pancho Villa spotted the soldiers the instant they came onto the road. It seemed like a bad dream.

Villa raised his right hand and skittered his stallion to a halt. His men bunched in the road, their horses difficult to handle. Both men and horses were tired and edgy. A sense of confusion ran through the mounted bandits as the distance between them and the soldiers quickly closed.

Sensing another ambush, Villa searched the low hills adjacent to the road with his binoculars. "There has to be more of them," he said.

The soldiers kept coming, and Villa struggled to calm his horse. The animal sensed danger. Villa considered his options. Last year, he would have charged with ruthless abandon. Now, he had no reserves, and he feared another trap. The soldiers were four hundred yards out and still coming.

Villa turned his horse and ran, scattering his men like coyotes into the brush-choked arroyos beyond the road.

The lieutenant stared in disbelief. Pancho Villa had fled. He turned in the saddle and shouted, "Boys, we don't care about anybody except Villa." Living the dream, the lieutenant spurred his horse, pulled his pistol, and galloped in pursuit of Pancho Villa.

Villa turned back and fired twice, and then vanished into the brush.

Charging into the thickest brush after Villa, the lieutenant struck a branch and fell from his horse. Dizzy from the blow, he scrambled to his horse and hustled back into the saddle. Panic stricken, the lieutenant hurried through the trees onto a low, graveled hill.

The general was gone. Pancho Villa had gotten away.

PART 5:
The Second Punitive Expedition into Mexico

Poor Hayduke: won all his arguments but lost his immortal soul.
— Edward Abbey, *The Monkey Wrench Gang*

CHAPTER 29

The Raid at Glenn Spring

THE LIEUTENANT SAT on his bunk inside the adobe fort at Glenn Spring and drank sotol. It was Cinco de Mayo, the Mexican national holiday honoring the French defeat at the historic battle of Puebla, and there was a lively fiesta happening down in the village. His soldiers were certainly enjoying the fandango, but the lieutenant sat alone in the redoubt cursing his hard luck, draining yet another glass of sotol.

"I was close enough to smell the bastard," grumbled the lieutenant. "How different things would be if I'd caught Villa."

When Captain Henry had learned about the failed and unauthorized attempt to capture Pancho Villa, he'd recalled the lieutenant to headquarters in Marfa and given him a royal ass-chewing. Threatening him with a formal investigation, Captain Henry had again ordered him to avoid all contact with both Irma and Daniel.

The lieutenant refilled his glass with sotol and stepped onto the veranda. He settled on a rock bench beneath the frail crescent moon and listened to the sound of guitars playing corridos, fanciful ballads of the war in Mexico. Music, and the laughter of people dancing, rose into the night sky.

Alone in his misery, the lieutenant watched the crescent moon fall beyond the broken mountains lining the western horizon. His troubled mind refused to stick on one problem long enough to properly consider it before jumping to another concern. Everything would have been glorious, if he had captured Pancho Villa. Had his failure to capture

Pancho Villa been his only mistake? Samuel had tried to kill him. If only he had sided with Navarro at the wedding dance, would that have changed anything? Arresting Samuel was the surest way to salvage his failed career, but he suspected that behind all his problems lurked that damnable Marshal Navarro.

Disgusted with himself and his situation, the lieutenant staggered back inside his quarters, lay down on his bunk, and passed out.

<center>~~~~</center>

"Wake up, Lieutenant!" shouted Sergeant McKinney, shaking him awake.

The lieutenant willed the man out of his dream and rolled onto his side hugging a pillow for comfort.

"Get up, Lieutenant! We are under attack!" The sergeant was relentless. He kept yelling, "Wake up, Lieutenant! Wake up, damn you!"

The lieutenant opened his eyes to see McKinney's face creased by a bloody slash. He sat up and puked in his own lap.

McKinney cursed, "Dammit, Lieutenant, we're under attack."

Having succeeded in waking his commanding officer, McKinney unlocked the gun rack. He grabbed two rifles and several boxes of ammunition and ran to the adobe wall near the gate.

Vomiting had had a sobering effect on the lieutenant, enabling him to rally to his duty. He staggered to his feet, grabbed a rifle and two boxes of ammunition, and joined McKinney.

From their defensive positions at the adobe wall, they could see the raiders looting the village. Armed men ran wild in the street, shooting indiscriminately, kicking in doors, and carrying away everything of value they could load onto their string of pack animals.

The lieutenant's mind raced. Who was raiding the village? Was it Villa? The thought calmed his mind. Maybe he could redeem himself. Wiping his mouth with a shirtsleeve, he asked, "Who is it, Sergeant?"

"Does that even matter, Lieutenant? Whoever it is aims to kills us."

McKinney aimed at two raiders running up the hill toward them and squeezed the trigger of his carbine. One of the raiders fell dead with a bullet in his chest.

The lieutenant fired at the second raider and missed. He adjusted his aim and fired a second time, hitting his target in the groin. The raider fell with a howl.

Wracked by the dry heaves, the lieutenant dropped to his knees and wretched.

Disgusted, McKinney cursed the lieutenant as he fired at the raiders who continued to make their way up the hill toward their position. The attack faltered, and the raiders scattered into a ravine that ran parallel to the trail leading to the soldier's redoubt.

Suddenly, a man appeared at the top of the adobe wall.

Chambering a round in his rifle, McKinney spun and faced the man. "Damn you, Owen, I almost shot you!"

"I'd apologize if it weren't me that damn near got killed, Sergeant." Owen grinned. He was barefooted and clad only in his woolen union suit.

"What happened to your boots and clothes, trooper?" demanded McKinney.

"I was as naked as the day I was born when those thieving bastards attacked. What happened to him, Sergeant?" Owen pointed toward the lieutenant, who was now sitting against the adobe wall holding his head in both his hands.

"He's drunk. Go get a rifle and protect that wall you just snuck over."

Owen went into the fort and returned with a rifle and several boxes of ammunition. "It stinks in there."

"Shut up and defend that section there, Owen," growled McKinney.

Owen settled against the adobe wall and loaded his rifle.

The lieutenant staggered to his feet. "You think its Villa, Sergeant? They say he raided Columbus, New Mexico."

"Again, I ask you, does it matter who it is?"

"Probably not," said the lieutenant. "What do you think we should do, Sergeant?"

"I think we can hold them off, sir."

"How's that cut?"

"It hurts, sir."

A rain of bullets smashed into the fort. The lieutenant collapsed onto his side and covered his head until he realized that McKinney was returning fire and that Owen had moved forward from his original position to provide supporting fire. Owen shouted every time he imagined one of his bullets finding its mark.

Gathering his wits, the lieutenant moved to resupply the soldiers with ammunition as a Mexican raider leapt over the wall and landed on all fours in the veranda with a pistol in one hand. Unarmed, the lieutenant turned and faced the raider.

The Mexican leveled his pistol as he scrambled to his feet but he was not quick enough. Owen shot the man twice in the chest. He made certain the man was dead before he returned to his original firing position.

In that moment, the lieutenant understood that he could die tonight. He took the dead man's pistol, tucked it into his britches, gathered his own rifle, and moved to the high ground at the back of the fort.

The higher perch provided a clear view of the hillside below as the raiders continued moving up the hill. The deep arroyo immediately north of the fort had allowed the raiders to sneak to within twenty yards of the outer wall. The glow of a fire appeared at the head of the arroyo.

"Why would they build a fire?" whispered the lieutenant.

A raider appeared in a crouched position at the cusp of the illuminated arroyo. He carried a fiery torch and quickly exploded to his feet and ran toward the fort. The lieutenant let the raider clear the arroyo before he shot the man.

The bullet hit the Mexican in his upper torso, yet the raider still managed to toss the burning torch onto the brush-covered roof of the veranda. The lieutenant fired in anger, preventing additional Mexicans from clearing the arroyo with more torches, even though the first torch had hit its mark.

A growing fire danced on the veranda roof, illuminating the night.

McKinney ran to battle the flames. Owen went to his aid, but McKinney shoved him back toward the wall and ordered him to keep firing. Owen did his best to defend their position while McKinney tried to extinguish the burning veranda. The heat of the roaring fire forced Owen to jump off the north wall, where a Mexican's bullet severed his spine before his feet touched the ground.

McKinney could not hear Owen call for help. The fire burned incredibly hot, and he kept at the flames, badly burning his hands when the roof collapsed.

The heat of the fire forced the lieutenant to move up the hill beyond the fort into the rocks. He called for McKinney to follow him as he escaped.

Two shots echoed from below, followed by an eerie silence. The lieutenant knew that McKinney was dead. It took several moments for the lieutenant to find the nerve to scramble back down the hill.

Back inside the fort, the lieutenant watched the raiders ride south. He counted four dozen horses, maybe more including the pack animals. The lieutenant walked to where McKinney lay in a bloody heap. The man had a gaping gunshot wound between his shoulders.

"Owen," called the lieutenant. "Owen, answer me." When there was no response, the lieutenant walked around the fort's perimeter until he found the man. Squatting, he checked for a pulse and found none.

Not knowing what to do, the lieutenant returned to the dead sergeant's side. Sitting in the ashes of the smoldering veranda, he buried his face in his hands and cried. He was afraid to go looking for more dead men. From the depths of his shame, he smelled himself and cursed. He had shit his pants.

"Is anybody alive in there?"

The lieutenant hesitated before he answered. "Yeah, I'm here." He recognized the voice. It was Ellis Wallace, the owner of the wax plant.

"You okay, son?"

"I'm okay," said the lieutenant. "Who was it?"

"Who was what, son?"

"Who were the raiders? Was it Villa?"

Ellis shook his head. "No, it wasn't Villa himself. It was one of his henchmen, Capitan Ramirez, and his thieving red-legged bastards."

"Oh," whispered the lieutenant, disappointed.

"Are you wounded, son?"

"No."

"Are there any other survivors here?"

"No."

"You sure you're okay?"

"Yeah, I'm okay."

"Is that McKinney?" asked Ellis.

"Yes."

Privates Harlow and Butler appeared from the darkness. They stood reverently next to the sergeant's corpse, coming to attention the best they could.

"Have you seen any of the others?" asked the lieutenant. "What about Hawkins?"

"Yes, sir," said Harlow. "We've seen Hawkins, sir. He got himself shot in the ass, but he's okay. We can't seem to find Owen, sir."

"Owen is dead," said the lieutenant.

"And so is Jones, sir. Johnson and Chandler grabbed two horses and went out trailing the raiders, sir. Including poor Sergeant McKinney, we can account for everyone, sir," said Harlow. "By the looks of the spent brass around here, ya'll put up a good fight."

"It seemed like forever," replied the lieutenant.

There was an eerie glow in the night sky from the fires still burning in the wood-frame buildings down in the village; armed men ran through the streets checking on family members and surveying the damage.

"Harlow," said the lieutenant, swallowing his pride.

"Yes, sir?"

"Make sure Hawkins gets looked at."

"It's already been done, sir. We carried him to the midwife's house. Like we said, he's going to be fine, sir."

"Good job," said the lieutenant. "Round up the men and dig some graves."

"Let me go with you," offered Ellis, following the two men.

The lieutenant grabbed Ellis by the arm. "Did you send for Navarro?"

"I did."

"Good. Thank you. I will ride out after the raiders as soon as we can get organized."

"I will send a horse for you. It appears all the army horses got stolen."

"Thank you."

The lieutenant walked into the burned-out redoubt and searched through the ashes until he found his bottle of sotol. It was going to be a long day; he sorely needed a hair of the dog.

CHAPTER 30

Boquillas Crossing

A DOOR SLAMMED, waking Daniel from a deep sleep. He heard the sound of boots crossing the kitchen floor and reached for the pistol beside the bed.

Ramona stirred in the darkness, waking to his quick, furtive movements. Startled, she sat up in bed.

Daniel put a finger to his lips and cocked the pistol. The hammer noise stopped whoever was moving through the kitchen. Silence engulfed the warm stuffy room as Daniel considered his options. He dropped his feet to the floor and moved toward the bedroom door.

"Put your gun away. It's me, Sergio."

Daniel relaxed.

Ramona sighed. "Make the coffee, please." She rolled into her pillow, pulling the sheet over her shoulder.

Daniel holstered the pistol where it hung on the bedpost, leaned down, and kissed Ramona's cheek. "Yes, my love." He pulled on his pants, slipped on a thin cotton shirt, grabbed his boots, and walked barefoot into the kitchen.

Sergio had lit a pair of oil lamps and was building a fire in the cookstove.

Daniel sat at the table and pulled on his boots. "What time is it?"

"I don't know, almost daylight?" said Sergio.

"What's going on?"

"Rodriquez Ramirez raided Glenn Spring."

213

"What?"

"Captain Ramirez raided Glenn Spring, robbed the payroll, and shot up the town." Sergio kindled the stove and put the coffee pot on to boil.

Rubbing the sleep from his eyes, Daniel asked, "What about the soldiers?"

"It appears the raiders burned down the soldiers' fort and killed three, maybe four, soldiers."

"How'd you learn all this? Who told you?"

"I was at José Torreón's house in San Vicente, Texas, when the raiders rode through. I personally saw Captain Ramirez eating at Señora Torreón's kitchen table, and I talked to some of the men while they were resting."

"You knew them?" asked Daniel.

"A few were from Jaboncillos. You know, several of the raiders were wounded and more than a few of them were shot up pretty bad."

"You sure it was Ramirez, and not Villa?"

"Sí!" Sergio laughed.

Daniel thought for a moment. "Where were they headed?"

"They will ride for Múzquiz. They will want to get as far from the border as quick as they can. They were frightened by their very success." Sergio took a tin of coffee from the cabinet and poured two handfuls into the enameled pot on the stove. "Captain Ramirez respects and fears both Mario and José. If Ramirez didn't molest San Vicente, Texas, after what they did at Glenn Spring, I don't think they will bother anyone here."

"What about the other Boquillas?"

"Who knows?" Sergio poured cold water onto the boiling coffee to settle the grounds.

"Go saddle my horse."

"I already did."

Daniel paused, seeing the boy in a new light. Sergio had matured a great deal since Chilicote. Nodding his approval, Daniel carried two cups of coffee to the bedroom where Ramona sat wrapped in the sheet. He handed her a cup and sat down.

Ramona made room for him on the bed and blew the steam off her coffee. "I don't think they will bother Toribio."

"No," said Daniel, agreeing with her. "But I should check on him."

"And?" asked Ramona, knowing he intended to do more.

"I should go check on the Deemers."

Ramona sipped her coffee. "You are going to check on the lieutenant, no?"

"Yes, I am."

"Be careful," pleaded Ramona.

Daniel kissed her on the forehead and said, "I will."

"We should take our golden eagles and leave this place."

"Where will we go?"

"I don't know, but we should make that decision ourselves before it's decided for us."

Daniel finished his coffee and set the cup on the bedside table. He adjusted the pistol in his shoulder holster and grabbed his rifle. "You want to leave Boquillas?"

"Yes."

"Let me think about it, okay?"

"Thank you." She smiled at him.

"We can talk about this when I get home." Daniel kissed Ramona on the lips, and then walked out the door.

~~~~~

Ramona went to the open bedroom window. The frail light of dawn softly illuminated the Rio Grande. She sighed as Daniel disappeared into the soft gray rain.

~~~~~

Toribio sat in the doorway with a shotgun in his lap. He watched Daniel appear from the drizzling rain and ride toward his store.

"How have you been, amigo?" called Daniel, adjusting his slicker against the rain.

"Good, thanks to the grace of God," replied Toribio.

"Have they crossed the river?"

"No." Toribio stood, cradling the shotgun in the crook of his left arm. Stretching his lower back, he cursed the rain. "Damn wet weather."

Daniel looked toward Toribio's unlit house. "Are you by yourself?"

"I sent my wife and kids to her mother's house."

Daniel wiped the rain from his neck with a black silk scarf. "How come you built this store up here so far from Boquillas?"

Toribio laughed. "I built the store here because of the automobile. Soon, only men herding cows and goats will ride horses. After the mine closes, which it will someday, they will quit using the cable tram and there will be no reason for anyone to live at the mouth of the canyon. In my mind, this is the best river crossing for commerce with Texas."

Daniel considered Toribio's forethought and smiled. "You need me to stay with you?"

"No offense, but it would be best if there aren't any gringos present when Ramirez rides through."

"I'm not offended. I understand." Daniel turned his horse to face the river and adjusted the brim of his hat to protect his eyes from the drizzling rain. "Somebody should check on the Deemers."

"I heard shooting from that direction just before you arrived."

"So the raiders have already reached the other Boquillas?"

"I think so."

Daniel sat on his horse and stared across the mesquite-covered floodplain, the river rising with the constant rain. "Where do you think they will come across?"

"They will come across down there," answered Toribio, pointing at the river with his chin. "You should cross the river farther upstream beyond Ojo Caliente."

Suddenly, three riders appeared from the brush on the Texas bank and plunged into the swollen river. Clinging to their horses' manes the riders angled upstream struggling against the current. In crossing the river, the riders washed quite a distance downstream.

Only after the riders emerged in Mexico did Daniel notice the lengths of rope they had dragged across the river.

"They're crossing an automobile," said Toribio.

"Is it Mr. Deemer's?"

"Yes."

"Damn. This ought to be something to watch."

The bandits pushed Deemer's Bearcat convertible automobile into the river. The car immediately swung downstream, putting tension on the ropes tied to the riders' saddles. The horses strained with their rumps low to the ground. The riders put quirts to horseflesh until the car rolled into Mexico. Daniel was impressed with the riders' skill and amazed by their luck.

Refocusing his binoculars through the rain, Toribio said, "Joe Buck is with them, as is Mr. Deemer."

"Hostages?" asked Daniel.

"Most likely," exhaled Toribio. "They are going to want coffee. I might as well get it made."

"I had better get going. You sure you will be okay?"

Toribio stepped out of the rain and into the doorway of the store. "Yes, I will be fine, thank you. It's you who must be careful."

"Thank you," nodded Daniel.

Toribio waved good-bye as Daniel rode toward the sand dune that stood west of town.

Daniel road upstream and crossed the rising Rio Grande at the settlement of Ojo Caliente. Cautiously, he rode the final distance to the Deemers' store in a constant rain, where a huddled crowd of concerned neighbors had gathered on the porch.

Mrs. Deemer walked from the house wringing her hands. "Did you see them?"

"I saw them when they crossed the river," said Daniel, sliding down off his horse.

"Did they take Mr. Deemer and Joe Buck across the river?"

"I saw them both, Mrs. Deemer. They are okay." Daniel calmly held both of Mrs. Deemer's hands. He considered her teary eyes and asked, "Were they hurt in any way?"

"No." Mrs. Deemer sobbed.

"The two men were in good health when the raiders took them?"

"Yes." Tears flowed down her face. "Neither man was harmed; however, Captain Ramirez compelled them to accompany him back into Mexico."

"Well, that is good to know. If Ramirez had intended to harm them, he would have done it already. We should get off this wet porch and out of the rain, Mrs. Deemer. I sure could use a cup of your fine coffee. The soldiers should be here soon, and you know they'll be hungry."

"You're right," said Mrs. Deemer with a sigh. "Those soldiers are almost always hungry, aren't they?"

Daniel helped Mrs. Deemer into the house, and then turned to the crowd of people gathered on the porch. "Everyone go home. There is nothing you can do until the soldiers arrive."

⁓ ⁓ ⁓

It was still raining when the lieutenant arrived at the Deemer's store. He was both surprised and relieved to see Daniel sitting near the potbelly stove drinking coffee. Mrs. Deemer ran to the lieutenant and sobbed as she explained how the bandits had kidnapped her husband and a local miner, Joe Buck. When Mrs. Deemer completed her story, the lieutenant told Private Harlow to interview anyone who had anything to say and to start a written report.

The lieutenant walked to the stove, poured himself a cup of coffee, and sat down. "How are you doing?"

"Okay," replied Daniel. "And you?"

The lieutenant shook his head. "A bit overwhelmed, but coping."

"What happened at Glenn Spring?"

"Ramirez shot up the place and rode off with everything of value, including Ellis's payroll."

"You okay?" Daniel asked.

"Yeah," whispered the lieutenant, a faraway look in his eyes. "I sure thought it was Pancho Villa himself."

Daniel nodded. It was easy to understand why the lieutenant would think it was Villa. "How many soldiers did you lose?"

"Three. They killed little Tommy Compton too. He was only nine years old."

"Both of the hostages appeared unharmed when I saw them at Boquillas Crossing, and Toribio doesn't think that Ramirez will do anything to hurt either of them, at least not intentionally."

"How do you know all this?"

"I watched them cross the river."

"How did you hear about the raid so quickly?"

Daniel clinched his coffee cup in an attempt to calm his rising anger. He took a long, deep breath and briefly told the lieutenant how he knew what he knew. "Sergio was at José Torreón's house in San Vicente, Texas, when Ramirez rode through. Sergio rode to Boquillas and warned us." Daniel leaned forward in his chair. "We can catch them if we move quickly."

"No," whispered the lieutenant.

"No?" said Daniel in surprise. "What do you mean?"

The lieutenant looked up from his coffee and scowled. "My current orders do not allow me to enter Mexico under any circumstances."

"Jack, although the past has brought us to this very moment, only in this moment can we choose to make everything new."

The lieutenant shrugged and said nothing in return.

"So be it," said Daniel, standing.

"Where are you going?" asked the lieutenant, startled by Daniel's reaction.

"I'm going after Deemer and Joe Buck."

"I can't let you do that."

"Excuse me?"

"We must wait on confirmed orders before we can make an organized push into Mexico."

"They will be in Múzquiz by then." Daniel sensed that no amount of encouragement was going to change the lieutenant's mind. "Either come with me or I will do this alone."

"I can't," whispered the lieutenant. Embarrassed, he left the house.

Daniel drained his coffee cup and found Mrs. Deemer in her bedroom. "I will be back with your husband and Joe Buck as soon as I can."

"Be careful," she pleaded.

Daniel pushed his way through the soldiers huddled on the porch and threw himself into the saddle. He rode to where the lieutenant stood beneath a giant cottonwood. The two men stared at each other for a long moment before Daniel said, "We should go after them."

"I don't have a choice."

"Pershing chased Villa all over Mexico and never caught him. What makes you think that you failed?"

The lieutenant examined the sodden sky for answers, finding none.

"Wait for your captain if you must. I'm going to rescue those men before they are harmed." Daniel spurred his horse and galloped toward the Rio Grande.

◦～◦～◦

Toribio stepped from his store into the rain.

"Are they gone?" Daniel asked, sitting on his horse, hunkered in his rain slicker.

"Yes."

"You okay?"

"They didn't bother me," replied Toribio.

"Did they steal anything from you?"

"No."

"Was Deemer okay?"

Toribio laughed. "Actually, they were treating him more like an honored guest than a hostage."

Daniel chuckled, "Well, I'll be damned."

"That automobile wouldn't start after crossing the river, and they had to pull it with horses."

Daniel looked south. "You don't think they might lie in wait for anybody riding their trail?"

"No," said Toribio. "Except for Ramirez and a few of his cousins, they were all boys. My guess is they will run as fast as they can to the Ocampo cutoff. From there, they will scatter. Are you planning on going alone?"

Daniel nodded.

"Neither Ramirez nor the other boys will harm those two men." Toribio glanced at the drenched sky. "The arroyos will flash, if they haven't already. Eventually, those men will get tired of pushing that old man's car, and they'll leave them alongside the road."

Daniel stared toward Mexico.

Toribio held up his right hand to his forehead in order to better see through the pouring rain and said, "Be careful. Marshal Navarro will likely use this as an excuse to cause problems for either you or Samuel or both."

"That he might," agreed Daniel, turning south after the raiders.

CHAPTER 31

Rescued

EVERY SIGNIFICANT ARROYO south of Boquillas was flooded. The larger arroyos required scouting and the utmost concentration for a safe crossing. Thankfully, the raiders were easy to follow, as they had left a wide trail of stolen goods and empty liquor bottles.

Daniel rode all night and reached the Ocampo cutoff at sunrise. The raiders had split into two groups. One group appeared to have taken the automobile south along the high mountain road toward Múzquiz. A smaller group had turned west. Daniel calculated that the raiders needed Deemer and Joe Buck to keep the vehicle running.

As Daniel climbed higher into the mountains, the vegetation changed. The grass savanna gave way to stringers of oaks in the drainages and open groves of giant yuccas, juniper, and piñon pine trees scattered across the hillsides. The fragrance of wet pine trees marked the down-canyon breeze.

It was midafternoon when Daniel discovered Deemer and Joe Buck. They were sitting in the convertible automobile beneath a crumbling outcrop of weathered granite smoking hand-rolled cigarettes. Two disheveled Mexican boys sat against the side of the car with their hands bound in their laps.

Joe Buck called out the moment he recognized Daniel. "Look here, Mr. Deemer. I told you they would come for us. Where are the rest of them?"

Daniel stopped his horse alongside the car, dropped to the ground, and asked, "The rest of what?"

"The rescue party," shouted Joe Buck.

"I'm it," said Daniel.

Deemer frowned. "You came alone?"

"Yes, I did. Where are the rest of the raiders?"

Deemer laughed. "They went on ahead."

"And you captured these two boys?" asked Daniel pointing at the two Mexican captives.

"We did." Deemer sighed. "I wanted to let them go, but people got killed."

"Why do you think Ramirez left you here?"

"The damn old radiator was acting up and overheating, and Ramirez was generally worried about the US Cavalry catching up with them," explained Joe Buck.

"Well, what really happened was that Joe here let most of the radiator water out and the car overheated," said Deemer.

"Can you get your car going again?" Daniel asked.

"What do you think, Joe?" Deemer asked.

"Maybe," said Joe Buck. "I'm still puzzled that Daniel came by himself. Is the cavalry coming for us, or not? You came all this way without any help?"

"I did, Joe. I came all by myself. Oh, the army is coming, all right, but not until they get organized." Daniel opened the radiator cap and examined the engine block. "I figure they'll be along in a day or two."

"Well I'll be damned," said Deemer, stepping alongside Daniel. He pushed back his felt fedora and wiped his forehead with a shirtsleeve. "I too can't believe that you came after us all alone."

Daniel nodded. "It seemed like the neighborly thing to do, Mr. Deemer. What do you say we get this car turned around and roll it down the hill? Maybe see if we can get it running again?"

"We're going to need gas soon," said Joe Buck.

"Oh, I'm sure the cavalry will have plenty of supplies, if and when they get to us." Daniel laughed. "You got some extra water?"

"We do," answered Deemer, handing Daniel a canvas water bag. "Use this to fill the radiator, and I'll kick those rocks out from the tires. Joe, you put those boys back in the car."

"I … I just can't believe you came after us alone," stammered Joe Buck, helping the two Mexican boys to their feet.

Even though both Daniel and Joe Buck were good mechanics, it was hard work keeping the car running. The men pulled it across a dozen flooded arroyos with Daniel's horse. Although they were exhausted, they kept at it, making decent progress on the road north.

Just when the automobile was yet again stuck in another flooded arroyo, they were all enormously relieved when Joe Buck jumped up and shouted, "Look, Mr. Deemer! The cavalry has finally arrived."

Still a few miles off, Marshal Navarro, Captain Henry, and Lieutenant Thompson rode at the head of a very large column of soldiers.

Daniel stepped from behind the automobile, and Deemer hurried to untie the rope between the car and Daniel's horse. "You should get out of here, son," Deemer said to Daniel.

Joe Buck let out another shout and ran to greet the forward elements of the Ninth Cavalry.

"You think Joe can keep his mouth shut long enough for me to get away?" asked Daniel, rising onto his horse.

"Those soldiers won't be able to make hide nor hair out of his version of any story. Go with God, son, but go now," said Deemer.

Daniel nodded a quick good-bye, and then escaped into the foothills of the Sierra Fronteriza.

Deemer sat on the front bumper of the car and waited on the Ninth Cavalry.

Navarro rode at the front of the column. He raised his right and the column halted.

"Hello, Marshal," said Deemer with a friendly wave of his right hand.

Ignoring Deemer, Navarro issued a command: "Secure those captives."

The first four enlisted men at the head of the column did as instructed. They dropped from their horses and escorted the Mexican prisoners north along the column toward the supply wagons.

"I'm going with these boys, if you don't mind, Mr. Deemer," said Joe Buck. "I need to find me something to eat, if I can."

"Go on, Joe. I'll be along in a minute," replied Deemer.

"You okay, Mr. Deemer?" asked Captain Henry.

"Yes, I am, Captain." Deemer did not complain about the army's slow response. He did not want to appear ungrateful.

"You unharmed, Mr. Deemer?" asked Navarro, eyeing the foothills beyond the road.

"I'm fine." Deemer saw where Navarro looked. It bothered him that Navarro would not stop looking toward the nearest arroyo leading into the foothills of the Sierra Fronteriza.

"How did you escape?" asked Captain Henry.

"It was nothing, Captain. The Mexicans quickly bored of us once the car became a liability. Thank you for coming after us."

"Our pleasure," bragged Captain Henry.

"And the raiders?" asked Lieutenant Thompson.

"They have scattered. You will never find them all in one place."

"We will do our best," said Captain Henry. Turning to Navarro he asked, "Should we turn back? It does appear that our quarry has scattered to the wind."

"When to return to Texas is your decision, Captain." Navarro answered.

"Captain," said Deemer. "Could you spare the lieutenant and a few soldiers with extra horses to help me get my car back to Boquillas?"

"Why of course," replied Captain Henry. "Lieutenant Thompson, tell the quartermaster that he should provide Mr. Deemer with whatever he requires."

Navarro spat and said, "Captain, now that we have secured the civilian hostages, I'm going hunting on my own before I turn back north."

Before Captain Henry could respond, Navarro spurred his horse into a gallop. He rode directly toward the arroyo that led southeast into the mountains.

⁓ ⁓

The lieutenant watched Navarro disappear into the foothills. He thought that he had seen someone ride into that same arroyo just before the cavalry had arrived at the stalled car. It had to have been Daniel.

"Lieutenant, you will ride with me?" asked Deemer.

Pulled from his thoughts, the lieutenant looked to the captain and said, "It would be my pleasure to be of assistance, Mr. Deemer. You are the reason that the Ninth Cavalry invaded Mexico, are you not?"

CHAPTER 32

A Matter of Choice

SOAKED TO THE skin, Daniel rode through a miserably cold and constant rain into the yard at Mario's mountain ranch house, where Samuel's horse stood alone in the corral. He tethered his horse in the corral and hurried through the pouring rain to the house.

Samuel greeted Daniel at the door with a pistol in his hand, wearing one-piece long johns and a pair of moth-eaten socks. He yawned and rubbed sleep from his eyes. "What are you doing out in this rainstorm?"

"Captain Ramirez raided Glenn Spring, and the cavalry is pursuing him on the road to Múzquiz."

"Was the lieutenant involved?"

"Of course he was."

"Is he okay?"

"Yeah, he didn't get hurt."

"Did you see him?"

"Yes," exhaled Daniel.

"What did he say?"

"Ramirez stole Ellis's payroll at the wax camp."

"Did anyone get killed?"

"Three troopers, including McKinney; they killed the Compton boy too."

"Dammit," cursed Samuel. "McKinney was a good man. I'd like to know what really happened," he mumbled. "Get in here."

Daniel followed Samuel into the kitchen.

Samuel took a pair of coffee cups, rinsed them in a basin of water in the metal sink and poured two cups of steaming hot coffee. "So why are you here? You think the soldiers will come looking for me?"

"Navarro is with them."

"In Mexico?" groaned Samuel. "Why is Navarro riding with the cavalry in Mexico?"

"Navarro thinks the cavalry works for him."

"Damn him!" cursed Samuel a frown crossing his face. "You don't think Navarro followed you here?"

"Most likely, wouldn't you agree?"

"Did he see you ride off?"

"No, I left before the soldiers arrived."

"Arrived? What soldiers arrived where?" Samuel asked.

"Goddamn it, Samuel, just get your ass dressed and packed. We need to keep moving."

"Not until you tell me what is going on!"

"Does Navarro know about this place?" Daniel asked.

"Of course he does, you idiot," exclaimed Samuel. "Navarro and Mario used to hunt together when they were kids."

"Damn," murmured Daniel. "Now that is an interesting twist."

"It might be, but why am I hurrying to get packed up and ride out into that weather?" asked Samuel.

"Ramirez returned to Mexico with American hostages, and Navarro has invaded with the Ninth Cavalry. You know Navarro is gunning for you, don't you?"

"Are you a dumb ass, or what?" said Samuel. "You honestly think that Navarro believes we have all those gold coins hidden up here like a bunch of stupid pirates?" Samuel laughed.

"This is personal, Samuel. It is not about the money any more. Get dressed!"

"It's always about the damned money. Where are we going to go?" He took his pants from a hook on the wall and put them on.

"Navarro has a legal reason to be in Mexico, and you're here—two facts that work to his advantage. I'm not sure where we're headed, but I do know that we can't stay here," insisted Daniel, handing Samuel his wool shirt.

"Maybe we should go north," Samuel said, buttoning his shirt. "Or maybe we should go to New Orleans, Daniel. Have you ever been to New Orleans?"

"I've been there a few times." Daniel laughed, his mind briefly considering what Ramona might think about living in New Orleans.

Samuel frowned as he pulled on his tight boots. "It's snowing up high, you know."

"I know. Our trail will be impossible to track."

Samuel laughed. "You always did like riding the hard road." Finally, he holstered his pistols and pulled on a rain slicker.

Daniel turned up the collar on his rain slicker and followed Samuel outside. Without a warning, a single shot pierced the air.

"Son-of-a-bitch!" cursed Samuel, falling to the ground holding his left thigh, blood oozing between his clenched fingers.

Daniel had flinched when Navarro shot Samuel, but he did not hide. He stood his ground not more than ten paces from the shooter.

"I'm here for Samuel," shouted Navarro, walking toward the men. "This ain't between you and me, Daniel. Leave that gun of yours in that fancy holster."

Daniel raised his hands away from his body.

"You're a fool, Navarro," yelled Samuel as he crawled toward the stone corral dragging his wounded leg. "The money is in the Marfa bank, not buried in Mexico!'

"This isn't about money." Navarro raised his pistol and pointed it at Samuel.

"You can't arrest me in Mexico, you imbecile."

"No, but I can kill you and leave you for the vultures, coyotes, and wolves."

"Marshal, put that gun down," shouted Daniel, lowering his shoulder and charging through the torrential rain.

Daniel collided against Navarro with his right shoulder. A shot rang out. The two men fell to the ground in a bloody heap. Navarro lay dead, shot in the back.

Confused, Daniel looked up to see the lieutenant standing in the rain holding a smoking pistol. "What did you do that for?"

"I couldn't permit him to kill you," whispered the lieutenant.

"And for that, I'm glad," agreed Daniel.

"He gave me no choice," said the lieutenant.

"That's not what happened. You made a choice. It's always a matter of choice," said Daniel, going to Samuel's aid. "How's that leg?"

Samuel was tying a bandana around his bloody thigh. He stood with Daniel's help. Testing the leg, he said, "It went clean through. You sure Navarro is dead?"

The lieutenant rolled the marshal onto his belly, exposing the gaping wound in his upper back. "He is dead all right."

"Yeah, he's dead," said Samuel. "You okay, son?"

"I killed a federal marshal," said the lieutenant, staring at the pistol in his right hand. "What now?"

"We take Navarro back to Texas, I guess," said Daniel.

"Or we could leave him here buried in a shallow grave," argued Samuel.

"That's not right," complained Daniel.

"Doing the right thing is likely to get some of us hung," said Samuel. "What do you think, Lieutenant? This is your situation."

"It's a temptation to leave the man. He did ride off into Mexico alone. Anything could have happened to him," mused the lieutenant.

"It's just not right to leave him here in Mexico," said Daniel.

"It's his choice," argued Samuel. "Leave the boy to decide his own fate."

"No," whispered the lieutenant. "Taking him home is the right thing to do. Unless God himself intervenes, we probably should take Navarro back to Texas and let the army sort it out."

"Then put that pistol away and let's get this done," said Daniel.

Samuel shook his head and cursed. "I say we bury the dead bastard in Mexico. Can't we just leave him here?"

"No," said Daniel. "We need to set things right, once and for all. You will see, Samuel. This will work itself out in the end. It always does. The lieutenant prevented a murder, and we didn't do a damn thing wrong."

"Except murder a federal marshal," sighed the lieutenant.

A bolt of lightning flashed, exploding in the top of a nearby pine tree. A simultaneous, resounding clap of thunder shook their very bones.

"This storm is making me nervous," said Samuel.

"You're just woozy because of the bleeding. Saddle your damn horse," commanded Daniel, pointing Samuel to his horse. Turning to the lieutenant, he said, "Give me a hand here and let's get the dead marshal secured and tied onto his horse before it starts raining any harder."

"It can't rain any harder," spit Samuel, saddling his horse with some difficulty. He tried to push himself into the saddle, but failed. "I'm going to need a boost up, I think."

Daniel helped Samuel into his saddle, and then finished helping the lieutenant tie the dead man into a bundle. Once the marshal was secure in his blanket, they tied him on his horse.

Without fanfare, the men turned north into the cold rain. They rode without speaking, each man contemplating his own thoughts.

"What will happen after we get to Texas?" Samuel murmured. "My damn leg is starting to hurt." Neither of the other men responded. Whistling a Mexican war corrido to calm his nerves, Samuel fidgeted in the saddle and studied the storm, which soaked the men and their horses.

"What about my career?" The lieutenant fretted. "I'm about to face serious consequences. Maybe even a court-martial—or worse."

Daniel huddled in his slicker. The rain pasted his pant legs against the mare's wet ribs. His thoughts drifted to Ramona in Boquillas as the bruised sky poured water onto the lonely savanna. He had never witnessed this much rain in the desert.

Mud clung to the horses' feet, and the trail from the ore tram terminal into the arroyo leading to Boquillas was too slick to ride in places; the men walked their horses down the steepest slopes. In the distance, the Rio Grande swelled with the constant rain. The river rose from its banks, swirling across the desert.

Riding the final mile into Boquillas, Daniel noticed how the Rio Grande arched toward Texas. He considered how the normally dry wash they were riding occasionally carried enough water to force the Rio Grande north into Texas. The simple movement of water was a terrible force to consider.

A rumbling sound interrupted his contemplation. The noise echoed from the nearest mountains. Assuming it was the ore tram, Daniel looked overhead. However, he saw nothing. The ground trembled as the noise increased. He looked toward the town of Boquillas. People were running from their adobe houses carrying children and armloads of possessions.

"What is that noise?" the lieutenant asked, searching for the source of the grinding sound that was causing the ground to shake.

"There!" said Samuel, pointing south in the arroyo.

Daniel recognized the fear of annihilation in Samuel's eyes, and then turned in his saddle to face the pulsating brown wall of water, rocks, and brush that churned toward them. Daniel's horse tried to run, but was overcome by churning, viscous mud of the flash flood. The roiling wall of water quickly swallowed the men and their horses.

Tumbling with the cresting flood, Daniel lost sight of everything. Pulled under by the floodwaters, he was nearly drowned as his pockets and boots filled with mud and rocks. Weighed down, he fought for his life.

Finding himself pinned against a limestone cliff, Daniel grabbed a tree root and pulled himself free of the swirling eddy that churned against the cliff face. He crawled onto the highest ledge rock he could reach on the Texas riverbank and looked downstream to where the ravenous shadow of Boquillas Canyon swallowed the raging Rio Grande.

The peaceful village of Boquillas appeared completely destroyed by the flash flood. Daniel prayed that Ramona had been anywhere but home.

CHAPTER 33

The Nagual's Gift

DANIEL STOOD AT the river's edge and mourned. It had been several weeks since the flash flood. His sorrow ran deep and stirred old emotions. He held a half-empty bottle of laudanum and stared at the dark crack where Boquillas Canyon swallowed the Rio Grande. In the past, the laudanum had served to erode painful memories of war and love lost. Now, nothing dulled the pain of losing Ramona to the flash flood that had totally swallowed the village of Boquillas. Many of the residents had miraculously survived, but Ramona had not. Samuel and the marshal's corpse had also disappeared in the flood.

A canyon wren sang a beautiful song from the nearest limestone canyon wall. These little wrens sing in the loneliest places on Earth. Out of habit, Daniel followed the tiny bird's song until he found the wren clinging to a vertical cliff face above the river.

From the darkest shadow in the maw of Boquillas Canyon, a man appeared leading a horse and rider. Even at a distance, Daniel noticed the older man's shoulder-length gray hair. The rider was a woman. Her bandaged leg stuck out at an awkward angle from the horse and saddle.

The old man walked the horse along the Texas riverbank, obviously reading the current. When he seemed satisfied that he had arrived at the right place, he gave a soft tug on the reins and calmly led the cinnamon-colored horse into the river.

By the time the old man and the woman rider had crossed the river into Mexico, Daniel recognized the man, the woman, and his long-lost horse. Overcome with joy, he dropped the laudanum bottle onto the graveled bank, where it shattered. He whispered his lover's name, "Ramona!"

Heart pounding, Daniel ran to greet them. He gently pulled Ramona from the horse, and they hugged each other tight. Incredulous, they released their initial embrace and gazed into each other's eyes. "You're alive!" Daniel shouted.

"I am."

"What happened?"

"I washed many miles downstream before someone pulled me from the river. My leg was broken, although it appears to be healing."

"Are you okay?"

"I am now," sighed Ramona, melting into his arms.

Daniel looked at Romero and asked, "How did you find her?"

"I stopped by a jacal for a meal and she asked me for a ride. Until now, I didn't realize that she was your woman."

The horse whinnied and nudged Daniel's arm.

Daniel laughed as he turned to the horse and rubbed the white star on the gelding's face.

"I see your horse also remembers you," smiled Romero.

"Romero brought you to me the first time," sighed Ramona. "Now he brings me to you."

"So it seems," agreed Daniel.

"Is everyone okay?" asked Ramona, her tentative voice exposing her fear of the unknown.

"Your entire family is fine," said Daniel. "Others in Boquillas weren't so fortunate, such as Samuel."

"Samuel?"

"He too is gone."

"Where is Mario?" Ramona asked, leaning her head against his chest.

"Over in Texas at San Vicente with Sergio and the girls," said Daniel, inhaling the smell of her hair. "I'm glad that you sent them to Texas after the raid at Glenn Spring."

"José is still down south?"

"Yes, he is still fighting his stupid war. José truly believes that he can avenge what happened to his son."

"What about the lieutenant?"

"He survived it all."

"Is he still at Glenn Spring?"

"No," said Daniel. "He was transferred to San Antonio."

"I thought I had lost you," said Daniel, staring into Ramona's green eyes.

"I, too, thought all was lost," whispered Ramona, studying her lover's face.

They kissed and turned to the old man. "Where have you been?" Daniel asked.

"I went to the ocean." Romero's eyes widened. "Have you ever seen the ocean?"

"Yes," answered Daniel. "Yes, I have."

"I have brought you your horse just as I promised that one-eyed man."

"You keep the horse as a gift for returning Ramona."

"Thank you." Romero smiled. "The peyote cured you, no?"

"Some folks believe that."

Romero touched Daniel's chest with an open hand. "Mescalito heals by illuminating, and then integrating lost or discarded portions of the human soul."

Daniel nodded. "I'm no longer sure what to believe."

"That is an important first step in moving from the known into the unknown."

"Daniel," said Ramona. "I want to take the children and wait out this damned war with Romero in his native village in the Sierra Madre."

"First we eat." Daniel smiled. "Decisions are always best made with a full stomach."

Daniel gently lifted Ramona back into the saddle and led them away from the river.

Rawles Williams is a yoga teacher and naturalist with thirty-five years of experience hiking, boating, and exploring the Big Bend region of far west Texas and northern Mexico. A wildland firefighter by profession, he has worked from Alaska to Florida, including most western intermountain states. In addition, Rawles helped Big Bend National Park organize a wildland fire hand-crew of Mexican nationals from the rural communities of northern Coahuila, Mexico; and he has guided adventurous travelers through the isolated canyons of the Rio Grande, high into the Sierra del Carmen, and back of beyond into the depths of Mexico's Copper Canyon region.

Because of these experiences, Rawles became an avid student of the Mexican Revolution of 1910, while traveling extensively in Chiapas, Mexico, and the war-torn highlands of Guatemala during the 1980s. In Guatemala, he learned firsthand about the effects of civil war.

During the years he spent living in Boquillas, Rawles developed a rich and rewarding relationship with Don José Falcon. Falcon served Boquillas as de facto mayor for almost thirty years. The tourists who ventured across the Rio Grande to visit Boquillas all loved Falcon—and his tacos and burritos, three for one dollar. The old man in the wheelchair was soft spoken, kindhearted, and a brilliant business executive. In truth, Falcon ran Boquillas with a tight fist. Falcon helped Rawles to see both local history and current events from a Mexican perspective.

Rawles lives in Alpine, Texas, where he teaches yoga while waiting on another fire season. He continues to work with Los Diablos, and he enjoys occasional walkabouts in Big Bend National Park and other remote places. Rawles is currently renovating several old houses, finishing his second novel, and assisting the citizens of Boquillas in preparing for the anticipated 2012 reopening of the Port of Entry at Boquillas Crossing in Big Bend National Park.

Made in the USA
Lexington, KY
30 April 2012